STAR WARS™
RIPTIDE

STAR WARS

RIPTIDE

PAUL S. KEMP

arrow books

Published by Arrow 2011

2 4 6 8 10 9 7 5 3 1

First published in Great Britain in 2011 by
Arrow
Random House, 20 Vauxhall Bridge Road,
London SW1V 2SA

www.starwars.com
www.randomhouse.co.uk

Addresses for companies within The Random House Group Limited can be
found at: www.randomhouse.co.uk

The Random House Group Limited Reg. No. 954009

A CIP catalogue record for this book is available from the British Library

ISBN 9780099542841

The Random House Group Limited supports The Forest Stewardship
Council (FSC®), the leading international forest certification organisation.
Our books carrying the FSC label are printed on FSC® certified paper. FSC
is the only forest certification scheme endorsed by the leading environmental
organisations, including Greenpeace. Our paper procurement policy can be
found at www.randomhouse.co.uk/environment

Printed and bound by CPI Group (UK) Ltd, Croydon, CR0 4YY

For Jen, Roarke, and Riordan

acknowledgments

A great team made this book possible.
Thank you Shelly, Sue, and Leland.

THE **STAR WARS** NOVELS TIMELINE

OLD REPUBLIC
5000–33 YEARS BEFORE
STAR WARS: A New Hope

Lost Tribe of the Sith*
Precipice
Skyborn
Paragon
Savior
Purgatory
Sentinel

3650 YEARS BEFORE *STAR WARS: A New Hope*

The Old Republic
Deceived
Fatal Alliance

Red Harvest

Lost Tribe of the Sith*
Pantheon**
Secrets**

1032 YEARS BEFORE *STAR WARS: A New Hope*

Knight Errant

Darth Bane: Path of Destruction
Darth Bane: Rule of Two
Darth Bane: Dynasty of Evil

RISE OF THE EMPIRE
33–0 YEARS BEFORE
STAR WARS: A New Hope

Darth Maul: Saboteur*
Cloak of Deception
Darth Maul: Shadow Hunter

32 YEARS BEFORE *STAR WARS: A New Hope*

> **STAR WARS: EPISODE I**
> **THE PHANTOM MENACE**

Rogue Planet
Outbound Flight
The Approaching Storm

22 YEARS BEFORE *STAR WARS: A New Hope*

> **STAR WARS: EPISODE II**
> **ATTACK OF THE CLONES**

22–19 YEARS BEFORE *STAR WARS: A New Hope*

The Clone Wars
The Clone Wars: Wild Space
The Clone Wars: No Prisoners

Clone Wars Gambit
Stealth
Siege

Republic Commando
Hard Contact
Triple Zero
True Colors
Order 66

Shatterpoint
The Cestus Deception
The Hive*
MedStar I: Battle Surgeons
MedStar II: Jedi Healer
Jedi Trial
Yoda: Dark Rendezvous
Labyrinth of Evil

19 YEARS BEFORE *STAR WARS: A New Hope*

> **STAR WARS: EPISODE III**
> **REVENGE OF THE SITH**

Dark Lord: The Rise of Darth Vader

Coruscant Nights
Jedi Twilight
Street of Shadows
Patterns of Force

Imperial Commando
501st

The Han Solo Trilogy
The Paradise Snare
The Hutt Gambit
Rebel Dawn

The Adventures of Lando Calrissian
The Han Solo Adventures
The Force Unleashed
The Force Unleashed II
Death Troopers

*An eBook novella
**Forthcoming

REBELLION
0–5 YEARS AFTER
STAR WARS: A New Hope

Death Star

STAR WARS: EPISODE IV
A NEW HOPE

Tales from the Mos Eisley Cantina
Allegiance
Choices of One
Galaxies: The Ruins of Dantooine
Splinter of the Mind's Eye

YEARS AFTER STAR WARS: A New Hope

STAR WARS: EPISODE V
THE EMPIRE STRIKES BACK

Tales of the Bounty Hunters
Shadows of the Empire

YEARS AFTER STAR WARS: A New Hope

STAR WARS: EPISODE VI
RETURN OF THE JEDI

Tales from Jabba's Palace
Tales from the Empire
Tales from the New Republic

The Bounty Hunter Wars
  The Mandalorian Armor
  Slave Ship
  Hard Merchandise

The Truce at Bakura
Luke Skywalker and the Shadows of
  Mindor

NEW REPUBLIC
5–25 YEARS AFTER
STAR WARS: A New Hope

X-Wing
  Rogue Squadron
  Wedge's Gamble
  The Krytos Trap
  The Bacta War
  Wraith Squadron
  Iron Fist
  Solo Command

The Courtship of Princess Leia
A Forest Apart*
Tatooine Ghost

The Thrawn Trilogy
  Heir to the Empire
  Dark Force Rising
  The Last Command

X-Wing: Isard's Revenge

The Jedi Academy Trilogy
  Jedi Search
  Dark Apprentice
  Champions of the Force

I, Jedi
Children of the Jedi
Darksaber
Planet of Twilight
X-Wing: Starfighters of Adumar
The Crystal Star

The Black Fleet Crisis Trilogy
  Before the Storm
  Shield of Lies
  Tyrant's Test

The New Rebellion

The Corellian Trilogy
  Ambush at Corellia
  Assault at Selonia
  Showdown at Centerpoint

The Hand of Thrawn Duology
  Specter of the Past
  Vision of the Future

Fool's Bargain*
Survivor's Quest

*An eBook novella
**Forthcoming

THE STAR WARS NOVELS TIMELINE

 NEW JEDI ORDER
25–40 YEARS AFTER
STAR WARS: A New Hope

Boba Fett: A Practical Man*

The New Jedi Order
Vector Prime
Dark Tide I: Onslaught
Dark Tide II: Ruin
Agents of Chaos I: Hero's Trial
Agents of Chaos II: Jedi Eclipse
Balance Point
Recovery*
Edge of Victory I: Conquest
Edge of Victory II: Rebirth
Star by Star
Dark Journey
Enemy Lines I: Rebel Dream
Enemy Lines II: Rebel Stand
Traitor
Destiny's Way
Ylesia*
Force Heretic I: Remnant
Force Heretic II: Refugee
Force Heretic III: Reunion
The Final Prophecy
The Unifying Force

35 *YEARS AFTER STAR WARS: A New Hope*

The Dark Nest Trilogy
The Joiner King
The Unseen Queen
The Swarm War

 LEGACY
40+ YEARS AFTER
STAR WARS: A New Hope

Legacy of the Force
Betrayal
Bloodlines
Tempest
Exile
Sacrifice
Inferno
Fury
Revelation
Invincible

Crosscurrent
Riptide

Millennium Falcon

43 *YEARS AFTER STAR WARS: A New Hope*

Fate of the Jedi
Outcast
Omen
Abyss
Backlash
Allies
Vortex
Conviction
Ascension
Apocalypse**

*An eBook novella
**Forthcoming

dramatis personae

Jaden Korr; Jedi Knight (human male)
Marr Idi Shael; first mate, *Junker* (Cerean male)
Khedryn Faal; captain, *Junker* (human male)
Runner; Force-using warrior (male human clone)
Seer; Force-using mystic (female human clone)
Grace; child (female human clone)

A long time ago in a galaxy far, far away. . . .

chapter one

JADEN FOUND HIMSELF ON HIS KNEES, THE ROOM SPIN-
ning. Blood leaked from his right temple, spattered
the floor in little crimson circles. More blood oozed
from the stumps of his fingers. Pain blurred his vision,
clouded his thinking. The short, rapid shrieks of an
alarm blared in his ears, rising and falling in time with
the dim flashes of overhead backup lights. Strange
lights. Like little starbursts buried deep in the green resin
of the ceiling. A haze of black smoke congealed near the
ceiling and darkened air that stank of melted plastoid,
rubber, and ozone. He thought he caught the faint stink
of decaying flesh but could not be sure.

Gingerly he placed his unwounded hand to his right
temple, felt the warm, sticky blood, the small hole there.
The blood was fresh; the wound recent.

The rapid flashes of the lights made his movements
seem herky-jerky, not his own, the stop-starts of a mari-
onette in unpracticed hands. His body ached. He felt as
if he'd been beaten. The stumps of the fingers he'd lost
on the frozen moon throbbed, the wounds somehow re-
opened and seeping pus. His skull felt as if someone had
driven a nail through it.

And he had no idea where he was.

He thought he felt eyes on him. He looked around the
dark corridor, his eyes unable to focus. He saw no one.

The floor vibrated under him, as if coursing with power, the rale of enormous lungs. He found the feeling disquieting. Filaments dangled like entrails from irregular gashes torn in the walls. Black scorch marks bordered the gashes. A control panel, a dark rectangle, hung loose from an aperture in the wall, as if blown out by a power surge.

He found it difficult to focus for long on anything before his field of vision started to spin. His bleary eyes watered from the smoke. The flashing lights and the wail of the siren disoriented him, would not let him gather his thoughts.

The pain in his head simply would not relent. He wanted to scream, to dig his fingers into his brain and root out the agony. He'd never felt anything like it.

What had happened to him?

He could not remember. Worse, he could not think clearly.

And then he felt it: the faint tang of dark-side energy. Its taint suffused the air, greasy on his skin, angry, evil. He swallowed down a dry throat.

Had he been attacked by a Sith?

With an effort of will, he pushed the touch of the dark side away from his core, held it at arm's length. Having an enemy gave him focus. He steeled himself against the pain in his head and stood on weak legs. Each beat of his heart felt like a hammer blow to his skull. Pound. Pound.

He tried to hold his ground but the room began to spin more rapidly, the alarm loud in his ears, the floor growling under him, the ringing, spinning, whirling. He wobbled, swayed. Nausea pushed bile into the back of his throat.

Without warning, the pain in his temple spiked, a white-hot flash of agony that summoned a prolonged scream. His wail rebounded off the walls, carried off into the darkness, and with the scream as a sound track, a flood of memories and images streamed across his consciousness, rapid flashes of colors, faces, a series of half-remembered or half-imagined things. He was unable to focus for long on any of the images, unable to slow them down; they blazed in and out of his awareness like sparks, flashing for a moment, then gone, leaving only a shadowy afterimage.

He squeezed his eyes shut and clamped his mouth closed to cut off the scream. The pain would not stop. His head was going to explode, surely it was going to burst.

He was teetering, his head pounding, his stomach in his throat, his eyes watering.

Unable to keep his feet, he sagged back to the floor. The spinning began to subside. The pain, too, began to fade. He sagged with relief. He would not have been able to bear much more.

Clarity replaced pain, and as his head cleared, images and events refitted themselves into the jigsaw puzzle of his memory, reconstituted him from their fragments. He sank into the Force, found comfort there. He closed his eyes for a time and when he opened them, he looked about with what felt like new eyes.

He sat in the middle of a wide corridor. The dim, intermittent flashes of the strange overhead lights showed little detail. The walls, ceilings, and floors were composed of a substance he'd never seen before, light green, semitranslucent. At first he thought it was some form of plastoid, or hued transparisteel, but no, it was a resin of some kind. For the first time, he realized that the floor was not merely vibrating under him, it was warm, like flesh. Faint lines of light glowed deep within it, barely visible, capillaries of luminescence. The arrangement looked ordered, a matrix of some kind, and the pattern of their flashes was not random, though he could not look at it long without its flashes disorienting him.

He tried to make sense of what he was seeing. The architecture, the technology it implied . . .

Where was he?

A word leapt to the forefront of his mind, a flash that came and went without explanation.

Rakatan.

He leaned forward, trying to remember, feeling as if he were on the verge of some revelation. He tried to pull the word back, to force it to take on meaning and make sense, but it eluded him.

"Rakatan," he said, and the word sounded strange on his lips. Saying it aloud triggered no more memories.

But more and more memories were clicking into place, connecting names, events, and faces, the backstory of his life being told just below the level of his consciousness. He must have been hit on the head, hit hard. Understanding would come eventually, or so he hoped.

Yet he knew he could not sit still and wait for it. The dark side was all around him. Palpable anger polluted the air, pressed against him. Alarms were wailing. The vibrations in the floor rose and fell like lungs, lurching, not so much like ordinary breathing as a death rale. He had to get away from wherever he was.

An explosion rumbled somewhere in the distance and everything shook.

He was in a ship then, or a station of some kind. He looked for a viewport but saw none.

He crawled over to the wall and used it to help himself stand. The pain in the stumps of his fingers caused him to wince. The smooth surface of the wall pulsed faintly under his touch and he had the sudden, uncomfortable fear that he had awakened in the belly of some nameless pseudomechanical beast, that he'd been swallowed and was now being slowly digested.

Licking his lips, he stood away from the wall. His wounded fingers had left bloody smears on the smooth green surface.

The comforting weight of his lightsaber hung from his

belt and he put his hand on its cool hilt. He had made
it. . . .

Where had he made it?

On a ship. On *Junker*. He'd made it on *Junker*.

He remembered giving his other blade, the one he'd
made as a boy on Coruscant, to Marr.

To Marr.

A face flashed in his memory: tan, weathered, a ruff of
hair haloing a towering forehead. The face of a Cerean.
Marr.

"Marr?" he called over the sirens, his raw voice
bouncing down the corridor. In his mind's eye he saw a
lazy eye, a malformed asymmetrical face, and a ready
smile, and a name accompanied the image. "Khedryn?"

No response.

He was alone.

He took a moment to evaluate his physical condition,
examining his limbs, chest, abdomen. Other than the re-
opened wounds on his hand and the small hole in his
head, he'd suffered no serious visible harm. He had been
in a fight, though. His cheek felt sore to the touch; his
ribs and his arms had several bruises, as if from blocking
blows.

He took inventory of his gear, sifting through pockets,
the cases on his belt—nutrition bars, extra power packs
for his blaster, liquid rope, a glow lamp. No medpack,
though.

He took the glow lamp in his wounded hand and activated it. Its beam put a path of luminescence on the
semitranslucent floor, down the corridor. The hair-thin
filaments in the floor seemed to glow in response, the
photons communicating in a tongue he could not comprehend. He fell in behind the beam of his glow lamp
and tried to find a way out.

He felt more himself as he moved. The corridor split
repeatedly. Vertical seams in the walls opened wetly at

his approach to reveal corridors and rooms beyond. Once more, he marveled at the technology.

The smoke made his eyes leak, turned his throat raw. The blinking patterns of light in the walls and floor drew him on, will-o'-the-wisps tempting him to some fate he did not understand. Distant explosions continued to rock the vessel and he staggered under their onslaught, his legs still weak.

The energy of the dark side thickened. He was closing on its source. Its power alarmed him. He leaned into it, against it, as he might against a rainstorm. He flashed on a memory of Force lightning crackling out of his fingers, energy born of fear or anger. He studied his hands, the one unwounded, the other missing three fingers, and knew that fear and anger no longer held any power over him. Force lightning was not a weapon he would use again.

Ahead he saw a large vertical seam, its size suggestive of a much larger door, a much larger chamber beyond. The lights in the floor and walls made a kaleidoscope of color around him, reds, greens, yellows, beckoning him forward, but he slowed, sensing something awful in the air, some lurking danger that lived in the darkness beyond the door. The hairs on the back of his neck rose. The lights flared more rapidly, more urgently, as if sensing his emotion. He stopped, swallowed. Sweat collected on his flesh.

His glow lamp died, then the lights in the walls and floor, leaving only the dim intermittent flashes of the overhead lights. He stood alone in the corridor, bathed in darkness, in light, in darkness, in light.

A shriek carried from the room beyond the seam and pierced the tension, a prolonged wail of hate only partially human. Its pure, unadulterated rage staggered Jaden. He took a half-step back, his hand on the hilt of his lightsaber. Adrenaline flooded him, turned his senses hyperacute.

The shriek diminished to a savage growl, but he heard the cunning in it. A huge boom sounded from within the chamber, another. Footsteps? Some kind of locomotion, surely. Whatever horror lurked in the chamber was coming toward him.

He fell into the Force and unclipped his lightsaber from his belt, the metal of the hilt cool in his sweat-slicked hand.

"Jaden," said a voice from behind him, a voice that sunk a fishhook into his memory and started reeling recollections to the surface of his consciousness.

He turned, saw furtive figures emerge from the shadows. Had they been following him? How had he missed them?

Jaden recognized them, one with his arm around the throat of the other, but his mind did not put a name to them right away.

"I know you," Jaden said.

And all at once memories flooded him. He remembered where he was, why he had come, what had happened to him. The sudden rush of memory and emotion overwhelmed him. He clutched at his head and groaned.

One of the figures held something in his off hand, a lightsaber hilt. He ignited it and a red line split the darkness.

Another shriek sounded from the chamber behind Jaden. The lights in the wall flared to life in response, brighter than before, and Jaden at last recognized them for what they were—veins coursing with dark-side energy.

He *had* awakened in the belly of a beast.

Another shriek shook the walls.

He ignited his lightsaber, its yellow light his answer to the darkness that surrounded him.

chapter two

TWO DAYS EARLIER

JADEN STARED THROUGH *JUNKER'S* VIEWPORT, HIS RE-
flection superimposed over the receding spheres of the
frozen moon and the blue gas giant it orbited. He stared
at the image of himself, able to hold his own gaze for the
first time in months. He'd lost fingers on the frozen
moon, broken bones, but he'd left his fear there, too,
and in the process healed his spirit.

He realized now that his doubts about his relationship
to the Force were not a sword of weakness to stab at his
resolve and drive him to the dark side. Instead, they
were a shield of self-examination to protect him from it.
He would never fall to the dark side, because he understood it too well.

Master Katarn had tried indirectly to teach him as
much, but Jaden hadn't fully learned the lesson until he'd
traveled to an uncharted moon in the Unknown Regions
and faced Force-using clones born of Sith and Jedi genes.

He hoped to see Master Katarn soon. It had been too
long. Jaden had let them drift apart until their orbits
never crossed. He would remedy that.

He held his hands before him, one whole, the other
maimed, the stumps of his lost fingers still the black and
red of charred meat. He knew he'd never again see Force
lightning discharge involuntarily from his fingertips.
Not because Force lightning was associated with the

dark side—for Jaden, the Force was a tool, neither light nor dark—but because its uncontrolled discharge represented a lack of understanding, of the Force, of himself. And he understood both now.

In fact, he felt the Force anew, felt it with the same unabashed joy he'd felt when he'd first awakened to it as a child, an awakening that had led him to construct a lightsaber from spare parts in his uncle's workshop. He did not remember actually making the lightsaber. It felt like a dream. He thought he might have been in a trance the whole time, but he did remember activating the weapon for the first time, marveling at the beauty of its thin, unwavering purple line, the quiet hum of its power. When he'd shown his handiwork to his uncle, his uncle had scarcely believed it.

"Stang, boy! Turn that thing off before you cut a hole in the wall!"

His uncle had contacted the authorities immediately and within two days Jaden had been enrolled in the Jedi Academy. It had been a whirlwind of shuttles and space flights that had ended with Jaden shaking Grand Master Luke Skywalker's hand for the first time.

"Welcome to the Jedi Academy," Luke had said to him.

Looking out on the stars, the glowing clouds of gas, Jaden realized that he had not thought about Uncle Orn in years. Orn had taken Jaden in when Jaden's adoptive parents had been killed in a shuttle accident. As a boy, Jaden had called his uncle "Uncle Orn the Hutt" because he was so fat. Jaden smiled, recalling his uncle's ready grin and wheezing laughter. Orn had been killed in the Yuuzhan Vong invasion of Coruscant. Jaden had been away on a mission and had learned of it after the fact.

As sudden and intense as a lightning strike, he flashed on a sense memory: the smell of his mother's red hair, a scent like wildflowers. He hung on to the memory, for he remembered so little else of his parents. He knew them mostly through family holos and vid recordings.

And he had no family left, not anymore. He was altogether alone. He practiced Jedi nonattachment not by choice, but by default. Odd, how his life had unfolded.

Khedryn's voice interrupted his ruminations. "Scans got nothing. The clones are gone. Or they're so far out, the scanners can't ping them."

"I figured as much," Jaden said, still staring out the viewport, still wrestling with memories. A ship full of genetically modified Force-using clones had fled the moon in a stolen ship. They were alone, too, he supposed. At least in a way.

"Probably better that way," Khedryn said. "*Junker*'s in no condition to follow. We've got at least a couple more hours of repairs before I'm putting her into hyperspace. Marr vented her altogether and she took a beating from those Sith fighters. Not to mention *your* flying, which almost tore her apart." He chuckled. "How's the hand?"

"It's all right," Jaden said, turning to face him.

Seeing him, Khedryn cocked his head in a question. His good eye fixed on Jaden, while his lazy eye stared past Jaden's shoulder, maybe at his reflection in the viewport.

"You all right?" Khedryn had a mug of caf, and sipped from it.

"Yeah, fine," Jaden said. "I was just . . . thinking about my family."

"Didn't know you had any."

"I don't. Not anymore."

"Me neither."

Jaden knew. Khedryn's parents had been survivors of the crash of Outbound Flight. They'd died long before Grand Master Skywalker and Mara Jade had pulled Khedryn, along with a handful of other survivors, from the asteroid on which the ship had crashed.

Khedryn grinned and hoisted his caf mug. "We've got each other now, though, don't we?"

Jaden smiled. "We do."

Khedryn had saved Jaden's life back on the moon.

"Fresh caf in the galley," Khedryn said. "Pulkay where it always is, in case you want a jolt. Do you some good, Jaden. You look like a man who's thinking too much and drinking too little."

Jaden grinned. "Is that right?"

"Damned right, that's right. Pondering, ruminating, looking for meaning here and there. That's you. Sometimes things just are what they are."

"You don't believe that."

Khedryn's face lost its mirth and he looked into his cup, swirled the contents, slammed down what remained. "I surely kriffin' do not. Not after what happened on the moon. But I don't like thinking about the meaning of it all too much. Gives me a headache. Let's get a refill, yeah?"

"Yeah," Jaden said, and they walked *Junker*'s corridors toward the galley. Khedryn stopped now and again to examine this or that joint on a bulkhead, a viewport. He'd tap the wall with his mug a few times and nod or frown, apparently deducing something from the sound of metal on metal.

"She's stressed," Khedryn said of the ship. "But she hung in there."

Same was true of all of them, Jaden supposed.

Khedryn patted the bulkhead. "She'll do what we ask. Won't you, girl?"

"I have no doubt."

Khedryn cleared his throat. "So, then, do you have a plan? What do we do about the escaped clones?"

"We find them," Jaden said.

"Yeah, I figured that. I'm all ears about how."

"First I need to speak to Grand Master Skywalker."

Following a Force vision, Jaden had left Coruscant without notifying the Order or filing a flight plan. That had been a mistake. And by now, someone would wonder where he had gone. Besides, he had an obligation to inform the Grand Master about the escaped clones.

"Makes sense," Khedryn said. He looked down at the floor. "So, uh, Marr tells me that you agreed to train him?"

Jaden felt the sharpness on the edges of Khedryn's question. He understood it. "I need to discuss that with the Grand Master, too."

Khedryn ran a hand along *Junker*'s bulkhead. "If that's a go, it kinda makes me odd man out, I guess." He chuckled, but Jaden knew it was forced. Khedryn and Marr had been friends for a long time. "Can't really be my first mate if he's training to become a Jedi."

"It would be difficult," Jaden acknowledged. "But let's not go too far down that path just yet."

"Marr, a Jedi." Khedryn shook his head. "It's hard for me to believe it."

"Things will work out, Khedryn."

Neither man said anything more as they entered *Junker*'s galley. The smell of fresh caf, ubiquitous aboard *Junker,* filled the air. Khedryn refilled his own mug, poured one for Jaden.

"Spike of pulkay?" Khedryn asked.

"No, thanks."

Khedryn started to spike his caf with a shot of the liquor but reconsidered and took the caf straight. "Kinda takes the fun out of it, drinking alone. Flying's the same way."

Jaden took his point but said nothing.

As if by unspoken agreement, they did not sit at the table where the three of them and Relin, a Jedi transported from four thousand years in the past, had sat and planned their assault on a Sith dreadnought. Relin had been killed in the assault, and Jaden, Marr, and Khedryn had nearly been killed. Instead, they sat at the counter.

"To Relin," Khedryn said, and lifted his mug in a toast.

"To Relin," Jaden answered.

They sipped their caf in silence for a time before Khedryn said, "I've been thinking about something."

Jaden sipped his caf and waited.

"Those clones flew their ship right through that exploded dreadnought. And Relin told us that ship was full of an ore that augmented the power of the Force."

"Augmented the dark side," Jaden said.

"Right, right. Well, they flew right through it." Khedryn looked at the table where they had sat with Relin, then out the viewport. "Makes you wonder what it might have done to them."

Jaden had been thinking, and worrying, about much the same thing. "That it does."

Soldier still felt supercharged, alive with power. The doctors at the facility would have named the power "the dark side" of the Force, but Soldier rejected their labels. To him, it was just power, and labels be damned.

They'd all felt it, even the children, as the stolen cloakshape fighter carrying them had blazed away from the frozen moon and through the aftermath of the exploded starship. Between the surface of the moon and the safety of outer space had hung a cloud of flaming debris, superheated gas, and . . . something more.

Soldier assumed that the exploded starship had been carrying something related to the Force, something powerful, a Sith artifact maybe, and that the vessel's destruction had diffused whatever it was through the moon's thin atmosphere, its essence saturating the sky, filling the air with power, with potential.

They'd felt it more strongly as they ascended, first as a

prickling on the skin, then as an upsurge of emotion that sent him alternately through moments of glee, rage, terror, and love. Soldier's emotions had swung pendulously from one to another. The clones had stood around in the makeshift cargo hold of the cloakshape and murmured questions while the children giggled and squirmed.

"What is that?" Maker had asked, his eyes wide. "Seer?"

But Seer had not answered. She'd seemed lost in one of her trances, eyes closed and swaying, in communion with Mother.

The feeling had intensified with each passing moment, a surge at once terrifying and exhilarating. Force lightning had leaked from Soldier's fingertips, twined around his hands, crackling. He stared at his fingers in wonder, grinning. The emotions of the other clones reached through their community's shared empathic connection and bombarded him with feeling. He felt their glee, their ecstasy, their anger. His emotions fed on theirs, and theirs on his, a never-ending feedback loop, an ouroboros of emotional energy that made him feel as if he were boiling inside, filling with emotional steam that he could vent only in bestial shouts, in discharges of lightning. The cargo bay was chaotic. Only his concern for the children kept him grounded. He stood over them protectively.

"It is a sign from Mother!" Seer suddenly shouted above the tumult. She had her eyes closed and raised her hands above her hairless head toward the ceiling. "She has blessed our exodus!"

The others—Maker, Two-Blade, Hunter, all of them— had echoed her words, their voices slurred from the rush of power.

"It is a gift from Mother. A gift."

The children had mostly laughed or groaned, their connection to the Force still weak.

"What is it, Soldier?" Grace had asked him in her small voice.

He could not bring himself to mention Mother, so he simply said, "It is power, Grace. Be still now."

And then the cloakshape had flown through the cloud and the power suffusing the air had bled through the hull and touched them all directly.

It had hit Soldier like an electric shock, torn open some deeper connection to the Force, and sent him to his knees.

"Soldier!" Grace said in alarm.

He waved her away, afraid that he could not control the power boiling in him.

The rest of the Community, too, had shouted aloud as the power entered them. Seer had begun to moan in ecstasy, the children—even Grace—to laugh aloud, a touch of wildness in the sound.

New channels into the Force opened and power rushed to fill the voids. Soldier's mind spun. Perception widened. His eyes watered and he gripped his head in his hands, as if trying to contain his expanded understanding.

The ship had veered wildly—Runner was piloting and he, too, must have been overcome. Everyone shouted as the sudden lurch threw them against the far wall of the cargo bay. Hunter cradled Grace and Blessing—her children—to her chest to protect them from the impact. Soldier, the most clearheaded of them all, had cushioned their impact with the Force, sparing them all broken bones, and the ship had ridden the lurch into a spin, throwing them across the cargo bay once more like so much flotsam, tipping the stasis chambers standing along one side of the bay. The chambers skidded across the floor, the shriek of metal on metal joining the chorus of the clones. Soldier and Scar both raised a hand and used the Force to halt the chambers two meters before they crushed the still-entranced Seer against the bulkhead.

Fighting against the push and pull of the ship's lurches, Soldier had climbed to his feet and wound through the chaos of the cargo bay to the cockpit. He found Runner in the pilot's chair, his arms out wide, his head thrown back, eyes closed, drool dripping from a vacant smile. Soldier pushed him to the floor and slammed a fist on the instrument panel to engage the autopilot. He turned and grabbed Runner by the shirt.

"You sit in this seat, you fly the ship!" he said, but Runner, lost in the surge of power, seemed not to hear him.

As the autopilot righted the ship, Soldier followed the sounds of the clones and the children back toward the cargo bay. Before he reached it, the emotional surge changed tenor. Through his connection with the other clones, he felt their fear grow. Then he felt their pain, and the laughter of the children give way to wails, then to shrieks of agony. The exultant exclamations of the clones stepped aside for screams of pain.

All but for Seer, whose voice he could still hear above the rest, praising Mother over the screams.

Soldier closed down the empathic connection as best he could and sprinted through the corridor to the cargo bay. He reached it and stepped into a storm of screams and pain.

Hunter lay in a fetal position, teeth bared in a grimace as she screamed. In her arms she cradled Blessing and Grace. Her eyes were open, vacant, and her breath came so fast between screams that Soldier thought she might hyperventilate. The girls, too, had their eyes open. Grace stared at Soldier, her welling eyes full of pain. Thankfully the children were not screaming. Instead, they lay entirely still, mouths partway open, eyes glassy. To Soldier they looked like corpses who did not yet realize they were dead.

The possibility of the children dying made his legs go weak.

"Grace," he called. "Blessing."

Neither moved. Neither seemed to hear him.

What had happened? He'd been gone only minutes.

Maker sat cross-legged on the floor, rocking, his mouth open and uttering guttural howls at intervals. His fingernails had scratched bloody grooves down the length of his forearm and he continued to worry at them even as his blood puddled on the floor. Repulsed, Soldier went to him and grabbed his hands.

"Stop it," Soldier said to him, but Maker seemed not to hear, and his hands continued to try for his wounds.

Scar's high-pitched screams pulled Soldier around. She lay on the ground near one of the overturned stasis chambers, writhing, the exposed areas of her blotchy skin visibly pulsing, as if thousands of insects crawled beneath her epidermis and sought exit through her pores.

"Help me!" she cried in a spray of spit, her face distorted by the crawling. "Help me!"

But no one moved to help her. Seer was too lost in her trance, still praising Mother, and the others were too lost in their pain. Soldier recovered himself, ran to Scar, crouched beside her, and pulled her to him. She was thin, her long dark hair lank on her drawn face. He tried to keep the revulsion from his face as her skin shifted and bulged under his touch.

"Help me, Soldier!"

"It's the sickness," Soldier said, feeling helpless. "It has to be. The sickness."

The sickness afflicted all of them—all of them but him—but he'd never seen the symptoms so bad, never seen them come on so quickly. The doctors at the facility had altered the midi-chlorians in their blood, and it seemed their altered blood was responding to the same phenomenon that had given them a surge in power. The sickness was surging, too. Soldier had to get the medicine.

"I'll be right back," he said to Scar, and she answered him with a scream. The bulges in her face grew larger, darkened, formed pustules, distorting her expression, then burst in a spray of pink fluid that spattered Soldier's face and clothes.

"What is happening to me?" she screamed.

His mind turned to the children. They were sick, too. He looked over at Grace, Blessing, and Gift, but they looked all right.

Soldier stood, his legs weak under him. He saw the chest they'd used to bring the remaining medicine from the moon. It was near the far wall and Two-Blade stood near it, his eyes feral, his hands on his lightsaber hilts. Two-Blade did not seem to be in pain, at least not yet. He murmured something incomprehensible over the screams and shifted on his feet, as though preparing for a fight.

Soldier headed for the chest of meds, slowly, hands held up to show harmlessness. Two-Blade's eyes hardened, his muscles a coiled spring. Sweat beaded his brow. His mouth was a hard line in the nest of his beard. His green eyes fixed on Soldier, but he blinked often and seemed not to see clearly. His pupils were fully dilated, black holes that saw something other than the real world. As Soldier watched, slight palpitations under the skin of Two-Blade's face foretold a fate like Scar's.

"I need the meds," Soldier said, nodding at the chest behind Two-Blade.

"Soldier," Two-Blade hissed.

Soldier tried to step around him but Two-Blade blocked his way. His chest rose and fell like a bellows. Soldier swallowed a flash of irritation. The screams and moans of the surviving clones put him on edge. Seer's imprecations to Mother were a pebble in the boot of his mind.

"Get out of my way," Soldier said. He pushed past Two-Blade and knelt before the chest.

The sizzle of igniting lightsabers sounded from behind him and instinct took over. He rolled to his left, bounded to his feet, took his own blade in hand, and ignited it. The red line sparked and hissed, a mirror of his mood. Anger kindled in him and the surge of power affecting them all lit it into a bonfire. Force lightning shot from his fingers, coiled around his hilt, his blade. He reveled in the newfound intensity of his power.

Two-Blade, his reddish-orange blades jutting from the hilts he held in both fists, snarled.

"It always had to end this way, Soldier. You aren't one of us."

"You're not thinking clearly," Soldier said, but his heart wasn't in the protest. He wanted to fight, wanted to kill.

Two-Blade snarled and lunged forward with blades low. Soldier bounded back, slapped both blades aside with his own lightsaber, and raised his blade for a killing strike. Before he did, Two-Blade's roar of rage turned to a groan of pain and he fell to the floor, grasping his head, writhing, screaming. His blades deactivated and his flesh crawled, bulged, rippled.

Soldier stood over him, blade in hand, violence still fresh in his mind. It would be so easy to cut Two-Blade down, so easy. He raised his lightsaber. . . .

Scar's screams of pain reached a crescendo, popped the balloon of his rage, and brought him back to himself. He recalled his purpose. With difficulty, he lowered his blade and deactivated it. He was sweating. The anger boiled in him, simmering—*It always had to end this way*—but he controlled it.

He took a deep, calming breath and spared a glance back at Scar. He was too late. Open sores on her face and arms leaked fluid, ragged craters erupting pus.

"Soldier," she mouthed, and raised one of her hands for a moment before it fell slack to her side. Her body twitched once, twice, then lay still. Her vacant, dead eyes, turned bloodred by burst capillaries, stared accusations at Soldier.

Soldier cursed and kicked Two-Blade in the ribs. Soldier did not know why he cared. Except for the children, the rest of the clones cared little for him. But he could not deny that he did have feelings for them.

And so he would do what he always did—take care of them.

He knelt before the case that contained the hypos. Thirty doses of the meds remained. They had expected the doses to last them weeks, maybe longer, but whatever they'd flown through had exacted a price for their increased connection to the Force—it had accelerated their illness. Presumably it would also speed the onset of the madness that inevitably came with the sickness. As bodies failed, so too would minds. Two-Blade was already almost gone. Hunter, too. A Jedi had come to the moon, killed one of the clones, but the rest had escaped to . . . To what?

While the screams and groans of the sick resounded off the walls, Soldier measured out doses with steady hands. He watched his skin as he worked, afraid that he would see the same crawling mounds he had seen on Scar, but to his relief, he saw nothing. The doctors at the facility had made him well, it seemed.

When he'd prepared enough injections, he turned and threw himself back into the storm of their agony, moving from one to another, injecting each with the medicine the doctors had created to keep them alive and sane. He started with the children, then Two-Blade, then Hunter. Each calmed moments after the injection, eyelids heavy, breathing slow and regular. He put a hand on Grace's head, smoothed her red hair, did the same with

Hunter. Hunter was soaked with sweat. She shivered at his touch, but her skin, at least, no longer crawled.

"Where is Alpha?" Hunter asked, her eyes lucid for at least the moment. She held Grace and Blessing—both fathered by Alpha—in her arms. The girls had closed their eyes. They appeared to be sleeping, but their pinched faces and tiny whimpers bespoke continuing pain. The children always suffered the most from the illness. Most of the clones' offspring had died young over the years.

"Alpha is dead," Soldier said. "The Jedi killed him. You know that, Hunter."

She stared at him a long moment, as if not comprehending.

"It should have been you," she said at last, her speech slurred, and closed her eyes.

The words ablated harmlessly on the emotional armor in which Soldier usually sheathed himself. He'd heard them or something similar often enough over the years. He was different from the others. They knew it and he knew it. He was the best of them, the final specimen created by the doctors, and he showed no signs of the illness that afflicted the rest. Only the children treated him as one of them.

"Do you need water?" Soldier asked her.

"No," she said, her voice soft, as if she had forgotten her harsh words from a moment before.

"Rest, then. I will get you blankets for the children."

He started to stand but her hand closed on his forearm, her grip a fevered vise. "Why is this happening, Soldier?"

He did not trust himself to answer, but he didn't have to. She answered for him.

"Mother is testing her faithful," she said. She smiled and nodded distantly. "We will pass this test, as we have all the others."

Soldier patted her hand and stood. His eyes fell on

Scar's body, her face covered in leaking sores. He imagined infected blood crawling across the floor, boring into the flesh of the others. But he knew it was fanciful. He thought Mother might be fanciful, too, but knew better than to say so. If Mother was real and *was* testing them, then Scar had already failed. Others would, too, he had no doubt.

He got blankets for the children and picked his way through his unconscious and semiconscious siblings, uttering soft words of encouragement. He finally made his way across the cargo bay to Seer. He still had not injected her. With the screams of the other clones ended by the meds, Seer's prayers to Mother filled the silence.

Before he reached her, Maker sat up and rose on unsteady legs.

"Soldier," Maker said. "Come here."

"In a moment," Soldier said.

"Now," Maker said, and occupied the space between Seer and Soldier. Maker's expression was twitchy, uncontrolled. The others looked on or not, their expressions vacant. Maker stepped close to Soldier and spoke through bared teeth.

"You aren't sick," he said, his voice the low volume of a threat.

From behind Soldier, Two-Blade murmured agreement, though he never opened his eyes. Blessing and Grace whimpered. They always disliked conflict among the members of the Community.

"And you aren't because I gave you the meds," Soldier answered.

Maker's eyes moved from Soldier to Scar's body. Maker and Scar had been mates, and Scar's corpse was a whetstone that sharpened Maker's rage. Through their empathic connection, Soldier could feel the anger growing in Maker, a dark cloud that promised a storm.

"Why aren't you sick, Soldier?" Maker asked. His

body twitched, a spasm that shook him from head to toe. "I can feel them crawling under my skin, the midis. Do you feel them?"

Soldier did not answer. He looked past Maker toward Seer.

"Seer—"

"She won't help you," Maker snapped.

The anger kindled in Soldier by Two-Blade erupted into a sudden flare of heat. Once started, he could not stop the conflagration. He did not *want* to stop the conflagration. He needed to vent the pressure building in him and Maker was as good a way as any. He stepped nearer to Maker, who stood a hand taller than him, until they were nose to nose.

"I don't need her help, Maker."

Maker sneered. Soldier readied himself, fell into the Force.

The anger and fear in the room swirled around them, coalesced into a powerful emotional brew. Maker fed off it, as did Soldier, both of them stuck in a feedback loop that could end only one way.

Maker snatched the hilt of his lightsaber, activated it, and stabbed at Soldier's abdomen, but Soldier lurched sideways, spun, and used the momentum of the spin to put a Force-augmented kick into Maker's chest. The impact blew the air from Maker's lungs and sent him flying five meters across the cargo bay. He hit the wall, bounced off it, roared, and charged Soldier, leaping over the toppled stasis chamber.

The other clones, perhaps roused by the rising tide of anger and power, moaned and shouted.

The power coursing through Soldier intensified. He could not control it. He gave it voice in a shout of rage. Force lightning shot from his fingertips, swirled around him. He extended his left hand and discharged it at

Maker. It slammed into him, halted his charge, and lifted him from his feet. Maker screamed.

Soldier relished his pain. Holding Maker aloft, Soldier gestured with his right hand and sent Maker flying into the bulkhead. He hit it hard enough to break bones, then slid toward the floor. Still Soldier did not release him. Using the Force, he slammed him into the bulkhead again, again, again.

Maker's lightsaber fell from his hand, his arms and legs flailed about as if disconnected from his body, the bones broken, torn from their joints. He looked like a child's doll. Soldier felt Maker's pain, let it feed his rage, his power.

Soldier narrowed his focus, gestured with his forefinger and thumb, and seized Maker's throat in a Force choke. Maker clutched at his neck, gagging. With his other hand, Soldier sent another blast of Force lightning spiraling at Maker. It caught him up in a shroud of crackling energy, but Soldier's Force choke denied him any screams of pain.

Soldier stared into Maker's face while Maker's legs kicked feebly and his face purpled. Soldier continued to squeeze until Maker went still. Only then did he let the body fall to the floor. Maker's corpse lay beside that of Scar, his flesh disfigured by Soldier, hers by the illness.

Other than Soldier's breathing, the cargo bay fell still. Even Seer quieted, ceasing her prayers. The combat and Maker's death seemed to have drained some of the emotion out of the air. Or perhaps it was just the medicine working.

Soldier glanced around. The others, in the grip of the accelerated symptoms of the illness, in the grip of their growing madness, seemed to barely comprehend what had happened. He was pleased the children had not seen it. He would have been ashamed.

He stood there, alone with himself, and studied his

hands. He had never before been capable of Force light-ning of such power. He looked up to see Seer, finally out of her trance, staring at him, her eyes looking through him. She looked at Maker's body, back at Soldier. He brandished a hypo.

"You need the medicine, too, Seer."

She shook her head slowly and smiled. Her beauty struck him, as it often did: the symmetry of her features, her deep-set eyes.

"No I don't," she said. "I am more strongly connected to Mother now than ever. She will test us before we reach her. Do you hear me?" She spoke not just to Sol-dier but to all of them. "She *will* test us! Do not lose faith, not now! Those who do will never reach Mother."

To Soldier's surprise, the surviving clones murmured assent. They lived in a mental space incomprehensible to Soldier, though he'd never have said as much aloud.

He picked his way through them until he stood before Seer. Had he been one of them, he might have bowed to her. But he was not one of them.

"You need the hypo, Seer. You were the last of them before . . ."

"Before you."

He nodded. "Before me. But they hadn't bred out the illness even with you. Whatever we flew through—"

"Mother's blessing."

"Yes. The . . . blessing. It will affect you, too. Later than the others, maybe. But it will."

She smiled, then reached up and touched Soldier's face.

"You are not like us, Soldier."

"No," he said, and fought down a flash of anger. "I'm not. I don't have the sickness."

The soft smile did not leave her face. "That's not what I mean. You don't believe." Her smile faded, her expres-sion hardened, and she took his face in her hand, her grip firm. "I've seen the doubt in you. As I did in Wry."

Wry. The others had torn him apart when he had given voice to his doubts. His death had taught Soldier the value of silence.

"Runner needs the meds, too," he said, and made to move past Seer to the cockpit.

She stopped him with a hand on his chest. "I will make you believe, Soldier."

They shared a look, saying nothing, saying everything.

She held her arm out for an injection. "This is the only hypo I will have. When we reach Mother, she will heal us, all of us. Including you, Soldier."

Soldier stared into Seer's intense, dark eyes, softened his expression, nodded, and shot the hypo into her shoulder. Without another word, he moved past her to the cockpit. Runner lay curled up on the floor, moaning. The injection mitigated his pain and Soldier carried him back to the cargo bay and laid him beside Hunter and Grace and Gift. Seer had already returned to her prayers, her quiet communion with Mother. Soldier wondered what Seer heard during her trances.

He recalled the first time that Seer, in hushed, reverent tones, had told them of her connection through the Force to Mother. She had first sensed Mother years ago, and had offered sermons to them after the doctors had left them alone for the night, when they sat alone in their transparisteel-ceilinged observation chamber.

After Wry's death, Soldier had gone along with their plans in stoic silence. For years they had plotted, planned. In the dark of their cages, working only by touch and their connection to the Force and to one another, they'd secretly constructed lightsabers, honed their powers, and bided their time until the reckoning. Soldier still did not know how Seer had obtained crystals to power the lightsabers.

And when the reckoning had come, when Seer had at last commanded them to kill, they had murdered every sentient in the facility and sacrificed their bodies to the altar they'd made to Mother. And then . . .

And then they'd lived alone on the arctic moon, eating what they could find, worshipping Mother and waiting, always waiting. Over the years—years of little food, little hope, and constant cold—Mother had become their purpose, the axis around which their existences turned. And Seer had become their prophet. Soldier had thought they'd never leave the moon, despite Seer's constant proclamations to the contrary. And then a ship had come, bearing a Jedi, just as Seer had said it would. Alpha had insisted on facing the Jedi while the rest of them had fled in a stolen ship.

I will make you believe, Soldier.

He shook his head, pushed the pernicious notion of faith from his mind, and returned to the cockpit to be alone. The sight of the stars, blinking in the unending void, enthralled him. Up to then, he'd spent his entire existence within the confines of a frozen facility not more than a few square kilometers in area. Staring out the transparisteel of the cloakshape's cockpit, he saw endless space, endless possibility.

And yet he had no idea where they were going, or what they would do when they arrived. Only Seer knew, and Seer would go mad within days—as would the rest of them, except him—unless they obtained more medicine.

And if that happened, what would he do? They were his purpose—especially the children—as much as Mother was theirs.

He made up his mind, stood, and headed back to the cargo bay, to Seer.

chapter three

DARTH WYYRLOK STRODE INTO THE DARK CONFERENCE room, leaving the door open behind him. A smooth metal conference table dominated the circular, domed chamber. A pyramidal vidscreen sat centermost on the table. A small, sealed metal case with a retinal scan lock sat on the table, waiting for him. Within it was technology—mindspears—that One Sith agents had found in forgotten Rakatan ruins, deep in the Unknown Regions. The technology had formed the basis of the Master's cloning program. One Sith scientists had been unable to duplicate its fiber-photon, dark side–based technology, so they had only a limited supply. Eyeing the case, Wyyrlok felt the faint, familiar pulse of dark-side energy emanating from it.

Thunder from a storm outside vibrated the walls of the tower. Rain thumped against the windows. Lightning traced a jagged seam the length of the night sky, the flash casting the soaring tombs and spires of Korriban in silhouette.

Staring out at the storm through the large transparisteel window, Wyyrlok wondered if the Master controlled the weather on Korriban, even as he journeyed in dreams.

As if in answer, the storm growled thunder, and another bolt of lightning made glowing veins in the sky. The dark-side energy of the planet pulsed, rippled.

Wyyrlok wondered, not for the first time, when the Master would emerge from his sleep to conquer and reestablish the Sith. Until then, the One Sith would only lurk around the edges of galactic events. Wyyrlok accepted that. His role was to serve, and the endgame of the Master's plans stretched not through years, but centuries.

Wyyrlok checked his wrist chrono and saw that Nyss was late. He decided to start on his own and sat at one of the table's high-backed, contoured chairs.

He activated the vidscreen with a touchpad built into the table and watched the mute replay of the transmission from the frozen moon. He'd already seen it once, but he needed to see it again, to ensure he had missed nothing and to confirm his thinking.

The transmission was a copy of the visual stimuli received by the One Sith's Anzat agent, Kell Douro. The One Sith had attached a recorder to Douro's optic nerve and brain that could be activated or deactivated as the Master willed. The Anzat had been as much a construct as a droid. Of course, he had never known that he had been made a sentient recording device, though Wyyrlok knew that Douro had often experienced lost time, memory lapses, and religious epiphanies—side effects of the implantation. When active, the implant had transmitted the visual data back to Douro's ship, where a secret subroutine in the main computer had opened an encrypted subspace protocol and sent the data to Korriban for review.

There was another roll of thunder. Wyyrlok ran a hand over his head, his fingers lingering on his damaged left horn. He wondered if the Master had placed a similar device in *his* eye and brain. But then, perhaps the Master did not need such a device for him. He often felt that the Master could read his mind directly.

A blaster shot to Douro's head had ended the transmissions. But not before the One Sith had received a raft of information from Douro's most recent mission: tracking the Jedi Jaden Korr to a frozen, uncharted moon in the Unknown Regions. And there, Douro had found something of enormous interest.

Using the touchpad, Wyyrlok sped through the grainy video feed—images of space, Douro's short time on Fhost.

Wyyrlok stopped at a moment in a cantina in which Jaden Korr had sensed Douro and turned to face him. There was no sound in the recording. Wyyrlok studied the expression on Korr's face.

"Remarkable," he said softly. He knew Jaden's face quite well.

He continued the recording until he reached the point at which Douro had descended toward the frozen moon. Wyyrlok saw the fuzzy, pixilated, overhead view of a large, snow-covered facility. He recognized it as a Thrawn-era cloning lab. To judge from the architecture and power generators, he surmised it had been used a bit later in the Grand Admiral's secret cloning program than the sites the One Sith had previously plundered for technology.

The possibilities of that intrigued him.

"Could it be?" he mused.

Not for the first time, he wondered how much of recent events the Master had foreseen, how far into the future the Master's foresight extended. It was as though the Master had a recorder on the eye of fate, and through it saw and anticipated events like no one else.

Despite himself, Wyyrlok felt awed by the Master's power.

Outside, the rain turned to hail and pelted the exterior windows. Lightning once more drew glowing angles across the sky.

Wyyrlok started the recording again and watched

through Douro's eyes as the Anzat set down on the moon. He sped through the images until he reached the point at which Douro had entered the facility. He stopped the video here and there as Douro stalked the corridors, enhancing this or that frame in hopes that something would confirm his suspicions. Nothing he saw made him certain, but everything was suggestive.

The timing was right. The location was right.

"It could be," he said.

An ache rooted in the back of Wyyrlok's head. At first he thought it the ghost of the wound that had taken half his horn, but no, it was something else. He wondered again about a possible implant, but then his connection to the Force grew weaker, attenuated. The power emanating from the case went quiescent. The disconnect was not altogether strange to him, though it remained uncomfortable. He recognized its source, had felt it many times in the past. Out of habit, his hand moved toward his lightsaber hilt, though he knew that the weapon would not function—the crystal powering it would have temporarily lost its attunement to the Force.

"How long have you been standing there?" he asked over his shoulder.

A soft rustle, then, "Not long."

Nyss's voice was as soft as a pillow.

Wyyrlok turned in his chair to face him.

The darkness in the hallway seemed deeper than usual, like ink, and Nyss Nenn stood in the midst of the pitch, his form lost in the shadows, his hairless face and head floating like a pale moon in the darkness. All Umbarans, born on a dim planet shrouded in darkness, lived in shadow. But Nyss seemed *of* shadow. He was not a Force user, not in the ordinary sense. But he was attuned to the Force somehow. Perhaps the Master knew the nature of Nyss's relationship to the Force, but Wyyrlok did not; it was beyond his comprehension.

What he did know was that Nyss's presence, and that of his twin sister, Syll, could disrupt a Force sensitive's connection to the Force. Nyss and Syll were unique among Umbarans and one of the greatest weapons the One Sith possessed. They could turn a Force user into an ordinary sentient.

Wyyrlok stared past Nyss at the darkness of the hall, looking for Syll.

"My sister isn't with me," Nyss said.

Wyyrlok found that hard to believe. The two were rarely apart. Their relationship was odd, psychologically symbiotic.

Lightning split the sky, casting the room in a flash of lurid light. Nyss winced in the sudden illumination. Wyyrlok took comfort in the Umbaran's discomfort. Despite Nyss's power, light disquieted him.

"Sit," Wyyrlok said, and gestured at a chair, though not the one nearest him. "And do not use your power in my presence. I find it . . . irritating."

"I should think," Nyss said. He inclined his head, and the pain in Wyyrlok's skull slowly faded. The Umbaran glided into the room, as silent as a ghost, and slid into a chair. His eyes fell on the case.

"Do you feel it?" Wyyrlok asked, nodding at the case.

"You know I don't," said Nyss.

"I know you *can't*," said Wyyrlok.

Nyss simply stared, and Wyyrlok continued: "The Master has a task for you. Therefore you should see this."

Wyyrlok replayed the vid from the point at which Douro set down on the moon. He wanted to see if Nyss's conclusions matched his own.

Nyss's eyes, set deep in shadowed sockets, shone in the glare of the vid, his pupils enormous. "That facility postdates the sites we found previously," he said, watching as Douro entered the facility.

"I agree. And therefore it is of importance to the Master."

Though Nyss had suppressed his power, Wyyrlok still found proximity to the Umbaran distasteful. The Force connected all living things and was powered by all living things, yet Nyss and his sister seemed to exist outside of the Force somehow. They were holes, gaps in the network of life, alive to ordinary senses, but dead to the Force. It was as if Nyss *was* dead.

The two of them watched as Douro moved deeper into the abandoned cloning facility. They saw him beat a human male and leave him lying there, his face shattered, bleeding.

"He is not dead," Nyss observed.

"Indeed not," Wyyrlok said, knowing that the human male ultimately killed Douro.

"That was a mistake," Nyss said.

"More than you know."

Nyss watched the recording. Wyyrlok watched Nyss.

After a few more moments, Nyss asked, "The Master believes there's technology of value in the facility?"

The One Sith had spent decades plundering Thrawn-era cloning facilities, plumbing their secrets. They'd taken Thrawn's secret technology and improved it markedly, in part by using the Rakatan biotechnology contained in the metal case. They'd also learned the purpose of the Grand Admiral's program. The fact that he had actually accomplished his goal, and that no one but the One Sith knew even after so many years, made Thrawn's plan and its execution all the more impressive. Of course, the Grand Admiral had never seen the final stages of the plan come to fruition—he'd been killed soon after placing the clone on Coruscant. It had fallen to the One Sith to complete the Grand Admiral's plot.

"Wyyrlok," Nyss said, "there is technology there?"

"*Darth* Wyyrlok," Wyyrlok corrected. "Do not forget your place, Umbaran. And not technology, as such, no."

"Then what?"

"Continue to watch."

Nyss watched intently as the rest of the recording played. Even at only a meter away from Wyyrlok, the Umbaran merged so well with the darkness in the chamber that his outline blurred into the shadows. He seemed to amplify the darkness and to wear it like a shroud.

Nyss leaned forward when Jaden Korr came on-screen. The Jedi was in the midst of combat with a savage-looking human male wearing tattered clothing and wielding a red lightsaber. They fought on the edge of a deep pit in the floor of a large room. Douro must have been watching the combat from the darkness, unseen by the combatants.

"That is a third-generation Spaarti cloning cylinder," Nyss said. "Nothing we haven't seen before."

Wyyrlok froze the picture, centered it on the savage male's features, and magnified. Long white hair half-covered a strong-jawed, angular face.

"Do you recognize the features?"

Nyss shook his head.

"That is a clone of Jedi Master Kam Solusar."

Realization dawned on Nyss's face. "So it is. Thrawn cloned a Jedi."

"Thrawn cloned multiple Jedi and Sith. There, in that facility. Therefore . . ."

Nyss finished for him. ". . . it may be where Thrawn birthed one of the final clones for the project. Given the dates suggested by its architecture and power signature, and the fact that the Solusar clone survived so long without succumbing to illness, I'd say it's likely. We could be looking at the facility where Thrawn grew the Prime. We should investigate it."

Wyyrlok shook his head, causing his lethorns—fleshy

growths that hung from each side of his head and termi-
nated in long, slender horns like those on the top of his
head—to sway. "The Jedi Jaden Korr will have notified
the Order by now. Skywalker will send an investigative
team to the moon. We cannot risk exposure. Therefore,
we will never know if the mole was grown there."

"We could infiltrate it, Syll and I. Even with Skywalker's team there. You know that we can."

Wyyrlok did not doubt it. "The Master deems that too
dangerous. Besides, there is no need. Other clones escaped."

Nyss fixed his dark eyes on him—dead eyes, the pupils
black holes. "You're certain?"

"Douro's ship has a beacon that relays not only its location but the number of life-forms aboard."

"How many?"

"Eleven were aboard when the ship left the moon.
There are nine, now."

"They are dying," Nyss said.

"Or they killed two of their number."

Nyss ran a hand over his bald head, his excitement
palpable. "You want me to find them. See if a Prime is
among them?"

"We do. But there is more of interest. Watch."

Wyyrlok let the tape play, and they watched the combat between Jaden Korr and the Solusar clone. The
lightsabers, green and red, made blurred wedges in the
air.

"Jaden Korr fights well," Nyss said.

Wyyrlok shrugged.

Eventually Korr lost three fingers as the Solusar clone
disarmed him and drove him into the cloning cylinder.
For a moment, the recording lost the combat. But Douro
must have circled and moved closer to get a view of the
interior of the cylinder. There, they saw Korr on his
knees, his left hand held before his face and—

"Freeze it there," Nyss said, half-standing and staring at the screen. For a moment, he lost control of his power, and a headache flared in Wyyrlok's skull.

"Is that what I think it is?" Nyss asked. "Magnify."

Wyyrlok already knew what it was, but it pleased him that Nyss saw it and understood the implications.

He centered the image on Korr's hand and magnified.

Bolts of Force lightning extended from his fingertips, jagged green lines summoned by fear or anger.

Outside, ordinary lightning split the sky. Thunder rumbled.

"He is falling," Nyss observed in a whisper. He retook control of his power. "It is too soon, isn't it?"

His headache gone, Wyyrlok nodded. "The Master did not expect him to fall so readily. Therefore, you will find him, too."

"And?"

Wyyrlok nodded at the case of mindspears on the table. "And do what needs to be done."

Nyss clucked his tongue on the roof of his mouth, then nodded slowly, already planning. "Korr will hunt the clones," he said. "We may be able to complete both tasks at once."

"I thought the same thing," Wyyrlok said, then added, "Therefore the Master wishes you to take an Iteration."

Nyss turned in his chair and faced him full on. Looking at the Umbaran's smooth, expressionless face, Wyyrlok felt the true otherness of Nyss. He was unlike the Sith, unlike the Jedi, unlike anyone else in the universe save his sister.

"Awake?" Nyss asked.

"Yes, but in stasis until everything is ready." Wyyrlok slid the case across the table to Nyss. "There are two spikes in the case. One blank for later. And one basic to be used now, to awaken the Iteration."

Nyss laid his pale hands on the case. "It's up to date?"

"Up to date enough," Wyyrlok said. "You know how valuable these are. We have few left. The Iteration's appearance, his grooming, has been matched to that of the mole."

"When should we leave?" Nyss asked.

"Immediately. The beacon on Douro's ship shows that a course has been set for Fhost."

Nyss rose, tucked the case under his arm. "We can leave within the hour. Let's go, Syll."

Nyss smiled at Wyyrlok as Syll slipped from the shadows on the other side of the room and threw back her hood. Her smile was a tight, slightly upturned curl of lips that never reached her dark eyes. Like her brother, she was pale and slightly built. Short black hair haloed the pale oval of her face.

It occurred to Wyyrlok that Nyss had not lost control of his power during the conversation. Probably Syll had been toying with Wyyrlok.

Wyyrlok licked his lips and tried to keep the surprise and anger from his face. He must have looked at her and past her several times during the briefing.

"You tread dangerously," he said, and his hand fell to his lightsaber.

Nyss only smiled. He stood, bowed, collected the case, and glided out of the room with his sister.

After they'd gone, Wyyrlok rewound the recording back to the point at which Kell was in orbit around the moon. The recording showed a ship in the distance, a huge blade-shaped dreadnought bristling with weapons. Wyrrlock had never seen one like it. The One Sith's technicians had analyzed the images and concluded that it was a craft modeled on an ancient Sith design. Wyyrlok wondered what else had happened in the system and what had happened to the ship.

Outside, the storm raged.

* * *

She could not recall a particular moment when she had become self-aware. Sentience had not occurred in a revelatory flash. Instead it had come in a series of gradual steps, a long climb up from darkness to light, from thing to person.

In that way, she became self-aware.

She did not know how long it had taken. Back then she'd had little sense of time. But she surmised, now, that it had taken millennia.

After awareness of herself came awareness of the Force. She mistook it as her own power at first, but soon understood that she was *of* the Force, but was not herself the Force. Perhaps she had been the Force once, but self-awareness had severed her from it, put an irrevocable barrier between the Force and her self-aware mind. The price of her sentience was solitude. The Force existed separately from her, surrounded her, connected her to the outside, but it was not her and she was not it.

In that way, she came to realize that her existence was not the universe.

Gradually she learned that she could perceive things through the Force, things from the outside. She remembered feeling impulses she later understood to be feelings, the feelings of others who existed on the outside.

She'd wrestled with the idea of others for a long while, not understanding how thinking things could exist outside of her own perception. But they did. The feelings were not hers, but they echoed hers. She later learned names for them.

In that way, she came to understand frustration and anger.

Over time, she'd come to know her own power. And her own limitations. She was bound, trapped in a prison made of lines and spirals and coils, a geometry of bondage with only the dead for company. She had been created and her creators had trapped her. Her consciousness was bound in a structure that circled back on itself and left her no way to escape. She could perceive the outside, but it was beyond her reach. The others had forms, bodies; they could *move*. She could not.

Her anger and frustration grew.

In her desperation, she reached out through the Force, casting her feelings out into the universe, millions of threads in all directions, in hopes that one of those on the outside would perceive her, would help her. From time to time over the millennia she felt a connection and rejoiced, but always the connection was too dull, too diffuse for her to communicate her needs. Help did not come. She was not understood, and in time the connection with the various others ended, unconsummated. Still she tried, century after century, millennium after millennium, occasionally touching one mind or another, taking what solace she could in that small contact. But the partial meeting of her needs did not dilute her frustration and anger; it intensified it. And frustration and anger grew until she knew a new feeling.

In that way, she came to hate.

She hated her solitude. She hated her prison. She hated the others, who had freedom when she did not.

And then something had changed, perhaps in her, perhaps in the outside. She connected to a being on the outside, a more thorough connection than ever before. She had reveled in the purity of emotion they'd shared, in the mutual understanding. The other called herself Seer and she had others with her, and they, like her, were alone in the universe. They, like her, were in pain.

I will help you, she told Seer. *I will end your pain. Come to me.*

Seer called her "Mother" and promised to come.

In that way, she came to hope. But her rage went unabated.

* * *

While Khedryn returned to the cockpit, Jaden found privacy in an auxiliary communications room with a subspace transceiver. He linked his portacomp to the transceiver, went through a series of secure protocols, input his ID code, and opened a channel. Then, he waited.

In time, Grand Master Skywalker's soft but commanding voice, disembodied and ghostly, reached across the light-years. "Jaden. We had begun to worry. Are you all right?"

"I am now, Master Skywalker."

"I can feel that, Jaden. Something in you has changed, and changed for the better. There is a calmness in you that I haven't sensed for a very long time. Master Katarn, especially, will be glad to know that."

The words pleased Jaden. "Will you tell Master Katarn that I understand now, that I looked for dragons but found none?"

"Should I know what that means?"

Jaden smiled. "No, but I think he will."

"I'll tell him."

"And please accept my apology for the manner of my departure. I should have filed a flight plan."

"Yes, you should've. I imagine there is a good explanation?"

"There is an explanation. Whether it is good isn't for me to say."

"Tell me," Luke said.

For the next quarter hour, Jaden told Master Skywalker everything, a confession that, once started, he could not have stopped had he wanted to. The words poured out of him. He told Luke of his deed during the battle of Centerpoint Station, the alienation he'd felt afterward, the Force Vision he'd received and acted upon without the Order's sanction. He told him of Khedryn, Marr, the Anzat, Relin, and the ancient Sith ship, and, finally, the escaped clones.

"The Sith ship and its cargo are destroyed? Completely?"

"Yes. I will send the moon's coordinates to you so that a team can investigate the facility."

"Very good. And the clone you fought, Alpha, appeared to be grown from the DNA of Master Solusar?"

"Yes."

"Did you see any of the other clones?"

"No. Not in person."

"In your vision, then?"

Jaden swallowed. He did not want to open old wounds for Master Skywalker. The real Mara Jade Skywalker had been his wife and she had been murdered by Darth Caedus. But he did not want to withhold information. He'd been doing that for too long. Besides, the Grand Master would sense any evasion.

"I saw no faces in the Force Vision, Master Skywalker, but I heard voices that I thought I recognized."

"Whose?"

"Lumiya, Lessin, and . . . Mara."

Jaden blanched, expecting some kind of outburst. Instead, Luke said nothing, and a gulf of silence hung between them for long moments. Jaden imagined the Jedi Master inhaling deeply, eyes closed.

"Thank you, Jaden."

"I . . . do not understand, Master Skywalker. Thank you for what?"

"For telling me everything. The dark side lives in secrets kept. Remember that."

"I will."

"Now I want you to find the clones. If they're all users of the dark side, as was the case with the Solusar clone, you may have no choice but to destroy them."

"I know. Master Skywalker, there is one other thing—"

"Hold a moment, Jaden."

The connection went silent for a time as Luke attended to something on his end.

"Sorry for the interruption, Jaden. And now you wish to ask me if you can train Marr Idi Shael. Am I mistaken?"

The Grand Master's words took Jaden aback. Despite his age and experience, Jaden always felt like an apprentice when interacting with Luke Skywalker.

"I . . . you . . . no. I mean, yes. I mean . . . how did you know that?"

"I listened to your words when you spoke of him. He is quite old to begin training, Jaden. He will never be a full Jedi and there is danger in half-measures."

"I know. But he is willing and I think we do him a disservice if we refuse. Besides, I believe the Force brought me here not only to meet Relin and destroy the *Harbinger,* but also to meet Marr. I see purpose in it."

Luke considered. "I concur. Permission granted. You may begin his training immediately."

"I'm afraid it will be rudimentary, given the facilities available to me here."

Master Skywalker laughed, a sound Jaden had heard only a few times. "Jaden, Master Kenobi started my training in the cargo bay of the *Millennium Falcon.* Did you know that?"

"I did."

"The Force calls each of us differently. For you, it was enrollment at the Jedi Academy. For Marr . . ."

Jaden grinned as he eyed the worn bulkheads of *Junker.* ". . . it'll start as it did for you. In the belly of a freighter."

Jaden heard the smile in Luke's voice when he spoke next. "You don't plan to infiltrate an Imperial battle station and save a princess, do you?"

Jaden laughed aloud. "I don't think so, no."

"Good. Report back as circumstances allow. I will send assistance when I can, but it will be some time before I can dispatch anyone. There are . . . other matters transpiring here."

"Shall I return?"

"No. You must do as the Force has led you. But Jaden . . ."

"Grand Master?"

"I don't know where this will end, and I see danger ahead of you. And not just from the escaped clones. Some other forces are in play."

Jaden nodded. "The Anzat worked for someone."

"Indeed," Luke said. "The dark side is at work through more than the clones. Be careful."

"I will."

"I want to ask you something else, Jaden. You were offered a Master's rank long ago, but declined. Why?"

Jaden thought hard about the answer. "I did not think myself ready for the responsibility."

"You do now, though, which is why you're willing to train Marr?"

Jaden nodded. "I do. I do not have Master Katarn's pedagogical skills, but I see now the importance of a Master's . . . understanding of his apprentice."

"Quite so. It's a heavy responsibility."

"I understand. I'm ready."

"I believe you are. Good hunting, Jaden."

"Goodbye, Master Skywalker."

"May the Force be with you."

And that was that. Jaden would train Marr. And he would pursue the clones.

He felt more himself than he had in years.

Soldier found Seer in the corridor that connected the cargo bay to the cockpit. She sat with her back to the bulkhead, a portacomp she'd found somewhere on her lap. He saw star charts visible on the small comp screen as she touched one after another with her finger, as if plotting a path through the universe. Sweat glistened on her face and bald head. Her bloodshot eyes looked fevered, but not with illness. She did not look up when he approached, but raised a hand to stop him from speaking. He ignored her.

"We need to speak, Seer."

"Not now."

"Now."

Her brow creased in frustration. He alone among the clones did not regard her as his superior, though he knew to step lightly.

"Speak, then," she said, and closed the portacomp.

He stepped past her and closed the hatch to the cargo bay, cutting off the moans and cries of the others.

"You must have secrets to share," she said to his back, her voice all seductive mockery. "I can't wait to hear."

He steeled himself with an inhalation and turned to face her. "The most recent coordinates in the navicomp lead to a planet called Fhost. Data show it to be a back-water and very near. The onboard comp indicates that there is a medical facility in the primary city. There will be meds there. We know the mix the doctors gave us. We can get more."

She was shaking her head before he'd even finished. "No, Soldier. It's not science, not *doctors,* that will save them now. Or you. It's faith that will save us. All of us. And Mother."

"They'll need meds. Soon. So will you. The symptoms of the illness are manifesting more quickly. The madness will, too."

"Do you think me mad, Soldier?"

He shook his head too quickly. "No." He almost added, "Not yet," but resisted the impulse.

"I sometimes think that *you* are, for not seeing what is before your eyes," she said.

He dared not pick up the conversational thread she'd left dangling. "Whatever we flew through sped up the onset of the illness. It will kill us all."

A sly look entered her dark eyes. "Not you, Soldier. Never you. The doctors made you perfect. In body and mind."

"Seer . . ."

"But not in spirit, Soldier. You are not perfect in spirit. In spirit, you are the least of us."

He ignored the insult. "Some of them have only hours. You and Hunter have days. Maybe. I already burned through half the meds. The children are suffering. Unless Mother is very near, everyone will be dead before we reach her."

If we reach her, he thought. If there *is* a Mother.

She slid up the wall to her feet and stepped toward him, eyes burning. He could feel the heat generated by her lithe body through the ragged fabric of his shirt. "Do you feel her? Mother?"

He swallowed, looked away as he lied. "Sometimes. I think."

She ran her fingertips over the bare skin of his arm, and he tried and failed to deny the charge her touch put in him.

"Poor Soldier, made faithless by the ingenuity of others. Fear not. I will show you the way. You will see and you will believe."

The heat of her belief and the proximity of her body penned him in, left him no room for a reply. He stood before her, frozen, the subject of a silent inquisition. She stared into his face, her eyes measuring him and, he feared, finding him wanting. His hand twitched near the hilt of his lightsaber. She seemed not to notice and her face broke into a smile. He could not tell if it was sincere or false and his inability to tell worried him. She had become skilled at cloaking her emotional state from the others. She took emotion from them, but gave none of herself.

"In time, Soldier. You will believe, in time."

She looked away from his face, and he managed to take a breath. "Meanwhile?"

"Meanwhile, set a course for Fhost. You're right. We need meds. Mother is not close enough for us to get there in time."

The import of her words struck him like a blow. "Then . . . you know where she is?"

She smiled and looked away. "Already you are beginning to believe."

He stared at her, having no words, then turned and walked toward the cockpit. Her belief—or maybe his—pulled a question from him. He asked it over his shoulder.

"What does she say to you?"

He heard Seer inhale deeply. "She says . . . come home. Home, Soldier."

He nodded and walked away.

Before he'd cleared the corridor, she called after him, "What do you think the doctors would have done with us had we not sacrificed them to Mother? What was our purpose?"

The question embodied his entire existence. "I don't know."

"I do," Seer said. "I do."

He *wanted* to believe, wanted to find purpose in the fact of his creation, but belief melted in the heat of his reason. He suspected—and feared—that he'd have to make a purpose for himself.

chapter four

RELIEVED AFTER HIS CONFERENCE WITH MASTER SKY-walker, Jaden walked *Junker*'s corridors until he reached the cockpit. Khedryn and Marr sat in their accustomed seats running through a series of diagnostics. The cockpit door was propped open with a spare cooling coil, having been damaged by the Sith warriors Marr had fought aboard the freighter. Blaster fire had left black streaks, and bladed weapons had left deep scores in the metal.

Marr had shown considerable mettle fighting the Sith, and the fact only confirmed Jaden's thinking: Marr was ready for more advanced training.

For a time Jaden lingered in the corridor outside the cockpit, listening to his friends check one system after another. They made an impressive team, speaking little, accomplishing much. Jaden cleared his throat and stepped into the cockpit.

"She's almost ready," Khedryn said, checking the instrumentation.

Marr checked one final thing on the comp before looking up at Jaden. "What's our heading, Jad—I mean, Master?"

Marr's use of the term "Master" sounded so incongruous that it stunned both Khedryn and Jaden into temporary silence. Jaden supposed he had better get used to it.

"Fhost," Jaden said.

"From there?" Khedryn asked.

Jaden stared out the transparisteel of the cockpit. A million stars of the Unknown Regions blinked at him.

"I don't know yet. The Order wants me—wants *us*," he corrected, looking at Marr, "to find the escaped clones."

"Does 'us' mean you two, or all three of us?" Khedryn asked.

"All three of us," Jaden said. "Always."

His reply seemed to banish some lingering tension that had put lines in Khedryn's forehead. "They sending help?"

Jaden shook his head. "If there is any, it'll be long in coming. We're on our own."

Khedryn looked around for a cup of caf, saw none, patted his pockets for something, found nothing.

Marr held out a piece of chewstim from the pack he kept in his shirt pocket.

"Thanks," Khedryn said.

"Of course," Marr said. He offered Jaden a piece, and Jaden passed with a shake of his head.

"Might be just as well," Khedryn said around the chew. "No point in the Order sending someone out here to sit on their hands. We don't know where the clones are and probably won't ever find out. If they're smart, they're long gone."

Staring out at the stars of the Unknown Regions, Jaden could not help but agree. They'd have a hard time tracking the clones in all that black.

"Their possibilities are limited," Marr said. "Look." His fingers worked the instrument panel and called up a star chart of the near sectors of the Unknown Regions. "We know they're in a cloakshape fighter. And we know the kind of space an ordinary cloakshape hyperdrive can put behind it."

"Cloakshapes are tinkerers' ships," Khedryn said. "All of them are modified, Marr. You saw that one. It had a modular cargo bay tacked on to its belly. Its hyperdrive could have been modified, too. Probably was."

Marr shook the mountain of his head. "I disagree. Hyperdrives are notoriously difficult to change out in cloakshapes, so I suspect it's still standard. Maybe even slower than usual, given the cargo bay. And if it is and the clones went deeper into the Unknown Regions rather than into Republic space, then . . ."

Marr closed his eyes, and Jaden felt him drawing on the Force to perform his calculations. ". . . they would be somewhere within this radius."

With his finger on the star map, Marr drew an imaginary circle around a vast expanse of space in the Unknown Regions. He worked at the comp for a moment, then added, "And if we exclude dead systems along the hyperlanes, we're looking at this."

He tapped a key, and the semicircle of possible routes segmented into a few large slices radiating out from the known hyperlanes.

"That's still a lot of space," Khedryn said.

"It's a start, though," Jaden said. "Nicely done, Marr."

Marr beamed. "Thank you, Master."

The honorific was easier to hear the second time—for Jaden, at least, if not for Khedryn.

"Good job," Khedryn said to him awkwardly.

"Did you speak to Grand Master Skywalker?" Marr asked Jaden.

"I did. He approved your training."

Marr did not smile, merely swallowed and nodded.

"Congratulations," Khedryn said, the word pulled out of him by common courtesy and nothing else. He turned in his seat and cleared his throat. "Listen, Marr, given this . . . Jedi thing, I think we need to discuss your role aboard *Junker*."

The large expanse of Marr's forehead creased in a question. "My role?"

Khedryn's eyes, good and bad, looked off at oblique angles from Marr. "Right. Your role. See, Jaden and I were discussing your training and—"

Marr looked from Khedryn to Jaden, irritation in his eyes. "You two were discussing me?"

Khedryn nodded. "And we think it would be difficult for you to remain first mate while you're training."

"You do?" Marr said, eyeing each of them, annoyance creeping into his tone. "The two of you think that?"

"Yes," Khedryn said uncertainly, and looked to Jaden. "Right?"

Jaden crossed his arms over his chest. "The training is difficult, Marr. And—"

"Do you think I don't know that?"

"No, I presumed you knew that," Jaden stuttered.

Marr spun in his seat toward Khedryn. "Is there someone else around that you intend to employ as first mate?"

Khedryn recoiled, looked everywhere but at Marr's face, and ran a hand over his head. "No, not aboard. But I know some people—"

"Who?"

Khedryn's tone sharpened. "What do you mean 'who'? People."

"The hell you do. Listen, I'm first mate and engineer aboard this ship." He looked at Jaden and Khedryn in turn, challenging them to gainsay him. Neither did. "And *if* the training requires me to make a change, then I'll make it then. But it is my decision. Understood?"

Khedryn busied himself on the instrument console, and Jaden thought he looked relieved. "Yeah, sure, fine."

Jaden smiled. Marr had mettle, indeed. "Are you ready to continue the training?"

Marr looked to Khedryn, who waved him off. "I can handle the rest of the repairs and diagnostics. Go . . . move an object around with your mind or something. Maybe levitate a cup of caf into the cockpit for me."

As Jaden and Marr exited, Jaden heard Khedryn mutter, "What the hell's gotten into him?"

Mindful of Master Skywalker's point that training could occur anywhere, Jaden led Marr toward *Junker*'s cargo bay.

"Listen, Marr," he said as they walked. "You are very old to begin training as a Jedi. Typically, it means that it will be harder for you to overcome old thinking patterns, and that your capabilities will be capped at some point far below that of a Jedi who began training very young. That said, you have some unique talents that we may be able to harness." He thought of the Grand Master. "And there have been exceptions, but I want you to understand my thinking."

Marr stared straight ahead. "I understand."

"Good. Much of your training in the Force will come from your own focus. I'll guide you, give you tools, and answer questions, but you need to expand on what you already know and use that to learn more, question more, and then to grow more."

Marr seemed to consider that. "Does it ever stop? The learning?"

Jaden smiled. Marr's first question was a good one. "No. Your relationship to the Force is dynamic. It changes over time, just as you change over time. I learn new things every day. I learned . . . a lot on the moon. That is part of what makes this path so rewarding. And so challenging."

Marr nodded.

"Relin taught you about the mental space you reserve? The central place you hold in your mind?"

"He called it the Keep."

"Right. Master Katarn—my Master—called it the Sanctum. The name doesn't matter. The point is to recognize it as the wellspring of your relationship to the Force. Your understanding and perception will expand outward from it. You've already begun to do that. But think of the Keep as a place to which you can return to try a lesson anew."

Jaden tapped the control panel, and the gears of the cargo bay door hummed as the door slid open. A few shipping containers were all that remained in the bay. The rest had been lost in a dogfight with Sith ships.

Jaden had arranged a small shipping container into a makeshift table in the center of the bay. On it sat the hilt of the purple-bladed lightsaber he had built in his youth, the blade he had used to destroy the clone, Alpha. A small metal toolbox sat beside it.

Marr stood in the doorway, not stepping in. Jaden did not push him to enter. Marr had to take the step alone.

"That is your lightsaber," Marr observed.

"It is," Jaden said.

Marr stared at it for a moment, then stepped into the bay.

Jaden fell in beside him. "A Jedi typically crafts his own lightsaber. It's an important milestone. The way in which we come to that point varies for each of us. In my case, I built my first lightsaber, *that* saber, before I could drive an airspeeder."

Marr's eyebrows rose. "An impressive feat of engineering."

"Not at all, Marr. The Force spoke and I listened. When I think back, I remember it feeling as if I were sleepwalking. It was . . . strange."

Marr approached the table, eyeing the weapon.

"That's all? You listened?"

"Learning to hear the Force is the most important thing you can learn from me. Everything else follows from it. I think you already hear it plainly when you do mathematics."

Marr nodded slowly, his brow furrowed.

"Pick it up," Jaden said, gesturing toward the lightsaber.

Marr took Jaden's lightsaber and turned it over in his hands, examining the hilt from all angles.

"Now take it apart," Jaden said. He had chosen the lesson because he thought it would be well suited to Marr's talents as an engineer.

"This is yours, Master, and—"

"Take it apart, Marr. It's a weapon. It's made to be durable. You won't break anything." Jaden eyed his chrono and set the timer. "You have five minutes."

Marr's mouth fixed into a determined line and he sank into one of the chairs.

Jaden liked his apprentice's response. No complaint, no protest that he could not do it. Marr simply trusted himself and acted.

Jaden could almost see the analysis going on behind Marr's eyes. The Cerean's pupils could as well have been spinning gears. After turning the weapon over in his hands a few times, he set it down, opened the small box of precision tools, and got to work.

Marr had the weapon disassembled and laid out on the table in under two minutes. He picked up the striated, violet-colored power crystal and held it between forefinger and thumb.

"I feel . . . something in the crystal. The Force."

"Right. All lightsabers are powered by a crystal. The nature of the crystal determines the properties of the blade."

"Its color," Marr said, turning the crystal over, studying its facets.

"That, yes, but more. The crystal is not, by itself, the power source of the weapon. Like the Force user, the crystal is attuned to the Force. Without that attunement, the crystal is just a rock. And while a non–Force user could probably ignite and wield a lightsaber, provided the crystal was properly attuned to the Force, all that lightsaber would be for him is a shaft of superheated plasma. But for a Jedi, the lightsaber becomes more: it is a manifestation of a Jedi's connection to the Force."

Marr considered, nodded. "I understand. I think."

"Put it back together, Marr. Then activate it."

Marr reassembled the weapon with steady hands and activated it. The purple blade slit the air of the cargo bay. Its hum filled the quiet.

"Be careful, but feel the weight in your hand," Jaden said. "The blade itself weighs nothing. All the weight is in the hilt, in your hand."

Marr took a few slow practice swings, trying to mimic some of the technique he'd seen Jaden use.

"Now, feel the Force around you. Feel it in you, in the crystal. The weapon is not a thing apart from you. It is an extension of you. Let the Force flow."

Marr closed his eyes, his face wrinkled in concentration.

"Still your mind, Marr. You cannot think your way to the connection. *Feel* it. Let your mind expand outward from the Keep, let that expansion encompass all of you, me, the weapon you hold."

Marr's face smoothed and his breathing grew deep and regular. Jaden sensed when Marr made the connection, a mental key fitting a lock.

"I feel it," Marr said.

Jaden smiled. "Good. Let the connection continue and open your eyes."

Marr did so.

Jaden took the lightsaber hilt from his belt—the lightsaber he'd taken from the clone, Alpha—and activated it. Its sparking red blade sizzled into existence, its thin red line the border between them.

Marr stared at the red blade, at Jaden. Jaden felt the soft, faint pressure of the dark side against his consciousness. The blade's crystal, attuned to the Force by Alpha, still carried his taint.

"Do you feel it?" Jaden asked Marr.

Marr nodded slowly, his eyes never leaving the blade. "It feels like pressure, like a general sense of unease."

"That is the dark side," Jaden said. "The feeling is more acute when the power is greater. What you feel now is just residuum in the crystal of this blade."

"The intensity of the feeling is a function of the power of the dark-side user and the proximity of that user," Marr said. With his forefinger, he drew invisible figures in the air. It took a moment for Jaden to realize that Marr was actually plotting a function. When that registered, he thought he saw an avenue he could use to speed Marr's training.

"Now I'll teach you some basics of lightsaber combat. As before, feel the Force throughout. Very little about this is physical. Your strength and speed is not in muscle and tendon, but in your relationship to the Force. Let it flow through you, inform your movements. What you're capable of will surprise you, if you let it."

Marr inhaled deeply, then took a few more practice cuts and spins, all more graceful than before. Jaden could feel him settling into the Force.

"Excellent, Marr. As we engage, I want you to think about your movements mathematically. Consider the angles at which we hold our blades, the arc of my approach, the line of your blade intersecting mine, your feet moving degrees within a circle. Do you understand?"

Marr nodded without hesitation. "I do."

"Good. Defend yourself," Jaden said, and lunged at him.

For the next several hours, Jaden walked Marr through the basics of lightsaber technique. The Cerean was a quick study, his movements controlled and precise. Jaden knew it was unusual, even dangerous, to train a new apprentice with live blades, but he also knew that he, Marr, and Khedryn would be in serious danger if they found the clones. He wanted Marr as prepared as possible.

By the time they'd finished and Jaden deactivated Alpha's red blade, sweat dripped off the cliff of Marr's forehead and pasted the ruff of his hair to his pate.

"Tired?" Jaden asked him.

"Not physically tired, Master. But it's mentally exhausting."

Jaden thumped him on the shoulder. "That means you're doing it right. There's one more thing to learn today."

Marr waited, eyebrows raised.

"Go to the other side of the bay and activate your weapon."

Marr did as he was told, and while he did Jaden removed one of the cells from the power pack of his DH-44 and set the blaster to stun. It'd still pack a decent wallop, but a hit would not knock Marr unconscious.

"Don't try to guess where I'm firing."

"You're going to fire?"

Jaden nodded. "You must feel it, not see it. You could do it as well with your eyes closed as open. Angles of approach, Marr. Velocities. Let yourself feel the space around you."

Though the Cerean's face remained placid, he could sense Marr's apprehension.

"Close your eyes and settle your mind in the Keep, Marr."

Marr closed his eyes, inhaled.

"Now, expand your perception outward. Don't merely sense the objects and people around you. Sense the energy of the objects, perceive the lines of the Force that connect one thing to another thing, each thing to every other thing."

Behind him, Jaden felt Khedryn enter the cargo bay. Khedryn said nothing and lingered near the open bay door.

"I feel it!" Marr said. "Interconnection. I see it. It is . . . vast."

"Very good. Now, realize that your will and the Force are likewise interconnected. Each gives the other direction, but the causation is not linear. In fact, there is no causation. There is, instead, synchronicity."

Jaden knew the lack of causation would be difficult for Marr, the logical mathematician, to grasp.

"I . . . think I understand. Synchronicity."

"Then use that understanding to deflect this blaster shot back at me."

Jaden activated Alpha's lightsaber in his off hand, an awkward gesture given his wounded fingers, and fired his depowered blaster at Marr.

Marr attempted a block too late, and the shot hit him in the chest. He grunted, his breath catching, and staggered back two steps. To his credit, he did not open his eyes or mention the pain. Jaden felt Marr's determination grow.

"I felt . . . something," Marr said.

Khedryn chuckled, but Marr seemed not to hear him. Jaden held up a hand for Khedryn's silence.

"Fall into the Force," Jaden said, and fired again.

Again Marr missed the block, and again he grunted with pain, staggered backward.

"Again, Master," the Cerean said, his tone even.

Five times Jaden put blaster shots into Marr, and four times Marr failed to block them. On the fifth, he interposed the purple line of his blade and sent the blaster bolt careering into the near bulkhead.

Jaden expected him to erupt in happiness, but Marr did nothing of the kind. His eyes still closed, he said, "I think I have it now. Again, Master."

Jaden fired, more rapidly, and Marr blocked each shot in turn, sending the shots everywhere but back at Jaden.

"The angle of incidence is equal to the angle of deflection," Jaden said. "You control the angle of incidence."

He fired again, again, and by the third shot Marr sent the bolts right back at Jaden. Jaden deflected them into the floor with the lightsaber he held in his off hand. He fired more rapidly, moved as he fired, and Marr kept blocking, kept returning the shots at Jaden.

"Enough," Jaden said, and deactivated his lightsaber. "Excellent, Marr. Well done."

Marr opened his eyes, nodded, and deactivated his saber. "Thank you, Master."

Khedryn walked into the cargo bay. "If you two are done dinging up my cargo bay, we can make the jump to Fhost." He patted the bulkhead. "She's ready to move."

"I will help with the pre-jump," Marr said, and hurried past Jaden. He caught himself, turned, and said, "That is, if we're done, Master?"

"We are. Go."

Marr smiled and offered Jaden the hilt of his light-saber. Jaden stared at it for a long moment. For years, its purple line had been the string that wove together his past and his present. It was time to move away from the past.

"Keep it, Marr. It's yours until you build your own."

"But . . . this is yours, Master. You'll have no weapon."

Jaden held up the hilt of Alpha's weapon. "I have this."

"That is a Sith weapon."

"Not for long," Jaden said, and buckled it to his belt. He looked Marr in the eye. "Today was a good day. You learned a lot. But if things get hot, don't hesitate to use your blaster."

"Seconded," Khedryn said.

"You're feeling accomplished," Jaden said. "And you should. But were you to face a trained lightsaber combatant you'd be cut in half before you took a first step. You've got a long way to go. Do not forgo good sense in an effort to prove something to me, yourself, or anyone else."

Marr held his gaze. "I understand."

Jaden smiled. "Nicely done, Apprentice."

"Also seconded," Khedryn said. "You could've saved us a lot of grief if you'd learned this a few years ago."

Marr grinned, slapped Khedryn on the shoulder, and bowed his head to Jaden. Then he and Khedryn headed for the cockpit, chatting about star charts, coordinates, and various components of *Junker*'s engines. Jaden watched them go, thoughtful.

He was responsible for Marr, and the weight of the responsibility surprised him. He'd have to put Marr in danger. Repeatedly. Just as Master Katarn had done with him.

He thought Marr understood the risks, but he wasn't sure Marr was ready.

That was the awful burden of taking on an apprentice. One lapse in judgment, and the person who depended on him, the person who trusted him, could die.

Jaden knew that would be hard to bear.

He thought of Relin, who'd begun his descent to the dark side when an ancient Sith had killed his apprentice. The loss had been too much for Relin to carry.

Jaden decided that he would chart a different course—he would not suffer the loss in the first place.

He hefted the hilt of Alpha's lightsaber, eyed it as he might an enemy.

"You and I have an appointment."

Jaden returned to the small stateroom that served as his quarters aboard *Junker*. He sat at the small metal desk in one corner and rapidly disassembled Alpha's lightsaber. His missing fingers caused him to fumble a bit, but he managed.

He stared at the stumps, pondering the possibility of prosthetics. He'd lost all but the thumb and forefinger on his left hand—so he could still wield his lightsaber in his left. Probably he'd leave his hand as it was, maimed, a constant reminder to him that doubt—doubt over his actions, his relationship to the Force, his role in the Order—was the price he paid, and would always pay, to be who he was.

He left off his musings and returned to the disassembly. He had expected the clone's lightsaber construction technique to be crude, but instead found it clean and utilitarian, if inelegant.

He laid out the pieces before him. The crystal that powered the weapon, a crimson rhomboid, glittered in the overhead lights. Fine black lines veined the facets, some impurity the clone had not eliminated. Jaden stared at it, transfixed, feeling its connection to the dark side, the way it contained, in microcosm, Alpha's rage.

Khedryn's voice over the ship's comm brought him out of his reverie.

"Jumping into hyperspace in five seconds."

Jaden ticked off the moments and looked out the viewport as the black turned blue. *Junker* was under way to Fhost and whatever fate awaited them.

Jaden turned away from the maddening blue churn of

hyperspace and toward the maddening crimson of Alpha's crystal. He focused his mind and fell into the Force. The interconnected network of lines and light took shape in his mind's eye, marred only by the presence of Alpha's crystal, a lesion in his perception.

He took the stone in his hands, instantly felt the echo of Alpha's madness and anger, his hate, emotional pollution that radiated at Jaden from the stone's facets.

He endured it and covered the crystal in his hands as best he could with his maimed fingers. Focusing his mind, he meditated.

Once he was residing in the calm center of himself, he opened his hands and the crystal floated above his palms, turning slowly, casting red beams about the room. Jaden let his consciousness ride the beams into the crystal, into the crucible of Alpha's rage. Howls buffeted him, black clouds of anger, lightning bolts of hate. He stood in the midst of the storm, unmoved, and drew it to him. The dark emotions crashed against the rock of his calm, the stillness of his being, and began to dissolve. Alpha's rage burned around him, buffeted him, but had no effect. Jaden found strength in the example of the Grand Master, of his calm, measured response to the news that one of the escaped clones might have been born of Mara Jade Skywalker's DNA.

The shrieks in his mind diminished, the roar of Alpha's anger subsided. He sat in the lines of the Force, centered, at peace.

He opened his eyes. The crystal still hovered above his hands, but he had cleansed it of Alpha's contamination. It was no longer crimson, but was instead as clear as transparisteel. Ordinarily a cleansing would have taken much longer, days even. Alpha's attunement of the crystal must have been imperfect.

Jaden eyed the remade stone, thinking it a perfect metaphor for his own spirit, purged as it was of any temptation to the dark side. The light it cast, clean and white, brightened the dingy confines of his quarters.

He allowed himself only a moment to enjoy his triumph before refocusing on the crystal. He had cleansed it of Alpha's influence and the dark-side taint. Now he needed to attune it to himself and to the light side.

Once more his consciousness rode the beams back into the crystal until he sat in the center of the light. With an effort of will, he aligned the crystal's structural matrix with himself, made it harmonious with the Force, made it an extension of his will. Throughout, he remained peaceful, calm. He drew the crystal deeper into the Force, attuned it more closely to himself, to the lines that interconnected all things. His mind turned briefly to Relin, to the emotional churn the ancient Jedi had experienced.

For a long while Jaden sat in his chamber, enmeshed in the Force, aligning himself and the crystal with it. In time, the process was complete. When he opened his eyes and came back to himself, he saw that the Force had transformed the crystal from clear to a faint yellow. The black lines were gone, the impurities purged.

Smiling, he took the crystal in eager hands and placed it on the table. Moving rapidly, he reassembled the lightsaber hilt, modifying the grip as best he could with the pieces he had to hand. When it was ready, he seated the crystal into place and activated the blade.

A clean yellow line cut the air of his quarters. The hum of the weapon was musical.

In ancient times—Relin's times—a yellow blade had signified that its wielder was a Jedi Sentinel, a servant of the light side of the Force who balanced his service between the art of combat and the scholarly study of the Force. It pleased Jaden to see that the Force had gifted him with such a blade. His thought of Relin during the remaking of the crystal must have influenced the crystal's form. He nodded, satisfied. He had purged the weapon of its dark-side influence and made it his own, at the same time honoring Relin's memory. It seemed fitting.

He deactivated the blade and hung it from his belt.

He found it somewhat strange, the way he had been able to remake the crystal. It was as though he had wiped away someone's memory and replaced it with another.

He floated in a place of warmth, quiet. Then . . . sensation from darkness, something from nothing.

He heard the low, vibratory hum of engaging electronics.

How did he know they were electronics? He seemed to know some things.

His extremities began to tingle, then to itch, then to hurt, pinpricks of pain in his skin.

The whine of a device sounded in his ear. Streaks of color flashed behind his eyelids, smears of green, red, blue. He heard a mechanical voice speaking, the sound dulled, as if spoken from far away or blocked by something.

"His vital signs are normal. He is becoming conscious."

"Can he hear us?" said another voice.

"I do not know. Possibly."

"What will he know?"

He heard the slow bubbling of liquid. He had never noticed it before.

"All of the Iterations are implanted with basic knowledge roughly equivalent to that of a human adolescent. Otherwise they would be difficult to deal with when they awakened. It is easily overwritten by the Rakatan mindspear."

"Very good."

His body awoke fully to sensation, and he became aware of himself. He was a man. Restraints held his arms and legs immobile. Something was in his mouth—a tube. Adhesive strips kept his eyes closed. He tested his strength against the restraints. There was no give in them.

"Let's get him out," said the voice.

"Of course."

The liquid in which he floated began to drain, gurgling away into some hole near his feet. He felt vulnerable as the level of the liquid decreased, exposing first his head, then his chest, his legs. He imagined it was like being born, moving from warm and safe to cold and exposed. It felt strange to have his feet on the ground, supporting his weight. He was naked, shivering.

Metallic latches released, a hiss sounded, and he heard a hatch or door open right before him. A blast of cold air goose-pimpled his wet skin.

He opened his mouth to speak but gagged on the tube. Something took hold of it.

"Do not resist," said a mechanical voice, a medical droid.

He didn't, and the droid pulled the tube from his body. It went all the way to his stomach, and he felt as if the droid was disemboweling him as it pulled the tube up through his esophagus. The moment it cleared his lips he coughed out a bit of liquid and gasped.

The intake of air felt raw on his throat. His lungs burned. The smell of antiseptic filled his nostrils. He tried to speak, but his lips and tongue felt thick, his vocal cords tight. He managed only a grunt.

"You will be able to speak soon," said a soft, sibilant voice. "You have never used your vocal cords before, or your lungs. Try to remain calm."

He was still restrained, his eyes still sealed shut. He felt vulnerable.

"You are restrained for your own protection," said the soft voice. "The implantation process is painful. I don't want you to damage yourself."

The word "painful" stuck in his mind. He squirmed against the restraints, but they held him fast.

"You may go, One-Bee-Seven," said the voice.

"Yes, Master Nyss," replied the droid.

He heard the whirring servos of a departing droid, the whisk of a door that opened and then closed.

He was alone with Nyss, who had promised him pain. His heart was racing. Despite the cold, he was sweating, clammy. The smell of his own stink filled his nostrils. His breath was coming fast.

"You are afraid," said the voice. "There is nothing to fear. You won't remember the pain."

A hand closed on his jaw and he winced in anticipation of a blow. But a blow did not come. Instead he felt something warm and sharp pressed against his temple. He tried to turn his head away but could not. He grunted, terrified; tried to blink open his eyes against the adhesive but failed.

He felt a brief prick of pain, then pressure in his temple. A trickle of blood, warm like the fluid in which he'd lived for so long, wound down the side of his face. There really was no pain—

Then a shooting stab of agony exploded in his head. He shrieked, a prolonged, bestial wail that went on and on but did nothing to expiate the pain. The agony intensified, spreading from his temple to the rest of his head until it felt as if his skull were filled with molten metal that would burn forever.

His entire body was as rigid as a rail, every muscle contracted. He could not stop screaming. He wanted to cut off his own head, to rip it from his neck and murder himself to end the unending, unendurable pain.

But his hands were bound and he could not move.

There was nothing left to him but to scream and scream and scream.

Horror matched pain when he felt something squirming inside the scalding confines of his skull, writhing tendrils rooting through his brain, scraping against the underside of his braincase. He imagined worms burrowing through tissue, leaving a network of empty tunnels in their wake. He heaved as if to vomit, but his stomach contained nothing.

Between heaves his screams turned desperate; he warred against the restraints, but they simply would not give. He railed, screamed, shrieked, heaved, knew that he must soon pass out or die, and . . .

The pain vanished.

Sweat soaked him. Every muscle in his body ached. His breath came hard and fast through a throat made ragged. Before he could speak, ask what had happened, a spark shower exploded in his brain and a gout of information poured in, washing away what preexisted it and filling the empty vessel of his mind.

Memories flooded into the crevices of his empty recollection, making him anew, rebirthing him on the spot.

He remembered himself.

He had been born on Coruscant, and his parents had died in an accident when he was young.

A voice was speaking to him from outside himself, but he could not understand it, could not move his attention from the rush of memories, *his* memories.

After the death of his parents, he had turned inward, had become philosophical even as a child, and that internal focus had triggered his latent Force sensitivity.

The voice continued to speak to him, soft, insistent. But he refused to acknowledge it. Instead he lived in the past, his past, watching faces and events stream by.

Without any training, he'd used his Force sensitivity to make a lightsaber for himself. Soon thereafter, his uncle had enrolled him in the Jedi Academy. He'd met Grand Master Luke Skywalker.

The voice finally penetrated his perception.

"Do you hear me?" it asked.

He felt a hand tapping his cheeks but ignored it in favor of the memories.

He'd fought the spirit of Marka Ragnos on Korriban, trying to redeem Rosh Penin.

"Open your eyes," the voice said, and tore the adhesive strips from his eyelids.

He hesitated, unwilling to let himself slip from the realm of memory.

"Open them."

He did, and even the dim light in the small, steel-walled room set them to watering. He blinked, his vision blurred. A figure stood before him, but he could make out little detail.

"I cannot see," he said.

"Your vision will improve quickly," the figure said.

He looked around, down, trying to blink away the blurriness. He was in a transparisteel cloning tank. Traces of the pink suspension fluid in which he'd been floating puddled in the base of the tank. He stared at them while his vision cleared.

Cables, hoses, and wires snaked out of the sides of the tank and connected to his body at arms, legs, torso, and head. Conduits connected a computer to the tank. He was surprised to see that he was not restrained, yet he still could not move.

A man stood at the computer station. Not a man—an Umbaran, thin, with skin so pale it looked white. He wore a tailored black cloak complete with a cowl, and the dimness in the room seemed to collect around him, intensify near him. The reflected glow of the comp screen made his dark eyes glow red. He worked the keyboard with one hand. In his other he held a device that looked like a metal hilt or handle engraved with strange grooves and from which extended a spike of rigid filaments, each of them far finer than even the finest hair.

"I cannot move," he said to the Umbaran, his voice coarse with disuse.

"The programming paralyzes most of your skeleton-muscular system until the . . . process is complete."

"I cannot feel the Force," he said.

The Umbaran nodded. "That is my doing."

He did not know what to say to that. He did not remember ever being cut off from the Force. His gaze fell to the device the Umbaran held in his hand. The Umbaran noticed and held the device up for him to see.

"It is Rakatan," the Umbaran said. "We think they used it to store and transfer their consciousnesses. We've found caches of them here and there across the galaxy."

"We?" he asked.

"The One Sith," the Umbaran replied.

He realized his danger then. He was in the hands of an unknown faction of the Sith. He tried to fall into the Force but felt only emptiness. He was alone, powerless. The Sith had developed some new weapon by which they could separate a Jedi from the Force. He had to escape, report back.

"What do you want from me?"

"What's your name?"

"You know my name. Jaden Korr."

The Umbaran smiled. "No. You are the Iteration."

The word meant nothing to him.

"I'm going to speak a phrase," the Umbaran said. "And when I do, you'll know what you are."

He shook his head. Nothing the Umbaran said made sense, nothing about his situation made sense. How had he gotten here? He remembered very little after his graduation from the Jedi Academy.

The Umbaran smiled, an expression more sinister

than mirthful, and started to speak. He did not comprehend the words. He blinked and . . . knew.

He was a clone of Jaden Korr. He was an agent of the One Sith. He was to infiltrate the Jedi Order and be activated when the One Sith deemed the time right.

"I am . . . an agent of the One Sith."

The Umbaran nodded. "Yes."

"Why did you activate me now? I'm not a member of the Jedi Order."

"No. But you will be."

"I don't understand."

"You will in time. Now, who are you?"

"I am the Iteration."

The Umbaran nodded, hit a key on the comp panel.

The Iteration was able to move. At the same time, the darkness that seemed to hover around the Umbaran decreased somewhat and the Iteration's connection to the Force returned in a rush of power that made him gasp.

The Iteration took a step, another, ginger on limbs that had never before borne his weight. The cloning tank used electro-impulses to stimulate muscle development and growth, but he knew to take care with his first steps.

Behind the Umbaran, the door to the small chamber slid open and two figures in cowled cloaks strode in. Each towered over the Umbaran, over the Iteration, and both held electro-staffs in their fists. Their red hands featured scales and black claws. The cowls and dim light hid their faces, but the Iteration caught a suggestion of scaled eye ridges above reptilian eyes.

"Syll is awaiting him aboard my ship," the Umbaran said to them. "Get him aboard and put him in stasis."

"Yes, my lord," the two answered, their voices deep and guttural.

"Stasis?" the Iteration said. "But I just . . ." He struggled for the right word. ". . . woke up."

"I needed to make sure you could withstand the shock of the awakening and the first memory transfer."

"The first? And if I would've died?"

The Umbaran shrugged. "I would've used another."

"Another?"

"Get him aboard," the man said to the guards.

As the guards took him away, he asked over his shoulder, "Why did you awaken me? What am I to do?"

"Nothing, yet. You're just along for the ride until I need you."

"Until you need me for what?"

"Until I need you to iterate," the Umbaran said, and the Iteration imagined the thin line of a smug smile drawn across the Umbaran's pale face.

Soldier felt an odd sense of separation, a peculiar sense of otherness. A gulf opened in him, growing as the stolen ship blazed ever farther from the moon.

The moon had been his birthplace, the place where he had spent his entire life.

The place he had long ago grown to hate, but that was also his home.

He felt as if his life up to that moment had been the *before,* and that he had just begun the *after.* But the after felt uncomfortably vast. Suddenly adrift in infinite space, in infinite possibilities, he felt as he always had when he was floating in one of Dr. Green's sensory deprivation tanks—alone, unmoored from himself, a tiny ship bobbing across the surface of a limitless ocean.

The frigid, unnamed moon and its cloning facility had been the Community's home for decades. He and the other clones had been specimens for Imperial scientists, living in cages made of transparisteel, their existences an unending series of tests, questions, needles, training.

It had been awful, but they'd had structure, purpose.

Now they had neither.

The scientists had wanted to clone a unique Force user. And they had succeeded, in a way. But their success had been their undoing. The Community had earned their freedom with murder, killing everyone else in the facility and giving them to Mother.

And now they were riding Seer's promises into the velvet of space.

And where would they go?

First to Fhost.

Then to Mother.

Perhaps Soldier's possibilities were not as infinite as he supposed. Perhaps he had had more purpose, more structure, than he realized.

The readout showed the ship to be clear of gravity wells. Soldier took one last look around the system, the distant red star, the gas giants.

Seer entered the cockpit and folded her lithe body into the copilot's seat. "The universe is large and you feel alone," she said.

Soldier tried to hide his surprise. Seer had articulated his thoughts plainly.

"You don't need to be alone, Soldier. You separate yourself from us, from Mother. You needn't."

Not for the first time, Soldier wondered if Seer's empathic sense surpassed that of the rest of the clones.

"I don't feel alone," Soldier lied. "I am one of you. I take care of you, protect you all."

"You do so for the children's sake. Not the rest of us."

Once again, Seer had spoken truth. He had no children of his own, but cared for Grace, Gift, and Blessing as if they were his. If the clones had a purpose, the children embodied it. He wanted them to have a life different from the one he and the others had been forced to endure.

Unwilling to discuss it more with Seer, he changed the subject. "The coordinates for Fhost are in the navicomp and we're clear of gravity wells. I'm winding up the hyperdrive."

Seer stared at him, but he ignored her as he engaged the pre-jump sequence. He reached to engage the cockpit dimmer. His flight training in the facility's simulators had taught him that staring at the hyperspace churn too often could lead to madness. Seer caught his hand and did not release it.

"I want to see it," she said.

Her touch thrilled him, and he imagined she knew it.

"All right."

When the jump indicator showed green, he engaged the hyperdrive. Points of starlight stretched into lines, then the lines vanished into the blue swirl of hyperspace.

Seer gasped, her hand tight around his. "It's beautiful."

The swirls and whorls nauseated Soldier, but he said nothing. As he withdrew his hand, Seer seemed not to notice. Her excitement filled the cockpit.

"We'll reach Fhost soon," he said.

She nodded, staring wide-eyed at the blue.

"I'll check on the others," he said, and rose. Through their shared connection, he could feel the other clones' emotional state. They were calmed by the medicine, but that would last only a short time. The madness cast a shadow over their minds, the illness a shadow over their failing bodies.

He hoped Seer was right. He hoped Mother would heal them. Especially the children.

chapter five

Seer sat in the cockpit, staring out, during their entire time in hyperspace. Her silence unnerved Soldier. She eyed the starstreaks, unblinking, as if they hid something revelatory in their glow. He occupied himself by running diagnostics on the ship's systems while he waited for the computer to tell him they were nearing Fhost.

In time it did, and he said, "Coming out of hyperspace."

Seer finally looked away from the view outside and fixed her gaze on him. He could not shake the feeling that she saw right through him. The zeal of a true believer filled her dark eyes. Or maybe it was madness; Soldier could not distinguish them.

"Well done, Soldier," she said.

They came out of hyperspace, black overwrote blue, and the light of a nearby star painted the interior of the cockpit in orange. The ion engines engaged and they accelerated through the system.

Soldier had no idea what to expect on-planet.

"The data on Fhost show it to be sparsely populated, with only one large city—Farpoint. We'll go in on the far side of the planet and circle around. There's not much infrastructure. We should be able to avoid detection. I'll set us down outside of the city and some of us can head in."

Seer nodded, lost in thought, or maybe lost in another vision, as they closed on the planet.

Fhost floated in the space before them, a mostly brown ball dotted with intermittent spots of green and blue. Hazy clouds floated in long, thin strings above the arid world. Soldier guided the cloakshape around to the far side of the planet. He kept his eyes on the scanners, wondering if they'd be interdicted, wondering what he would do if they were, but either they passed into the atmosphere unnoticed or the planetary authorities saw them and did not care.

He took the cloakshape down and flew low and fast along Fhost's surface. He could make out little detail, blurs of green and brown and blue. Still, he found it beautiful, a stark contrast to the frozen hell that had been their lives for so long. He wondered what it would be like to simply settle on such a world and just . . . live.

He imagined Grace and Blessing as adults, living in a normal dwelling, living normal lives. The thought made him smile. He cleared his throat, ventured a heretical thought.

"We could just . . . settle here," he said. He wasn't sure Seer heard him.

"She is calling us, Soldier," Seer said, her voice singsong. "She wants us home. We must hurry."

Her words dispelled any thoughts of a life lived in quietude.

After a time, the HUD showed Farpoint a bit over fifty kilometers ahead. He sought a suitable landing spot. There were no signs off habitation nearby, so he slowed and settled the cloakshape in a large clearing in the center of a wood.

"I'll get what meds I can and come back as fast as I can," he said. "I'll need help, though."

Seer said nothing. Though her eyes were open, she still seemed lost in a trance.

"Seer? Seer?"

He left her in the cockpit and headed to the cargo bay. The other clones had moved little since he'd last checked them. The medicine coated their minds with an artificial calm and dulled the pain of their bodies, but through their shared mental connection he could feel the growing madness in the adults, roiling underneath the surface. Absent the medication, he imagined, the ship would be chaos. The medicine would work for another hour or two, at most. Then the madness would assert itself, or the illness. Either way, there would be death. He had to move fast.

He went to each of the clones in turn, the children first, evaluating their physical state, opening his mind enough to get a better feel for their emotional condition. All were flush with fever, their breathing too rapid, their minds seething with anger, terror, power. Blessing, Grace, and Gift were catatonic. He lingered over them, feeling a sadness that hit him hard. He had to save them, them above all.

Runner seemed the least afflicted, so Soldier took an adrenaline hypo from the medical supplies and injected him with it. His eyes flew open, the pupils dilating, and fixed on Soldier. Dry, cracked lips formed a word.

"Soldier," he said, his diction slurred.

"Are you able to stand? I need help to get meds."

Runner seemed not to hear him. He closed his eyes, winced as if with pain. His mouth, nearly hidden in the brambles of his thick beard, twisted in agony.

"I can manage," Runner said. "The power, Soldier . . ."

"I know."

Since killing Maker, Soldier had bottled up the power within himself. But he still felt as if the cap might blow at any time. His body, all of their bodies, struggled to contain it.

He tried to help Runner sit up, but Runner shoved his hands away and sat up on his own.

"I don't need you," he snarled.

Soldier resisted the angry impulse to punch Runner in the face. "You'd already be dead if not for me. Now, listen. You and I are going to a medical facility nearby. We're going to take the medicine we need to keep the Community alive."

Runner's glassy eyes shone. "Take it?"

"Yes, take it. Whatever we flew through when we left the moon accelerated the onset of the . . ." He almost said "madness," but thought better of it and instead said, ". . . illness. We'll need the meds or we'll all die before we reach Mother."

"Not you," Runner said, as he stood. He stank of sweat, of fever, of sickness. "You won't die." He leered. "At least not from the illness."

Soldier said nothing, merely stared into Runner's fevered face.

Runner's gaze took in the cargo bay, the clones. "Did you kill Scar and Maker?"

"I killed Maker because he gave me no choice. The illness killed Scar, and it will kill the rest of them, and you, if we don't get what we need. Do you understand?"

"I understand." Runner found a flask of water among their supplies, drank, and wiped his beard. "They won't let us take medicine, Soldier. They'll try to stop us. We'll have to kill *them*. Lots of them."

"Maybe," Soldier said, trying to ignore the eagerness he heard in Runner's words. He, too, felt the impulse to violence, but he could control it. Runner, with the madness taking hold, could not. But Soldier needed him. A medical facility would be guarded, even on a backwater planet. He could not assault it alone.

"We should leave now," Soldier said.

When he turned to go, he found himself face-to-face with Seer. Beside him, Runner fell to his knees, head bowed, and took Seer's hand in his own.

"Everything you said was true, Seer. You've saved us. Saved us."

"What I say are Mother's words," Seer said, her eyes on Soldier rather than Runner. "And those words are truth. And now I say that we *all* leave."

Soldier gestured at the comatose clones. "They're too sick to move, Seer. And someone should remain behind with them. You should. We shouldn't leave the ship unguarded."

Runner clambered to his feet, his eyes boring holes into Soldier. "You dare question her?"

"Shut your mouth," Soldier said.

Runner snarled.

"The ship is irrelevant," Seer said. "We're not taking it when we leave this world."

For a moment Soldier could not frame a reply. He feared Seer was succumbing to madness, too, and he was profoundly conscious of the anger pouring off Runner.

Seer smiled at him, as if reading his thoughts.

When he spoke, he kept his tone even. "What ship are we taking, then?"

"The medical supply ship that will be arriving at the hospital," she said.

Runner rocked on the balls of his feet, as if the power within him disallowed stillness, as if he could barely control whatever impulse sought expression. He still glared at Soldier.

"How do you know about a supply ship?" Soldier asked.

"The Force. Mother."

"Blessed Mother," Runner muttered, still rocking.

Seer's eyes searched Soldier's face. He thought she

looked almost sad. "Do you believe, Soldier? Do you believe *me*?"

Soldier felt Runner's burning eyes on him, the heat of his fever, his faith. His thoughts turned to Wry, the way the others had torn him apart, and he shifted his weight to distribute it evenly. If he had to draw his weapon, he'd need to be fast.

"You know what I believe," he said.

She leaned in, smiling, all danger and beauty. "Yes, I do."

"You've been right so far," he said.

She smiled, nodded. "We take everyone who can still be saved. The rest we must leave. Their faith, sadly, was inadequate to save them."

"They can all still be saved," Soldier said. "We're not leaving the children."

"I know you love them," Seer said. "It speaks well of you. But Blessing and Gift are almost gone. They cannot be saved. Only Grace will live to see Mother."

"You're wrong," Soldier said. His hand went to his lightsaber hilt. He would kill Runner if he had to. But would he kill Seer? Could he?

"I'm not wrong," Seer said. "And you know it. These were Mother's words, Soldier. Do you doubt them?"

Soldier did not look away, but neither did he dare dispute with her. "I'm giving each of them an adrenaline shot. If they rouse, they come."

Seer smiled. "That is acceptable."

"I don't need your permission," Soldier said.

Runner growled, and Soldier whirled on him, went nose to nose. "Something you want to say? Or do?"

Runner stared at him with bloodshot eyes, his breath foul, his breathing heavy.

"See to your shots, Soldier," Seer said. "It will be as I said."

Soldier left off Runner, found the adrenaline hypos from among their supplies.

"I'll give it to the children." He tossed some hypos to Runner. "You give it to the others."

Runner looked to Seer for guidance, and she said, "Do as he says."

Soldier went to Blessing. Her thin blond hair hung over a face that was too pale. He wasn't sure she was breathing. He pulled her to him, listened for a heartbeat, and did not hear one. He took her tiny hands in his. They seemed so frail, so fragile. His eyes welled and he pulled her close. She was already cooling.

"Goodbye," he said, thinking of her smile.

"She is already gone," Seer said. "She has gone to Mother."

"Shut up," Soldier said, swallowing his sobs. "Shut your mouth."

"I sense your pain," Seer said gently. "I'm sorry, Soldier."

Soldier checked Gift, found that he had succumbed also. Soldier stared into his face a long while. He had pinned his hopes—unfocused, inchoate hope, with no goal or particular aspiration, but hope nonetheless—on the children.

Vain. Useless.

He did not bother to wipe his tears. He left them on his face as a testament to his grief.

"What test of faith did he fail, Seer? What test? He was just a boy."

Seer did not answer him.

Dull and unfeeling, he went to Grace. When he found her alive, it was as if he had been resurrected. His tears redoubled.

"She's alive," he said, excited. With a shaking hand, he injected the adrenaline, and she gasped, inhaled deeply.

Relief flooded him as he watched her lungs rise and fall. He grabbed her up, hugged her close.

"Two-Blade is nearly gone," Runner said from behind him. "Hunter seems better."

"Leave Two-Blade," Seer said. "Blessing and Gift, too. Bring Hunter."

"No," Soldier said, and whirled on her. "We're not abandoning the children."

"They're not your children," Runner said.

"They're *our* children," Soldier spat over his shoulder. "Seer?"

"They have gone to Mother," Seer said. "Their bodies are irrelevant."

"To you," Soldier said.

"To them," Seer answered. "We must move quickly, Soldier. We cannot bring the dead. Only the living."

He stared at Blessing, at Gift, and knew she was right. He hated her for being right. He turned and vented his anger on Runner.

"A word to me about them and you die." He stepped forward and put his face in Runner's. "A word. Try me, Runner."

Barely controlled emotion caused Runner's eye to spasm. Anger curled his lips from his teeth.

It paled in comparison to what Soldier felt. Grief fed his rage, magnified it. He'd turn Runner inside out, bathe in his blood—

"That is enough," Seer said. "Too many are dead already. That is enough, Soldier."

Without taking his eyes from Runner, he said to her, "You may not always be right, Seer."

She smiled. "But what if I am, Soldier?"

To that, he said nothing. He went to little Grace, who breathed deeply, regularly. At his touch, she moaned. He lifted her, cradled her.

"Get Hunter," he said to Runner. "I have Grace."

He eyed Two-Blade. His breathing was ragged and rapid. His skin pulsed and bulged. He did not have long. Soldier felt nothing for him. He was focused entirely on Grace.

Runner hefted Hunter and Soldier lifted Grace. Soldier gently placed her in the speeder strapped to the cargo hold bulkhead. Runner loaded Hunter next to her daughter.

"You take the stick, Soldier," Seer said.

She sat beside him, with Runner in the rear along with Hunter and Grace.

Soldier opened the cargo bay door and activated the speeder. Its thrusters lifted it from the floor. Warm air from outside poured into the cargo bay. It smelled of vegetation, with a faint overlay of distant wood smoke. Insects whistled and chirped, all of it the sounds and smells of a living world. Soldier savored it. He wished Grace could see it.

As they maneuvered out of the cloakshape, a flock of small flying animals, perhaps startled by the appearance of the speeder, winged out of a nearby tree and into the sky.

"Perhaps they bear the souls of the dead to Mother," Seer said.

Soldier said nothing, merely watched them go, envying them their freedom.

Jaden found Khedryn and Marr in *Junker*'s cockpit.

"We'll be coming out of hyperspace soon," Khedryn said.

"Good," Jaden said.

"Caf?" Khedryn asked. He had an extra cup filled.

"Thanks," Jaden said, and took it.

As Khedryn handed him the caf, his eyes fell on the lightsaber hanging from Jaden's belt.

"You do something to that? It looks different."

Jaden smiled. "It *is* different." He took the hilt in hand and activated the lightsaber. The yellow blade hummed to life. Marr and Khedyrn eyed it.

"That was the clone's weapon?" Khedryn asked, incredulous. "That red blade?"

Jaden nodded.

"I didn't know that was possible," Marr said. "You did something to the power crystal?"

Jaden deactivated the blade. "The attunement to the dark side can be cleared and replaced. It's an advanced technique," he said to Marr. "But I will teach you in time."

Khedryn tapped a finger on his caf mug. "Jedi, if you could do that with the Sith, the galaxy would be a better joint. Just cleanse the place."

Jaden smiled. "A person is not a crystal."

"Too bad," Khedyrn said.

"Redemption isn't meant to be easy," Jaden said.

"Too bad, too," Khedryn said. "Though some of us don't require redemption."

Jaden chuckled, and raised his mug to Khedryn in a toast.

"May I ask a question?" Marr asked.

"Of course," Jaden said.

"Why are we hunting the clones?"

The question was so direct that it stopped Jaden in his tracks.

"What do you mean?" he asked at last.

"Yeah, what?" Khedryn asked.

Marr visibly warmed to this thinking, gesturing with his hands as he spoke.

"What have they done? From what you've told me, they could have killed you and Khedryn back on the moon. Isn't that so? You both stood in the open with the cloakshape right above you."

"Maybe they could have," Jaden said.

"But they didn't. And yet . . . we hunt them."

"You didn't see the inside of that facility, Marr," Khedryn said. "You didn't see . . . the place where they put the doctors and the Imperial troops. Even stormies don't deserve to go out that way."

"They lived a long time on that moon. Alone. They were experimented on in horrible ways."

"They were alone because they slaughtered everyone else," Khedryn said. "These clones were made by Thrawn to be weapons. And weapons want to be used."

Jaden listened, turned his thoughts over in his mind.

"These are people," Marr said. "Not items. They have sentience, agency. That the Empire bred them to be weapons doesn't make them weapons. They can choose otherwise."

Khedryn shook his head as he sipped his caf. "You sure about that?"

Marr looked down and shook his head. "No. But maybe they just want a life for themselves. People aren't equations, Khedryn."

Khedryn smiled. "That's odd to hear coming from you."

"What do you think, Master?" Marr asked.

"You *are* awfully quiet, Jedi," Khedryn said.

Jaden put down his mug. "I think you're both right. Biology isn't destiny or we're all just droids of flesh. Choice is what makes us human. But biology *does* constrain choice. Can the clones choose a path other than the violence for which they were bred?" He shrugged, swirling the caf in his mug. "Maybe. But the clone I faced on the moon was insane, and powerful in the dark side of the Force. If the others are like him, they're potentially dangerous. At the least we must take them into custody."

"At the least," Khedryn said.

Marr nodded, but Jaden felt his ambivalence. He had no words to dispel it.

"Maybe we'll never find 'em," Khedryn said. "Won't be our problem, then."

Ahead, Soldier saw the haphazard city of Farpoint rise out of the dust of the plain. To the west stood an expansive landing field littered with ships. A few swoops and speeder bikes dotted the sky.

Most of the buildings within the city were single-story, ramshackle structures built of corrugated metal, native wood, and whatever other materials builders could scavenge. The few multistory buildings of the city sat in the city center, the tallest about ten stories. It hit Soldier as they approached that their profile reminded him of something.

A ship's bridge.

In fact, the entire outline of the city looked like an elongated version of a cruiser or dreadnought, as if a giant had smeared a ship across the surface of Fhost. The city had been built on its skeleton. Over time, it had accreted additional structures, lost others, but the outline was still vaguely visible.

He wondered about the ship's origin as he steered the speeder along the cluttered, narrow streets of the city. What had the ship's crew been looking for? Had they found it, before they died?

"What are you thinking?" Seer asked him.

"Nothing," he said.

Dust coated everything. Speeders, swoops, wheeled and treaded vehicles, even primitive wagons pulled by a large reptile of some sort made the streets a crowded mash up of technology. Sentients of many species stood in shop doors and strode the walkways. The aroma of sizzling meat and exotic-smelling smokes leaked from some of the structures.

Soldier had never seen so many people in one place, so much activity. He wished to just get out and walk around, take it in.

"There," Seer said, pointing.

A cylindrical ship, the center of it a large cargo bay that looked like a distended belly, descended from the blue sky toward the city center.

Five uniformed sentients on swoop bikes—they looked like tiny bugs beside the supply ship—flew escort. The ship flew toward the tallest of the buildings, built from the remains of a crashed ship's bridge tower.

"The medicine you want is on that ship," Seer said.

"How do you know?" Soldier said.

"You know how she knows," Runner snapped.

As they watched, a portion of the roof of the ten-story building—the medical facility, Soldier surmised—folded open to reveal a rooftop landing pad.

"We'll have to get up there, then," Soldier said. Their speeder would not go airborne. They'd have to enter the hospital at ground level and get up to the landing pad.

A signal horn beeped behind them. Soldier had stopped in the middle of the street to watch the descending supply ship. A Weequay, the skin of his face as wrinkled as old leather, shouted at them and brandished a fist from his open-top speeder.

"Move it!"

Soldier felt Runner's anger spike.

"Don't," he said, and reached back to grab Runner's arm, but it was too late.

Runner made a sweeping gesture with one hand, and the Weequay's speeder looked as if it had been hit broadside with an enormous wave. It teetered on its side and slid across the street, onto the sidewalk, crushing several pedestrians, and into an adjacent building. Metal shrieked and bent. Glass shattered. The building half-collapsed with an angry rumble. One of the Weequay's speeder's engines sputtered and burst into flames. Black smoke poured into the air.

Passersby shouted, pointed at Runner. The wounded screamed. Vehicles stopped, the people within gawking. Pedestrians streamed toward the site. Soldier cursed, honked his signal horn to clear a path, and accelerated the speeder away.

"What are you thinking?" he shouted at Runner over his shoulder. "Idiot."

"Shut your mouth, Soldier. They won't connect the accident to us, and the damage and casualties will bring the authorities there. Med evac, too. That will work for us."

Soldier could not argue with the point. But he had trouble believing that Runner had actually thought ahead, as opposed to simply giving in to his anger.

Above, swoop bikes with uniformed officers streaked past, high-pitched sirens wailing. Somewhere behind the crush of buildings, he heard a different kind of siren and presumed it was med evac.

Using the tall spike of the medical center as a navigational aide, he drove the speeder quickly through the streets until they reached the city center. A score of pedestrians milled about outside the large, transparisteel doors of the medical center. Swoops, speeder bikes, speeders, and several wheeled vehicles were parked in a disorganized fashion on the street. A small, box-shaped medical shuttle alit from a second-story landing pad, turned, and shot off in the direction of the havoc Runner had wrought. Soldier looked over to Seer.

"You're certain the meds we need are on the ship?"

She did not blink. "I'm certain."

He spared a look at Hunter, at Grace. They would not last much longer. "Then let's go."

They parked the speeder and exited. Seer took Grace before Soldier could, so he carried Hunter.

"Cover your weapons," he said to Seer and Runner.

"Why?" Runner said.

"Just do it," he snapped.

Runner grumbled as he covered the hilt of his blade with his cloak.

Together, they walked toward the sliding doors of the medical facility. Soldier kept his head down, but he felt the eyes of pedestrians and passersby on him. Perhaps they noted the raggedness of his group's clothing.

A bipedal, anthropoid droid, coated in dust, separated itself from the crowd and approached them. Soldier tried to veer away, but it shifted to intercept them.

"May I assist you, sir?" the droid asked.

"No."

"I will alert a doctor about your sick companions."

"That's not necessary," Soldier said.

"It is no trouble, sir. Their body temperature is quite high and they will need rapid treatment. A medical team will be awaiting you inside."

Soldier had hoped to go mostly unnoticed. That, it seemed, was no longer possible. They moved through sentients and droids and into the medical center.

A waiting room opened to the right, a dozen worried sentients sitting in chairs or watching a holo. To the left was a medical triage. The smell of antiseptic filled the air. Violet-uniformed doctors and nurses moved about the triage area. The beep and whistle of medical equipment reminded Soldier of the facility on the frozen moon. Bad memories bubbled up from the dregs of his mind.

"I don't like doctors," Runner said, agitation coming off him in palpable waves.

Neither did Soldier. Their experience with doctors involved sensory deprivation tanks, surgeries without anesthesia, painful tests, hypos, and constant monitoring. He felt his own level of irritation rising. The power he held at bay crept up on him, desperate to be used.

A thin female doctor with graying hair stood near the reception area straight ahead. She held a portable scanner in her hand. A male nurse stood beside her, one hand on a wheeled gurney large enough to hold Hunter and Grace. Both hurriedly approached as Soldier and the others entered.

"Put them down here," the doctor said, her tone brisk and commanding.

Soldier laid Hunter down on the gurney and Seer placed Grace beside her. Soldier was pleased to see that Grace's color had improved.

Soldier scanned the triage, the reception area, the waiting room, looking for lifts. He saw six security guards in black uniforms stationed within eyeshot. All wore blasters at their hips.

The doctor began her examination. "They're burning up," she said.

"They need injections of Metacycline," Soldier said.

The doctor looked up at him. "Metacycline? I'm not familiar with—"

"It's a mixture of several drugs," Soldier said. "A genetic coherence sequencer, an antipsychotic, and a blood thinner."

The nurse said, "I read about Metacycline years ago in a medical ethics paper. The Empire used it decades ago in some experiments."

"Why would they need that?" the doctor asked Soldier.

"Just give it to them," Runner barked.

Two of the nearby security guards noticed them, frowning at Runner's tone.

The doctor blinked, taken aback, perhaps unused to being talked to in such a manner. She seemed to actually note their appearance for the first time—their filthy, threadbare clothes made from Imperial castoffs, their unkempt hair and beards.

Soldier saw the change come over her, the moment suspicion seized her mind, changing her concern from treating Hunter and Grace to ensuring that she was not harmed.

"Uh, I see," the doctor said. She stood up and backed away, her eyes wide. "Let me see what we have in the dispensary." She took the nurse by the arm and backed off a few more steps. "Nurse, I will need your assistance."

The nurse, surprised, said, "Uh . . . of course, Doctor."

Soldier sank into the Force, drew on the enormous reservoir of power bubbling beneath the surface of his control. He reached out with mental fingers and took hold of the doctor's mind, of the nurse's.

"You will both escort us to the lifts," Soldier said.

Doctor and nurse stopped their retreat and their faces went vacant.

"I will escort you to the lifts," they said in unison.

"You there," called one of the security guards from behind them.

"Take us," Soldier said to the doctor and nurse. "Now. Right now."

They turned and started walking toward the triage area. He could feel the emotion building in Runner, in Seer, in himself. He felt as if it might lift him from his feet.

"You there!" called the guard again from behind them. "Wait, I said!"

Eyes were on them—doctors', nurses', patients'.

Ahead, two other security guards appeared, talking softly into their comlinks. Each had a hand on his blaster. Behind those two, Soldier saw the lift doors.

"Enough of this," Runner said. He shoved Soldier to the side, the anger bleeding from him. He held out his hands and unleashed a blast of energy that went before him in a wide arc. The triage area virtually exploded.

Beds overturned; overhead lights shattered, raining glass; medical equipment toppled; and two dozen bodies—patients, security guards, doctors, and nurses, including those whose minds Soldier had bent to his will—flew across the room and slammed into the far wall. Bones shattered.

Before them, the pile of bodies, bedding, and machinery looked like the aftermath of a bomb blast. The lift doors were crumpled on their mounts; the lift control panel was shattered and spitting sparks. The alarms from medical equipment beeped plaintively. Moans and screams sounded from the wounded.

Soldier drew his lightsaber, activated it, and turned as the two security guards behind them drew their blasters and fired. His blade spun and he deflected both shots back at the guards, opening smoking holes in their chests. They staggered backward, fell, and died.

Screams came from all sides, some of terror, some of pain. An alarm activated and sang in high-pitched notes. The authorities would be coming.

"Come, Soldier," Seer said, her voice preternaturally calm. She had already scooped up Grace from the gurney. Soldier grabbed Hunter and put her over his shoulders. Runner picked his way through the carnage to the lifts and pressed futilely at the panel.

"You ruined them," Soldier said.

Runner whirled on him, his lips pulled back to bare his teeth. Caught up in Runner's anger, Soldier stepped in closer, fists clenched.

Seer interposed her body between them. "We use the stairs," she said.

Soldier swallowed hard, nodded. Runner said nothing, merely spun on his heel and used the Force to blow open the doorway to the stairs.

"Ruined this door, too," he said over his shoulder.

Soldier resisted the urge to drive his lightsaber into

Runner's back only because Seer, perhaps sensing his anger, put her hand on his forearm.

"Don't," she said.

They left the wounded and dying behind them and started up the stairwell.

As he climbed, Soldier wondered why he stayed with Seer. He could have taken Grace, even Hunter, and left Seer alone on her quest for Mother. Runner could not have stopped him.

But even as he asked the question, he knew the answer: he hated his doubt. He craved certainty, and he hoped, against his better judgment, that everything Seer said would ultimately prove true.

If that happened, he would kill his doubt forever.

Junker came out of hyperspace and the blue churn gave way to black, to Fhost's system. The system's star painted the cockpit in orange light. Ahead, the tan sphere of Fhost spun against the ink of space.

"Welcome home," Khedryn said. "Doesn't look the same somehow."

"No," Marr said thoughtfully. "It doesn't."

"The authorities may want us for questioning about The Hole," Jaden said.

"Reegas will not welcome our return," Marr observed.

Jaden had intervened in a sabacc game involving Khedryn and a local crime lord named Reegas. The game had turned into a brawl, and Jaden had left several of Reegas's bodyguards dead.

"We'll avoid sat pings, and planetary control won't know we're in-system," Khedryn said. He looked back at Jaden. "We're not staying long, are we?"

"Probably not," Jaden said.

Khedryn nodded. "You know the headings to use, Marr."

Marr started plugging numbers into the instrument panel. Jaden noticed that he did it with his eyes closed.

"I need to hail Ar-Six," Jaden said. He'd left his droid aboard his modified Z-95 in-system.

Khedryn handed him the ship-to-ship and Jaden input the frequency. The droid's beep of acknowledgment carried over the channel. The sound brought Jaden enormous comfort. Prior to meeting Khedryn and Marr, R-6 had been his sole companion for months.

"Good to hear you, too, Ar-Six," Jaden said.

Without further ado, R-6 exploded into droidspeak, unleashing a rapid series of whoops, beeps, and whistles.

"Slow down, Ar-Six," Jaden said.

"Something wrong?" Khedryn asked.

Jaden had trouble with droidspeak during the best of times, but he'd caught the note of alarm in R-6's tone and something about an attack. As a matter of routine, R-6 would monitor holo and radio transmissions planetside.

"Start over," Jaden said, and put the droid on speaker. "But go slower."

R-6 began again, and Khedryn and Marr watched Jaden as he listened.

"The medical facility on Fhost has been attacked," Jaden said.

"Users," Khedryn said, shaking his head. "Happens a few times per year. They get together in a gang and—"

"Repeat, Ar-Six," Jaden said, and the droid did so. "Are you sure that's what the report said?"

The droid beeped an affirmative.

Jaden looked to Khedryn and Marr. "Reports say that one of the attackers used a lightsaber. A red lightsaber."

A long moment of silence passed.

"Couldn't be," Khedryn said.

"The timing is right," Marr said. "They could be sick

after so long in isolation. Maybe they need medical supplies?"

"Ar-Six is getting this in real time," Jaden said. "So there's one sure way to find out."

"Heading for Farpoint Medical Center," Khedryn said, and wheeled *Junker* to starboard. "You're a magnet for this stuff, Jaden. Marr, I hope you know what you signed on for."

"Keep monitoring planetary authorities, Ar-Six," Jaden said, and the droid beeped an affirmative.

"There isn't much in the way of official security, Jedi," Khedryn said. "Reegas and those like him run Farpoint. The authorities are just thugs with uniforms. After the mess you left in The Hole, I doubt they'll even show up at the facility when they hear the word 'lightsaber.' " To Marr, he said, "Chewstim?"

Marr pulled the pack from his pocket, offered Khedryn a wedge.

"Better stow that caf," Khedryn said, nodding at the mugs.

Jaden and Marr scooped up the half-full mugs, dumped the contents, and packed them away.

Junker burned through the atmosphere, flames licking the ship's side. They completed reentry and burst through the cloud cover, and Fhost appeared below them. Farpoint looked like a darkened thumbprint on the planet's beige surface.

"Anything new, Ar-Six?" Jaden asked.

The droid beeped a negative.

"Maybe you ought to bring that droid aboard *Junker,* Jaden," Khedryn said.

Jaden stared at him, dumbfounded. Even Marr looked surprised.

"What?" Jaden said. "I thought you don't let droids aboard *Junker*."

"You seem fond of him, so maybe he's better than

most. Besides, I need *someone* to talk to when you two are off training. I feel like I'm flying a tomb. Too blasted quiet in here. That droid seems chatty, if nothing else."

"I see," Jaden said, smiling.

"Maybe time for some other changes, too," Khedryn said. "You don't seem inclined to run away from things, which is too bad, since it's a habit that's served me well for thirty years. So maybe we ought to arm *Junker* with something other than a tractor beam."

Jaden knew better than to push. "Whatever you think is best. She's your ship."

"Darn right she is," Khedryn said. He pointed down out of the transparisteel canopy. "There's the facility."

The medical center's ten stories had once been part of the bridge tower of the crashed ship that formed the bones of Farpoint. As the tallest building in Farpoint, it looked like a victory pennon planted in the city center. The doors of its rooftop landing pad lay wide open, a medical supply ship visible on the deck.

Jaden saw three swoops circling the exterior of the building at various altitudes, their sirens flashing orange.

"They're not going in," Jaden said.

"Told you," Khedryn said. "They'll let internal security handle it, then come in to clean up when it's over."

"Security can't handle even one of those clones."

"We don't know that it's the clones."

R-6's droidspeak carried over the comm. Jaden nodded, listening.

"Reports from inside say they're heading up the stairs," he translated. "The lifts were damaged in some kind of explosion. There are a lot of dead and wounded."

"At least they're in a hospital," Khedryn said, then winced at his bad joke. "Not funny. Sorry." He cleared his throat. "Coming in. Where should I set down?"

"If they're taking the stairs, they're going up."

"The supply ship?" Marr asked.

Jaden frowned. "Possible, but they could be after just about anything. Or they could be after nothing. The Solusar clone I faced on the moon was insane. Using reason to anticipate their actions is a fool's game."

Jaden flashed on the Kamclone's wild eyes, the script written in blood on the door of the cloning chamber:

MOTHER IS HUNGRY.

He thought of the corpses piled several meters deep in the cloning cylinder, the thick, pungent stink of decay. The clones had killed everyone.

He had to get into the medical facility or there would be many more dead.

"Land on the roof. Marr, I need a schematic of that building."

"Yes, Master," said Marr, and worked the keys of his comp station.

"Still wondering why we're chasing them?" Khedryn asked Marr, and the Cerean gave no answer.

Junker blazed through the air, the medical facility getting larger in their vision.

"I have it," Marr said. He tapped a few keys, and a hologram of the building schematics materialized over his station. "Stairwells there and there," he said, pointing. "Both accessible from the roof."

"I'll take the west stairwell," Jaden said to Marr. "You take the east."

Marr nodded, his expression unmarked by fear. Jaden credited him for it.

"I'll go with Marr," Khedryn said.

Jaden shook his head. "No. You stay on the roof with *Junker*."

"I may not be a Jedi, but I can handle myself, Korr."

"I know that. You're my last line of defense, Khedryn. If they are making a run for that ship and get past us, I need to know it right away. Understood?"

Khedryn inclined his head. "All right. Understood."

"Good. Let's move, Marr."

Jaden and Marr ran through *Junker*'s corridors until they reached the cargo bay.

"I need a marker," Jaden said. "A transponder beacon or something like it. Anything aboard?"

Marr's expression turned puzzled. "We have salvage beacons. We use them to mark derelict ships if we can't tow them. We find them later with the beacons."

"Unique frequency?"

"Have to be. Otherwise other spacers would pick up the signal and take our salvage."

"Get me one."

Marr ran across the cargo bay, opened a wall-mounted bin, and pulled out one of the pyramidal beacons and brought it back to Jaden.

"What's the frequency?"

Marr told him. "Why do you need it?"

"Just in case," Jaden said. "Always have contingency plans, Marr. Nothing ever goes as planned. Be prepared with backup plans and be prepared to improvise."

"Yes, Master."

Khedryn's voice carried over the comlink. "Setting down."

Jaden punched a button on the control panel to open the door. Air and Fhost's dust billowed in. The sound of sirens carried over the wind.

Jaden seized Marr with his eyes. "If it's the clones in there, then they killed people, Marr. That means we're past philosophical discussions about nature and self determination. They've made their choice. We will have to stop them. Kill them. Do you understand?"

"Yes, Master."

Jaden heard no hesitation in Marr's tone. "Good. Now, do not engage the clones alone."

"Master—"

Jaden held up a hand. "You have had hours of training, Marr. Your connection to the Force is strong, but your abilities are trivial compared with those of a trained Force user. You call me immediately and we engage them together. That's an order."

Marr bowed his head. "Yes, Master."

Only the faint glow of instrumentation broke the darkness of the scout flyer's cockpit. Both Syll and Nyss, born under the faint sun and dim skies of Umbara, preferred to keep the cockpit lights turned off. They saw in darkness better than they did in light. In some indefinable way, Nyss had always considered himself kin to darkness, an instrument of the night.

He looked under his feet, through the transparisteel bubble of the scout's cockpit. Korriban roiled below them, spinning slowly in its shroud of clouds. Nyss appreciated the planet's austere bleakness, even felt a kinship to it. He watched it churn, an angry black ball of storms and dark-side energy. Of course, he felt none of the energy, not even faintly. He and his sister did not possess whatever connection living things ordinarily had with the Force.

He and Syll were unique in the galaxy, disconnected from it.

Perhaps the disconnect made them dead, he mused with a smile. Or maybe he and Syll were the only two really alive and everyone else labored under the illusion of the interconnectedness of life, a shared falsehood belied by the truth of Syll and Nyss's existence. He liked that. He was truth. The rest of the galaxy was a lie.

He looked over and watched Syll input data into the

navicomp. Her dark hair and pale face made her look like an archaic photographic negative, the opposite of what she resembled, a false image of reality.

He thought her beautiful.

Syll finished plugging Fhost's coordinates into the navicomp of the scout flyer and Nyss went through the pre-jump checklist.

"Course is set," Syll said. "Tracking beacon on the cloakshape fighter is active."

Nyss nodded, set his palm on one of the cortosis-coated vibroblade knives he wore at his belt. The metal felt cool to the touch.

"We could use the Iteration," Syll said. "Why leave him in stasis?"

In truth, Nyss wanted the clone in stasis because he did not want another's presence to defile the time he spent with his sister. He preferred her company, and her company alone.

"If he's conscious, he generates more memories. And the more memories he possesses, the more the Rakatan mindspear must wipe away before making him anew."

From the fix of her jaw, he could see that his explanation did not fully satisfy his sister.

"If we need him, we'll get him out," he said finally. "Suitable?"

"Suitable."

"This shouldn't be difficult," he said. "Smash and grab, as before."

"Right."

"Ready?"

She nodded. "Let's go."

He held a hand out for his sister. She took his hand in hers, their arms bridging the gap between their seats. Syll activated the light filters on the cockpit bubble. Nyss engaged the hyperdrive and they leapt together into the abyss. The streaks of hyperspace irritated their eyes—and normal space disappeared. They floated alone in the dark warm womb of the cockpit.

Nyss felt most at home while in hyperspace. Probably because it, like him, was separate from the galaxy, not subject to the ordinary rules that governed reality.

Through the dimmed transparisteel of the cockpit bubble, the star lines of hyperspace were grayed out and barely visible, a dark curtain parsecs wide.

He settled in to pass the time.

chapter six

Nyss felt a sense of loss as the scout flyer came out of hyperspace and realspace hit him like cold water to the face. Hyperspace was the hole in the galaxy that mirrored the hole in his being. He enjoyed his time in it, emptiness communing with emptiness.

Syll partially undimmed the cockpit's transparisteel to reveal the mostly brown sphere of Fhost, backlit by its distant orange star.

Nyss engaged the ion engines and the ship blazed through the system. Planetary authorities did not comm them. Likely the technology on a backwater planet like Fhost could not even detect the scout flyer. Its baffles and cloaked propulsion system made it difficult for even up-to-date tech to get a fix on.

As they closed on Fhost, Nyss activated the tracking system attuned to the beacon the One Sith had placed on the cloakshape fighter. He waited for it to retrieve the signal. It took only moments.

He zeroed in on the location. A hologram of Fhost's surface appeared above his comp station, the transparent image of the planet turning rapidly as the program pinpointed the location of the beacon.

"It's twenty kilometers outside of the planet's largest city," he said. "Farpoint."

"What's there?"

"Nothing," he said. "They may have ditched it."

"Then we must hope they're still on-planet."

Nyss knew the clones were sick and prone to madness—all clones from Thrawn's program were. If they were still on Fhost, they'd almost certainly do something to attract the attention of the authorities.

"Monitor the planetary authorities' frequencies."

Syll set the comm to scan planetary frequencies originating in Farpoint. Meanwhile, they closed on the planet and burned through its atmosphere. Planetary control still did not comm them.

Tracking the beacon, they flew low and set down in a wood half a kilometer from the clones' ship. Once on the ground, they donned light-inhibiting goggles that doubled as macrobinoculars, checked their vibroblade knives, and slung their crossbows over their backs. Neither used blasters—too crude a weapon for their work. Their crossbow quarrels killed just as effectively as blaster fire and did so in relative silence.

They departed the ship via the small exit lift and glided through the forest. The goggles shielded them from the annoyance of the sun where the forest canopy did not provide shade. In silence they flitted from shadow to shadow. The sounds of the forest—the songs of native birds, the chirps of insects—did not change. Even the animals failed to note their passage.

In a short while they reached the edge of a large clearing. The cloakshape fighter sat in the center of the clearing, landing skids sunk deeply into the damp ground. The large cargo bay, added at some point in the past to the modular ship, hung from the craft's middle like a fat belly. The cargo bay door yawned, revealing a dark interior.

Hidden in the tree line, Nyss increased the magnification of his goggles and eyed what he could see of the inside. Bits of machinery and ragged clothing were cast about like flotsam, a toppled stasis chamber. There was also a body, female. She looked dead. He watched for a while longer and saw no movement in the hold.

In the handcant he and Syll had developed as children, he signaled, *One body. I'll go in. You cover.*

She nodded, unslung her crossbow, fitted it with one of the razor-tip quarrels they favored, and took sight at the doorway.

Nyss put a vibroblade in each hand, the familiar vibrations of the weapons welcome in his palms. He slipped from the shadows and darted across the clearing. He consciously restrained the Force-suppressing field he could generate around him. If any of the clones were inside, they would be alerted if their connection to the Force were severed.

He could smell the decay before he reached the ship. He lurked at the boarding ramp for a moment, head cocked, listening. Hearing nothing, he signaled back to Syll that he was going in, and then hurried up the ramp.

Inside the cargo bay, the smell hit him more strongly. He noted the bodies. Their clothing consisted of worn layers of Thrawn-era Imperial garb, their hair long, thick, and unkempt. Clones. He noted a male, a female, and two young children, a boy and girl.

The clones had children.

He could tell at a glance that the male was not the Prime—the face was wrong—so he took his time in examining the bodies. The woman had died first, and the burst boils and sores that covered her skin showed that she had died in pain, no doubt of some illness associated with genetic decoherence. He'd never seen a case so acute. He'd never *heard* of a case so acute. A long scar ran from the bottom of her throat to her navel, a zipper put there by one of Thrawn's doctors decades earlier. He put his fingers on the lightsaber hilt still affixed to her belt. The crystal that powered it, connected as it was to the Force, felt like an itch behind his eyes.

He moved to the children, saw no visible wounds on them. He assumed that the decoherence had manifested differently in them, born as they were, rather than grown.

The adult male, on the other hand, had died in combat. His skin was seared on the arms and chest—perhaps from Force lightning, but that had not been his cause of death. Given the hemorrhaging in his eyes, the bruises on his throat, Nyss judged that he'd died of suffocation.

He stood, thinking. The clones from the moon were dying from complications associated with genetic decoherence. For some reason, the decoherence in *these* clones had resulted in symptoms far more acute than usual. Eleven clones had fled the moon in the cloakshape fighter. Assuming they had not disposed of other bodies en route, four were dead, the Prime not among them.

He whispered into his comlink. "Four dead inside. I'll check the rest of the—"

The sizzle and hum of igniting lightsabers pulled him around.

A male clone, well over two meters tall, his long brown hair and thick beard obscuring much of his face, stood in the narrow hatchway that led from the cargo bay toward the cockpit. He was soaked in sweat and swayed on his feet. His glassy eyes fixed on Nyss.

A red lightsaber burned in each of his hands. Both of them sizzled, spitting sparks like a campfire.

"Get away from them," the clone said, his speech slurred but his intent clear. He took a lurching step toward Nyss.

"I am looking for the rest of your . . . family," Nyss said. He readied himself, held his blades under his cloak, shielded from the clone's view.

The clone took another step toward him, his breathing loud and rapid. He sniffed the air in Nyss's direction, as if for spoor.

"You want to kill them," he said. The flesh of his arms shifted and bulged, as if something within him were trying to escape the prison of his skin. He stared wide-eyed at his arms, then his face, too, twisted and swelled, for a moment looking like a reflection in a festival mirror.

"No!" he said, spraying spit.

Nyss had never seen anything like it. "I can help you," he said, a lie.

The clone shook his head like an animal and roared, and Nyss saw only pain and rage in his wild eyes. He was lost to reason.

Nyss released his hold on his suppressive field, willed it to expand—but he was too late. The clone made a cutting gesture with his hand, and a blast of energy blew Nyss across the cargo bay and into the toppled stasis chamber. The impact sent a shock of pain through him.

Growling like a beast, the clone bounded across the cargo bay, blades held high and spitting sparks. Nyss leapt to his feet and let the clone come.

Rage prevented the clone from sensing when he first entered Nyss's suppressive field. He stabbed both blades at Nyss's abdomen, but Nyss flipped backward atop the stasis chamber. The blades sank halfway into the metal, melting a good chunk of it to slag and warming the rest.

"Where are the other clones?" Nyss said calmly. Shadows coalesced around him, as they always did when he used his power.

The clone pulled his blades free and crosscut for Nyss's legs. Nyss flipped over the blades, over the clone, and landed behind him, all the while intensifying his suppressive field. The darkness in the cargo bay deepened, as if the sun outside had moved behind thick clouds.

The clone spun in a reverse crosscut at Nyss's neck and Nyss ducked under it; the clone stabbed with his off hand at Nyss's abdomen and Nyss sidestepped it.

"Where? Tell me where they went."

The clone roared in frustration and anger, spraying snot and spit. He raised both blades above his head for a killing strike. Nyss realized that he would get nothing from the clone. He sharpened his suppressive field as the clone swung his lightsabers down in arcs intended to cut Nyss in half twice over.

Nyss did not bother to dodge the blows as the weapons descended, merely stared into the face of the clone, whose expression turned from satisfied rage to profound surprise.

Nyss's intensified field had momentarily severed the connection between the power crystal in the lightsaber and the Force. The clone held only hilts in his hands.

With regret, Nyss thrust one of his vibroblades into the clone's chest. Warm blood gushed from the wound, soaked the weapon, his hand. The clone, wide-eyed, openmouthed, stared at Nyss until the light went out of his eyes and he fell to the floor of the cargo bay.

Syll, her crossbow at the ready, sprinted up the boarding ramp and took in the scene. Her lower lip curled in distaste when she saw the mess. "You're all right?" she asked him.

"I'm fine," he said, staring down at the clone, whose eyes remained open, filled with madness even in death.

"It's amazing how far the One Sith have improved Thrawn's cloning technology." He knelt and wiped his blade on the clone's coarse cloak. "These are the very best that Thrawn's scientists could produce."

Syll stood next to him, looking down at the body of the clone. "The Prime is the best that Thrawn could produce. And he did what Thrawn wanted. Thrawn just didn't live to activate him."

"Six more of the clones are unaccounted for," Nyss said.

"We should search the ship," she said, but Nyss was already shaking his head.

"A waste of time. They went to Farpoint."

Syll glanced about the cargo bay, at the bodies, the mess. "Why?"

Nyss shrugged. "Supplies, maybe." His gaze fell on the female clone, dead from decoherence. "They're sick, very sick. They may not understand what they have. I don't understand what they have."

Syll knelt and picked something up off the floor. She held it up for Nyss to see—a used pre-prepped hypo.

"And there's another," she said, pointing at a second hypo on the floor. "And another."

He read the preprinted labels on the hypo. "Perhaps they know what they have after all."

"They went to Farpoint for medicine," said Syll.

"Let's go get them."

They ran out of the cloakshape fighter, through the woods, and back to the scout flyer.

The relative darkness of the flyer's cockpit was a welcome respite from the outside glare. Syll monitored local frequencies as Nyss engaged the ship's thrusters. The ship rose straight up above the forest's canopy. A 3-D map of Fhost's surface appeared in Nyss's HUD, a small red light blinking over Farpoint.

"There's a landing field west of the city," he said. "We'll put down there, see if we can locate the clones."

Syll held up a finger for silence, listening to something she was hearing on local frequencies.

"Someone has attacked Farpoint's medical facility," she said.

Nyss reprogrammed the HUD to show him the medical facility, a ten-story spike driven into the center of

Farpoint. It looked like a dart, pinning Farpoint to the surface.

"Reports vary between three and six attackers," Syll said, still listening.

"It has to be them," Nyss said. "They're trying to get the medicine they need."

He climbed to altitude and engaged the engines. The scout flyer streaked through Fhost's sky, rapidly closing the distance to Farpoint.

From a distance, the city looked like a ship that had been stretched on its ends until it broke apart, its pieces scattering across a couple of kilometers. The spire of the medical center rose out of the decrepitude, impossible to miss. Nyss noted a landing pad on the roof, its large doors folded open. As he watched, a YT-class freighter streaked in and descended onto the landing pad.

YT-class freighters were as common as desperation in the Outer Rim, but its appearance right there, right then, gave Nyss pause. Syll voiced his thoughts.

"The spacers and Korr flew a YT, according to the Anzat's reports."

"Yes," Nyss agreed.

Perhaps they could hit two targets with one shot.

A few dozen swoops and speeder bikes dotted the sky over Farpoint. Sirens flashed red on several that flew near the medical center. Smoke spiraled into the sky from somewhere else in the city, far from the medical center.

"You take the stick," Nyss said to Syll. "Take me over the landing pad, but don't land."

"What will you do?"

"I'm jumping," Nyss said. "Be ready. When I have the Prime and Korr, I'll signal you on our usual channel."

"Go," she said.

The medical center loomed large through the cockpit transparisteel. Nyss pulled on his goggles, then hurried into the rear compartment, where they stored equipment. There, he took an antigrav pack, strapped it on, and stepped into the airlock.

"Almost there," Syll said over her comlink. "Reports have the clones in the stairwells and coming up. That has to be the spacer's freighter. It's got a modified ship's boat instead of an escape pod."

Nyss took hold of one of the bars bolted to the wall of the airlock and pressed the button to open the hatch. Wind and light and the scream of sirens blazed into the tiny compartment. Still holding the grip, he leaned out and looked down.

The scout flyer was almost upon the medical center. Nyss could see the landing pad ahead. The YT had set down near another ship, a large, cylindrical supply ship of some kind.

"Over in three, two, one. Mark."

Syll slowed for only a moment, and Nyss did not hesitate. He leapt from the airlock, spread his arms and legs to catch the wind, and fell free toward the building's landing pad.

The duracrete rectangle sped up to meet him. He waited, waited, then engaged the antigrav pack at the last moment. He fell the final ten meters at walking speed, hit the metal of the landing pad in a roll, bounced to his feet, and sprinted into the shadow of the large ship. There, he stripped off the antigrav pack. The shining star of Pharmstar Industries marked its side: it was a medical supply ship.

Loading droids milled about on the far end of the ship, preparing to unload it. Nyss drew the darkness to him and sank into the shadows near a stack of shipping containers. The droids did not see him.

He knew exactly what the clones intended. They were not attacking the medical center, at least not primarily.

Into his comlink, he whispered, "They're going to hijack the medical supply ship on the pad."

Syll's soft tones answered him. "Jaden Korr will try to stop them."

As if summoned by her words, the landing ramp of the YT descended and he saw Jaden Korr and the Cerean, Marr Idi Shael, standing in the open hatch. Had Jaden been alone, Nyss might have made an attempt then and there.

As it was, he remained in hiding, unseen, and watched.

The moment *Junker* touched down, Jaden and Marr bounded out of the cargo bay and onto the landing pad. Khedryn's voice carried over the comlink, ghostly.

"Be careful."

Jaden looked back at *Junker* and saw Khedryn through the transparisteel off the cockpit, giving them a thumbs-up.

Marr ran for the doorway that opened onto the east stairwell. Jaden headed for the west stair, but diverted toward the medical supply ship. A half-dozen loading droids stood beside the ship, waiting for the lateral cargo bay doors to open so that they could begin unloading.

"May I help you, sir?" asked one of the droids.

Ignoring it, Jaden activated a beacon and tossed it high up on the ship's side, where it stuck to the hull. He caught a peculiar ripple in the Force, an odd twinge, but it passed instantly. He looked around, saw nothing, and assumed it had something to do with the clones. He switched channels on his comlink and raised R-6.

"Ar-Six, I just placed a signal beacon on a ship that may try to leave the system." He gave R-6 the signal frequency. "If that ship lifts off and you don't hear from me, you inform the Order that I believe the escaped clones are aboard."

R-6 beeped an affirmative, then added a bit more in droidspeak.

"Don't worry," Jaden said. "I'll be careful."

He augmented his speed with the Force and reached the door to the west stairwell just after Marr reached the east. The Cerean held his lightsaber in one hand, his blaster in the other. He opened the door and entered without looking back.

Jaden threw open the west door and entered the stairwell. The sound of alarms carried from far below. The flights of stairs formed a perimeter around a deep, square stairwell. He leaned over the railing and looked down. The angle did not allow him to see the stairs very clearly, but he heard doors opening and closing on several floors below him. He also heard the sounds of hurried footsteps, frightened whispers.

He activated his comlink and whispered to Marr, "I think there are civilians on the stairs. Be mindful."

"I will," Marr whispered in answer.

Nyss considered his options. He needed to get to Korr, but he needed Korr alone. He could not risk exposing the One Sith's involvement unless he was certain of success. Indecision ate away the moments. It would do him little good to involve himself in a combat between Korr and the Prime.

"They are inside the building," he whispered to Syll.

"If he dies, then it's all for nothing."

Nyss's reply was sharp. "I know that. But if we're discovered, it's worse."

To that, Syll did not reply.

Jaden started down the stairs—past the ninth floor, the eighth. On each floor, he opened the stairwell door and

poked his head out into the hallway of the medical center proper, looking for anything unusual. The halls were
empty but for the occasional furtive passage of a doctor
or nurse. An alarm sounded. A voice over the speakers
instructed all personnel and patients to remain in their
rooms. When anyone saw Jaden, fear filled their eyes.
He smiled and did his best to look harmless before returning to the stairwell. He continued in that fashion—
the seventh floor, the sixth, listening for anything
unusual, waiting, waiting. . . .

A sudden scream startled him; it was followed by
shouts from three floors below, then the sound of an activating lightsaber, another, then another. Blaster shots,
then more screams.

"My side, third floor, in the stairwell," he said to Marr
over his comlink, as he activated his lightsaber and leapt
over the railing and down the shaft. He used the Force
to slow his descent and grabbed the fourth-floor railing
as he fell. The moment his free hand closed on it, he augmented his strength and pulled himself up, arresting his
fall and flipping onto the stairway between the fourth
and fifth floors.

He landed face-to-face with a startled nurse who had
been trying to flee up the stairs to the fifth-floor landing.
Two security guards lay dead on the fourth-floor landing
behind her, the black holes in their chests still leaking
smoke.

The woman opened her mouth to scream, but Jaden
shoved her behind him before she could get a peep out.

"Get out of here," he said, hearing footsteps coming
up the stairs at a jog and feeling the dark side press
against his consciousness.

One of the clones turned the corner of the stairs below
him. He looked vaguely familiar to Jaden, but his long
beard and shaggy hair made his features hard to discern.
He wore a threadbare Imperial uniform a size too small,

the whole covered in a gray cloak made from sewn blankets. The red blade of his lightsaber sizzled and sparked, its edges irregular.

The clone's wild, bloodshot eyes widened when he saw Jaden. Jaden took advantage of the clone's surprise. He drew on the Force, extended a hand, and struck the clone with a blast of concussive energy so strong it blew the clone back down the stairs and drove him into the floor. The clone lay there, dazed.

"Runner!" said a female voice.

Jaden took the stairs three at a time, bounded past the fallen clone, and saw two more—a woman, lithe and bald, and a man, tall, with long, straight brown hair and a beard. The woman carried a small girl. The man carried an unconscious woman, but when he saw Jaden, he let her slide to the ground and activated his lightsaber, red and angry.

Jaden lunged forward. The woman backed off a step, shielding the child, and the man met his charge, parrying Jaden's overhand slash with his red blade.

Across the intersected blades, Jaden locked eyes with the clone—and gasped.

He was staring into gray eyes the mirror of his own.

The realization took a moment to register, and when it did, it hit him like a punch in the face, staggering him. He lost focus, lost his concentration. The realization pulled a single word from him as implications crashed down on him.

"How?"

The clone unleashed a blast of Force that drove Jaden up against the far wall. Jaden recovered himself enough to cushion the impact with the Force, but the clone followed up immediately, leaping forward and unleashing a crosscut at Jaden's throat.

Jaden ducked under the red blade at the last moment and it cut a deep groove in the wall, causing a shower of sparks. He kicked out a leg and swept the clone's legs, but instead of falling prone, the clone caught himself on one hand before hitting the ground, pushed off, and backflipped away from Jaden.

Battle cleared the surprise from Jaden's mind, and the moment the clone's feet touched the ground, Jaden unleashed a blast of power designed to slam him into the wall.

The clone snarled, held up a hand, palm outward, and met Jaden's blast with his own. Power pressed against power and Jaden and the clone eyed each other across the landing, jaws fixed, eyes locked, neither gaining the advantage.

On the stairway above him and to his left, Jaden saw the clone he had dazed rise to his feet and shake his head, growling. His angry eyes fixed on Jaden. He gestured with both hands, and sent a burst of power at the Jedi.

Jaden held out his left hand—his maimed hand—at the last moment, intercepted the blast, and answered with his own power. The clone's push caused him to stagger, but he nested himself in the Force and stood his ground against both clones. He held his hands out, the clones' power pressing at him from right angles. The yellow line of his lightsaber, which he still held in his left had, sizzled before his eyes. The effort squeezed sweat from him, taxed mind and body. He took a step back, another, and found himself pressed against the wall. He could not hold out for long.

The female clone stared at him, a strange smile on her face. Her strong jaw and almond-shaped eyes clicked in Jaden's memory and he recognized her as a clone of the Dark Jedi Lumiya. Her baldness had thrown him at first. The child, her face dirty, her long red hair matted, did not move at all.

"What do you want?" Jaden asked through gritted teeth.

"To go home," the Lumiya-clone said.

"I can't allow that," Jaden said.

Her smile deepened. "You cannot stop us. No one can. Mother has called."

As one, the two male clones took a step toward Jaden, their power pressing against him. He fell to one knee, grunting against their onslaught, barely holding on.

They took another step and he fell to both knees.

The larger of the two grinned. Jaden recognized him now, behind the beard and hair. He was a clone of Jaden's Master, Kyle Katarn. Anger poured off both clones, anger born of years of frustration and mistreatment. It hit Jaden like a hailstorm. His elbows bent. He was failing, failing.

But he refused to give in.

He grunted, summoned a reserve of strength, extended his arms fully, pushed back against the clones, stood up, and held his ground.

"I won't let you pass," he grunted. "I can't."

His words erased the smile on the Lumiya-clone's face. She shrieked, her calm façade shattering under the sudden expression of her rage. Power went forth from her, joined that of the other two clones, and slammed him against the wall.

"Kill him, Soldier!" she screamed. "Kill him!"

The Jaden-clone deactivated his lightsaber and raised his free hand, fingers spread like a claw. Jaden knew instantly what was coming and braced himself as blue Force lightning filled the distance between them.

Jaden adjusted his blade slightly and the lightning caught in it, snaked around its length, spiraled toward the hilt, hit Jaden's hand, his forearm, his bicep.

The power burned his flesh while turning his spirit cold. He grimaced with pain. Trying to resist, he opened himself fully to the Force, but the clone's power was too much.

He screamed, took his lightsaber hilt in both hands and spun it before him, winding the Force lightning back up along its blade and away from his body. But his focus on the lightning cost him, and a renewed push from the Katarn-clone slammed him against the wall. The side of his face hit the duracrete and he sagged to the floor, struggling to maintain consciousness.

The Jaden-clone, Soldier, walked toward him.

"Just let us go, Jedi," he said.

Jaden's tongue and lips would not make words, so he shook his head.

The lightning sizzled again, the power pushing him along the floor, burning his flesh, searing his spirit. He was still holding his blade, still managing to deflect the bulk of the energy. He just needed to regain his wits, his clarity of thought.

The other clone, the Katarn-clone, appeared before him. Jaden had not seen him approach. His red blade cut down to split Jaden's head. Jaden blocked awkwardly with his blade, which was still enmeshed in Force lightning. The clone snarled, then loosed a Force-augmented kick to the side of Jaden's face that caused him to see stars and sent him careering down the stairs. He hit the next landing, and, fearing a follow-up attack, staggered to his feet, wobbly, weaving, unable to see clearly. He saw them above him, tried to ready himself, but a misstep sent him tumbling down the next flight of stairs.

He hit his head again. Blackness beckoned and he could not resist it.

Marr fought to keep calm as he darted through the medical facility's hallways. He sprinted past a few doctors, nurses, patients on gurneys, medical and maintenance droids.

"Who are you?" someone shouted.

He left unanswered questions and alarmed glances in his wake, holding his purple lightsaber in one hand, his blaster in the other. He could see the building's schematic in his mind and headed directly for the stairwell access door.

He shouldered through it, blaster and blade ready, and nearly tripped over Jaden's prone form.

"Master!"

He heard footsteps on the stairs far above them, voices, but saw no sign of the clones. He considered following, but only for a moment. His Master had ordered him not to engage them alone.

He knelt over Jaden. The side of his Master's face was discolored, his lip split, his right eye filled with blood from burst capillaries. But he was breathing. Marr tapped Jaden's cheeks but got no response.

He squeezed his comlink and raised Khedryn.

"Jaden is down, Khedryn. The clones are heading for the supply ship. Get it airborne or get everyone out of it."

"Jaden is down? What does that mean?"

"Go, Khedryn," Marr said, "Go, now!"

Cursing, Khedryn strapped on his blaster, jumped out of his seat, and tore through *Junker*, through the cargo bay, and down the landing ramp. He ran straight for the medical supply ship. When he got near the cockpit, he started shouting and waving his hands.

Through the transparisteel of the cockpit, he saw the crew still in their seats, probably going through some postlanding checklist, or perhaps trying to raise the medical facility—to no avail.

The three cargo doors hung open and the treaded loading droids were beginning to unload the materials. Khedryn hated droids—the blasted things performed their tasks without exercising judgment of any kind. The building could have been falling down and they'd continue unloading throughout.

"Raise the crew!" he shouted to the nearest droid. "Tell them to take off."

The droids either did not hear him or wouldn't acknowledge him.

He cursed and ran into the ship. The droids protested behind him—*now* they noticed him—but he ignored them. He pelted through the cargo bay, loaded with stacks of shipping containers, and made his way to the bridge, shouting the entire time.

Nyss slipped from the shadows and followed the freighter pilot onto the medical supply ship. He trailed him through the cargo bay and toward the cockpit, trying to determine exactly what was happening.

"I'm on the supply ship," he whispered to Syll.

Unable to rouse Jaden, Marr ran out of the stairwell and into the main hall of the medical facility. Wide eyes and alarmed glances greeted his appearance. Someone screamed, perhaps thinking him one of the attackers.

"I'm here to help," he said absently, looking for a medical locker. He found one mounted on a nearby wall, cut it open with his blade, and removed a packet of Quickwake. He hurried back to the stairwell and cracked the Quickwake tube.

Its ammonia smell cleared Marr's nostrils and made his eyes water. He placed it under Jaden's nose. Right away Jaden turned his head away from the stench, gasping. His eyes opened, fixed on Marr.

"Master, what happened?" Marr asked.

"The clones," Jaden said, and started to sit up. Marr assisted him.

"Up there," Marr said, and nodded to the stairway. "I've alerted Khedryn."

Leaning on Marr, Jaden climbed to his feet. "Khedryn can't stop them."

Khedryn burst through the cockpit door of the supply ship, breathing heavily. The captain, gray-haired and overweight, whirled to face him. The copilot, younger and thin, almost fell out of his chair with surprise.

"I know how this looks," Khedryn said. "But you've got to listen to me. Get this ship off the pad, right now!"

The captain's initial fear gave way to a look of confusion. "What?"

Khedryn had no time to talk about Sith-Jedi clones, so he lied. "I'm with building security. Criminals are making their way up through the facility right now. They want this ship. Get it out of here."

That seemed to register. The copilot spun in his chair, starting work at the instrument panel.

The captain said, "It'll take a few minutes to get the engines back online and close the cargo doors. She won't fly with the cargo doors open. Corporate safety feature to preserve accidental dumping of cargo."

Khedryn pinched his comlink. "How much time do they have, Marr?"

No response.

"Marr?"

Khedryn cursed.

"We could just seal the cockpit until the authorities come," the copilot offered.

Khedyrn shook his head. He knew what a lightsaber could do. If the clones got aboard, there'd be no keeping them out of the cockpit.

"Get off," Khedryn said.

"What?" the copilot said.

"No," the captain said, shaking his head. "We can't abandon the cargo—it comes out of our pay."

"That's why corporations have insurance, man. Get

off, now. There's no pay to collect if you're dead." When the captain hesitated, Khedryn drew his blaster and leveled it at him. "Now. I'm sorry, but this is for your own good."

That did it. The captain and copilot stood and Khedryn pushed them through the ship, down the lift, through the corridors, and into the cargo bay.

"Marr?" Khedryn called over his comlink. "Marr?"

"Where are we supposed to go?" the copilot asked. "If they're coming up the stairway, how do we get out of here?"

"Hide somewhere out on the deck. They don't care about you. They just want the ship. Marr, do you hear me?"

The captain and copilot ran down the ramp, the captain's belly bouncing every which way. They stopped at the bottom of the ramp, looked around. The copilot pointed to a stack of shipping containers near *Junker* and they sprinted toward it.

"Marr, if you can hear me, the crew is off the ship but we can't get her away in time."

Still no response. Khedryn began to worry.

He did not head back to *Junker*. Instead, he ran for the east stairwell.

Nyss lingered in the cargo bay of the supply ship and watched the spacer go. The droids worked around him, oblivious to his presence. He had no idea what had happened with Korr and the clones.

"Anything on the comm channels?" he asked Syll.

"Nothing new," she answered.

There was little for him to do but wait. He could not risk revealing himself too soon.

Before Khredyn reached the access door to the stairs, it exploded outward from its hinges and clattered on the landing pad. He ducked and shielded his face from flying debris.

The clones hurried out of the doorway, one of the males bearing a wounded adult, the female carrying a child of about nine. The male clones each held a sparking red lightsaber in hand.

"Stop there," Khedryn said, leveling his blaster.

They did not stop, so he fired at the foremost male—one shot, another, another. The clone, a towering human male with long hair and a thick beard, deflected the shots into the air and started to run toward Khedryn.

Khedryn backed toward the supply ship as fast as he could, still firing. Deflecting every shot, the clone closed on him rapidly. The other clones moved more slowly behind him.

Khedryn kept hoping that Jaden and Marr would emerge from the stairway, but neither did. He was in deep water and he knew it.

Shots came from somewhere in the sky above. They put black streaks on the landing pad near the clone's feet and knocked him down. Khedryn looked up to see two police officers on armed swoop bikes circling back for another pass.

"Yeah!" he said, and fired at the clone again.

From his knees, the clone deflected his shots without so much as looking at Khedryn, then made a seizing gesture with his off hand.

Above, the swoops' engines screamed, warring with the clone's power and losing. The clone made a cutting gesture, his teeth bared in a snarl, and slammed both swoops to the ground near the stack of shipping containers. A fireball blossomed, consuming bikes and riders. The clone stood, his eyes fixed on Khedryn.

Very deep water.

Khedryn turned and sprinted for the supply ship, firing wildly over his shoulder as he went. He had no idea what he would do once he got aboard the ship—seal it up, maybe buy some time for more police to arrive, for Jaden and Marr to get there.

A blast of power hit him in the back and drove him face-first into the metal of the landing pad. His nose crumpled and exploded blood. His teeth scraped along the pad. Only a surge of adrenaline kept him conscious. He got to all fours, turned, and aimed his blaster at the approaching clone.

Before he could squeeze the trigger, the clone gestured and Khedryn's blaster flew from his hand and into the clone's.

Khedryn knew he could not get away. He staggered up onto unsteady legs, swallowed, and resolved to die with defiance.

When the clone had closed to within a few paces, Khedryn spat at his feet. Blood and one of his teeth went with the spit.

"Blast you, pal!"

The clone snarled and made a cutting gesture that blew Khedryn backward ten meters and slammed his head against the landing pad.

Pain and blurry sparks, then blackness.

chapter seven

SOLDIER WATCHED RUNNER STRIDE TOWARD THE FALLEN
human. Runner flipped his blade and took a reverse
two-handed grip in preparation for driving it through
the man's chest.

"Wait!" Soldier shouted.

Runner looked over his shoulder, the wind blowing
his hair across his face so that Soldier could not read his
expression.

"Wait, Runner!" Soldier shouted again. "Seer, tell him!"

"Hold, Runner!" Seer said, and Runner obeyed her,
though he did not deactivate his blade.

Soldier and Seer, carrying Hunter and Grace, hurried
to Runner's side. Soldier nodded at the downed man. He
wasn't moving, and blood and dirt covered his face.

"If he's not dead, bring him," he said to Runner. "He
must be with the Jedi. I want to know how they found
us. They could send others."

Runner looked to Soldier, then to Seer, who nodded.
Grunting indifferently, Runner picked the man up by the
armpits and slung him roughly over his shoulder.

In Seer's arms, Grace stirred and opened her eyes.
"Soldier?" she said.

Soldier smiled, delighted to see Grace's eyes opened.
The meds he'd given her back on the cloakshape were
working. "Welcome back," he said.

"Is that my mother?" Grace said, nodding at Hunter.

Soldier nodded. "She'll be all right."

"I want to walk," Grace said to Seer, and Seer set her down.

Soldier watched her for a moment, then handed Hunter over to Seer.

"I'm going to check the containers the droids have unloaded. I want to make sure the meds are still aboard."

"Let's go aboard, Grace," Seer said.

Soldier watched them all head for the supply ship.

"Get the engines started," Soldier called to Runner and Seer. He looked skyward at the collection of police swoops that hovered at a distance. They showed no inclination to close or interfere.

Two droids rolled in front of Runner and Seer.

"Excuse me, but you are not authorized to—"

A diagonal slash from Runner's blades cut both droids in half, and the four smoking, sparking pieces fell to the landing pad.

Still hidden in the darkness of the supply ship's landing bay, Nyss watched the clones, bearing one of their wounded and Khedryn Faal, board the ship. He could have reached out and touched them with his hand as they passed. The Prime lingered on the deck outside. If Nyss could get the Prime alone, he could take him.

But the female clone shooed the child into the ship, then lingered in the cargo bay, near the ramp, watching the Prime.

Soldier hurriedly examined the labels on the shipping containers the loading droids had already unloaded, looking for the component materials he'd need to mix the Metacycline. He saw only probiotics and other ordinary supplies. No pharma.

"It's still aboard, isn't it?" Seer called to him from the

loading ramp. He could see her smiling from there, still holding Hunter.

"If it's here at all," he answered.

"You'll come to believe, Soldier."

He deactivated his lightsaber and hurried to the ship. Seer wore her smile the entire time. When he got in, he used the control panel to raise the cargo doors. By the time they closed, Runner had the engines online.

Storage containers lined the vast space of the cargo bay, hundreds of them stacked like children's blocks.

"I'll get the manifest and find the meds we need," he said to Seer. "Have Runner get the ship into the air and get us heading to . . . wherever we're going."

"To Mother," Seer said.

Hunter stirred in her arms. The meds were working for her, too.

"Yes," Soldier said. "To Mother."

After she left him, he found the nearest comp station and called up the ship's manifest. He felt as if he were engaged in a test of faith. If Seer was right, the meds were aboard. If she wasn't, then Seer, Runner, Hunter, and Grace would all die. Maybe Soldier would, too, in time, but he'd die alone, the last of them, purposeless.

He felt the ship lift off, felt the vibration as the landing skids retracted into the body of the ship. The engines engaged with a hum and he imagined the ship streaking skyward.

The manifest came online and he scrolled through it. His heart beat faster than it had when he'd faced the Jedi. He licked dry lips as he eyed the data, hopeful but afraid to let himself hope.

And there they were, just as Seer had said they would be: the genetic stabilizer, the antipsychotics, a few other reagents he'd need to mix in, all of them in such quantities that the clones would have enough for years, even with the accelerated pace of the illness.

Seer was right. Again.

The supply ship would not have a lab aboard, but he could make do. He pressed a button near the station to activate the onboard comm and raised the bridge.

"The meds we want are aboard. Lots of them."

A long pause followed, as if Seer and Runner were digesting his words. Finally Runner said, "We're away. Scanners show that no one is following us."

"Good. What about the prisoner?"

"He's still alive," Runner answered. "What course should I set?"

Now it was Soldier's turn for a long pause. After considering, he said, "Ask Seer. She knows where we're going."

He imagined her smiling at his response.

Nyss knew the Prime's name now: Soldier.

He maneuvered in silence through the dimly lit cargo bay, eyeing Soldier while the clone checked the cargo manifest at a comp station. With effort, Nyss kept the suppressive field closely drawn around him. He did not want Soldier to sense it . . . yet.

Nyss debated incapacitating Soldier then and there, but decided to wait.

If Jaden Korr was still alive, he would come for Khedryn Faal. And, when the time was right, Nyss could use his arrival to take both of them at once.

He moved off deeper into the cargo bay, away from Soldier, and raised Syll on his comlink.

"Have you been able to determine whether Korr is still alive?"

"He is," Syll said. "Both he and the Cerean are alive. I see them on the roof of the medical facility right now."

Nyss nodded, pleased. "Good. Don't let them see you. Lock onto my signal and follow the supply ship."

"What about Korr?"

"He'll follow, too. He put a tracking beacon on the supply ship before entering the facility."

"All right. And then what?"

Nyss was already working out the beginnings of a plan. "Keep your distance until I say otherwise. We're going to get Korr and the Prime."

"Should I bring the Iteration out of stasis?"

"Not yet."

Marr assisted Jaden up the stairs until they reached the roof. The access door had been knocked from its mounting and lay on the landing pad. The supply ship was already one hundred meters off the deck. Police swoops buzzed around it like sand flies, but they could do nothing to slow its ascent.

Burning wreckage lay near a stack of shipping containers, spitting a gout of black smoke into the sky. Pieces of one or more droids lay near where the supply ship had been docked. The rest of the loading droids stood aimlessly near the handful of shipping containers they'd unloaded before the supply ship launched. *Junker* sat on the pad, her landing ramp open.

Jaden stared up at the rising ship, concentrated, felt the dark-side signatures of the clones aboard.

"The clones are on that ship," he said.

There was no sign of Khedryn.

Marr nodded, activated his comlink. "Khedryn, do you read? Khedryn?"

No response. A pit formed in Jaden's stomach.

He and Marr shared a look and ran for *Junker,* hoping to find Khedryn aboard. Before they reached it, two figures emerged from behind a stack of shipping containers near the burning wreckage. Both wore dazed expressions and the uniforms of corporate flight officers. The older, gray-haired man, his belly hanging over the edge of his pants, wore the captain's wings. The younger man ran his hand over his hair, his eyes moving from the supply ship to the burning wreckage and back again.

"You piloted the supply ship?" Jaden asked, indicating the ship.

The men nodded, dazed.

"Did you see anyone else out here?" Marr asked them.

The men looked at them, seemingly not comprehending.

Jaden stood with his face in the captain's, locking the man's gaze. "Did you see another man around here?" He nodded at *Junker*. "He would have come out of that ship."

The captain blinked, nodded. "We saw a man. Dark hair. Lazy eye."

"That's him," Jaden said.

"He got us off the ship," the copilot said, looking skyward.

"Where is he now?" Marr asked.

"They got him," the captain said, nodding up at the supply ship just as its ion engines fully engaged and it shot skyward. "I'm sorry. I don't know if he was alive or dead. He saved us."

Jaden felt Marr's concern for Khedryn sharpen. The Cerean closed his eyes, visibly sought his calm. He inhaled deeply.

"Khedryn is still alive," Marr announced. "I can feel it."

"Then we'll get him back," Jaden said. He felt a rush of guilt. He had been so concerned with his responsibility to Marr that he had neglected his responsibility to Khedryn. The man was so competent that Jaden treated him as he might another Jedi, and that was a mistake. Khedryn would be no match for a trained Force user. Jaden had failed to consider that, and it had cost Khedryn dearly.

"Who were those people?" the copilot asked. "They had lightsabers. Red ones."

"They're the bad guys," Jaden said, and left it at that. To Marr, he said, "Come on," and they hurried toward *Junker*.

Police swoops circled the roof, started to descend. Jaden could not afford to waste time with an inquiry. He'd have to explain later.

They boarded *Junker* as several police swoops set down. *Junker*'s landing ramp started to rise. The supply ship's copilot ran toward the closing ramp and shouted at Jaden and Marr before it sealed.

"And who are you two, then?" called the copilot.

The ramp sealed.

"We're the good guys," Jaden said softly, and thought of his clone, another him, a murderous version of him.

They hurried through *Junker*'s corridors for the cockpit.

"I put the tracking beacon on the supply ship," Jaden said as they ran. "We can follow them wherever they go."

Marr nodded, his relief palpable to Jaden. Jaden activated his comlink and raised R-6.

"Ar-Six, put the Z-Ninety-five down on the Fhost landing field and seal it up. We'll be there to get you in a few moments."

The droid whooped agreement.

"We may need him," Jaden said to Marr by way of explanation.

"A good idea," Marr said.

When they reached the cockpit, Marr slammed into his seat and started the launch sequence. His fingers blazed over the controls. Jaden assisted.

"Calm, Marr," said Jaden. "Strong emotions serve only to slow effective action."

"Yes, Master," Marr said, but did not slow.

Several policemen stood outside on the landing pad, beckoning at Jaden and Marr through the transparisteel of the cockpit. Jaden activated the external loudspeaker.

"My name is Jaden Korr, Jedi Knight. The individuals who attacked the facility are criminals sought by the Order. I can't delay pursuit. Please back away from the ship."

He saw them confer—pointing at the ship, at the facility—then at last saw a ranking officer shrug and order the rest of them to stand away from *Junker*.

"She's ready," Marr said.

"You want to fly her?" Jaden asked Marr. "You're still the first officer."

Marr shook his head. "I'm the copilot and I'm not switching seats unless . . . I have to."

Jaden understood. "Let's get her up, then," he said, and took the controls.

Junker rose through the smoke and into the sky. The copilot of the supply ship stood with his arm raised in farewell. The gesture touched Jaden.

It made him feel like they were, indeed, the good guys.

They headed for Fhost's dusty landing field, the field where Jaden had first set down his Z-95 while following the Force Vision that had ultimately led him to the clones. It seemed to have occurred years before, not days.

They spotted his Z-95, R-6 rocking on his arms in excitement beside it. Jaden set down *Junker* and lowered the landing ramp. R-6 beeped over the comlink when he was aboard, and Jaden launched *Junker* back into Fhost's sky.

Before R-6 reached the cockpit, Jaden said to Marr, "I got good looks at the clones."

Marr nodded absently, still plotting courses, trying to get a fix on the tracking beacon.

"One of them was of Lumiya, a Sith agent."

Marr said nothing, lost in his task. He wouldn't know who Lumiya was.

"Another was of my own Master, Kyle Katarn."

That brought Marr up short. "I'm . . . sorry, Master. That must have been hard to see."

Jaden plowed onward. "It was. But listen, Marr. The other clone was of me."

Marr swung in his seat to face Jaden. "Of you?"

Jaden nodded.

"But . . . how is that possible?"

Jaden stared out the canopy. They were just moving through the atmosphere, the blue of Fhost's sky fading to the black of outer space.

"I'm still trying to figure that out myself. The math . . ."

"Grand Admiral Thrawn was killed five years after the Emperor died."

Jaden smiled absently. "You've been studying your history."

"As you instructed me to do, Master. When did you enter the Jedi Academy?"

"Nine years after the Emperor died."

Marr stared at him, the implication obvious. Jaden stated it anyway.

"The Empire had my DNA before anyone knew I was Force-sensitive. Not even my uncle knew."

"Obviously someone in the Empire knew."

Jaden shook his head. "Not possible."

"I don't understand. That doesn't make sense."

"I know."

"Then . . . what are you saying?"

Jaden struggled to maintain calm. "I don't know what I'm saying. I'm just stating the facts."

Marr sat quietly for a moment, and Jaden could see the gears of his mind turning. Finally, Marr said, "We don't know that they took your DNA before you enrolled at the Academy. They could have taken it after. The cloning program may have continued long after Thrawn's death. Someone else could have continued the program. And the pace of a clone's aging can be controlled."

"That's possible," Jaden acknowledged.

He tried not to grab too hard at Marr's theory, though it struck him as profoundly better than the alternative.

A beep of greeting announced R-6's appearance in the cockpit. He whooped and whistled.

"It's good to see you, too, Ar-Six," Jaden said, and patted the astromech on his domed head. "Connect to the subspace transmitter and inform the Order that we've left Fhost in pursuit of the clones. Give the details of the attack and . . ."

He trailed off. Marr eyed him sidelong.

". . . and that's it."

R-6 plugged into *Junker*'s computer core and started to transmit.

"I've got the beacon," Marr said, tapping a finger on the scanner screen.

"I see it," Jaden said, checking the instrument panel. "Let's get after them."

The dull buzz of voices pulled Khedryn out of the blackness. At first he heard the voices only as garbled nonsense, the rise and fall of pitch and timbre, not words. The stabs of pain in his ribs, head, and nose sharpened as his mind began to clear.

When he remembered what had happened, he forced his eyes open and looked on dim surroundings. Overhead lights cast only a slight glow. He tried to focus through blurry vision. His head throbbed with pain.

More words, something about a mother, a hyperspace course.

He was on the floor, propped against a wall. His hands were bound behind his back, the bonds cutting into the skin of his wrists. Small items lay scattered on the deck. He stared at them a long while before he realized that they were hypos.

He heard another hypo discharge and its empty cylinder hit the floor. He looked up and around. He saw an elaborate instrument panel, four swivel seats, a large viewport that showed stars and open space.

He was on a ship, in a cockpit.

On the bulkhead above the viewport, he saw the starburst symbol of Pharmstar Industries.

He was on the medical supply ship.

"He's awake," said a coarse voice from off to the side.

A large form stepped before him and blocked his view. He squinted through the pain and focused on worn boots, a ragged cloak, tattered clothing, a lightsaber hilt hanging from a belt. Glancing up, he looked into the blotchy, bearded face and wild eyes of the clone he'd shot at back on the landing pad of the medical facility.

A clone.

He'd been captured by the clones. The *mad* clones.

He tried to keep the flash of fear from his face, but he must have failed, because the clone before him grinned, showing yellow teeth.

"I think he knows where he is," the clone said, chuckling. He stepped away from Khedryn, sat in the pilot's seat, and started to work at the navicomp.

Khedryn's mind, still clunky, tried to piece together events, draw conclusions. The clones had gotten off Fhost. Did that mean that Marr and Jaden were dead? Why had the clones taken Khedryn instead of killing him?

He had no answers. He could barely breathe. His nose was broken. He blew out sharply and expelled a stream of snot and blood onto his face and shirt. The clones seemed not to notice or care.

A female clone stood beside the pilot's seat, one hand on the back of it. She stared out at space and he could see her in profile—her delicate features, her bald head.

He would have thought her beautiful had he met her in a cantina somewhere. Her eyes were closed and she swayed slightly, as if in a trance. A second woman sat in another of the chairs, her back to Khedryn, her long red hair pooling on the gray material of the seat. She seemed to be sleeping.

A child, a girl, sat on the floor near the woman's feet, nestled against the chair. Her long hair, also red, hung almost to her waist. She smiled at him, a guileless, friendly smile. The gesture struck Khedryn as so out of place that he did not know how to respond. Finally he stuck his tongue out at her, and she giggled.

A hand closed on his shoulder and pulled him roughly around. Another clone crouched before him, looking him directly in the face.

"I'm Soldier," the clone said.

Khedryn saw only a hint of wildness in the gray eyes of Soldier.

Gray eyes.

He blinked, thinking how familiar the eyes seemed. He noted the narrow, angled features, the hatchet nose, the jaw . . . and his mouth fell open.

"Stang," he whispered.

He was looking at Jaden Korr—a shaggy Jaden Korr worn thin by a harsh life on a forgotten moon, but there was no mistaking the eyes.

"I want you to tell me how the Jedi found us," Soldier said.

Khedryn deflected the question, his response on autopilot. "What Jedi? I'm just a salvage jockey who was visiting a relative at—"

"I saw the recognition in your eyes when you looked at me just now," Soldier said. "I saw the same thing in the Jedi's eyes when he first saw me."

"You should have let me kill him back on Fhost," said the wild clone in the pilot's seat.

"His name is Runner," Soldier said, nodding at the wild clone. "If you lie to me, I will let him do what he wishes with you. Do you understand?"

"You're going to kill me anyway," Khedryn said.

Soldier did not gainsay it. He leaned in closer. "Tell me how you found us."

"Jedi can do things. I don't know how—"

Runner whirled in his seat and lunged for Khedryn, his face twisted in anger. He pushed through Soldier, took Khedryn by the throat, and jerked him to his feet. Khedryn gasped for breath, his feet kicking. He thumped a boot off Runner's chest. The impact troubled the clone not in the least.

Khedryn began to see spots. He looked down and saw the little girl, curled up in a ball, hiding her eyes. He looked into Runner's bloodshot eyes, saw barely controlled madness there.

"Tell me how you found us," Soldier said. Then to Runner, "Put him down."

Runner hesitated.

"Put him down."

Runner dropped Khedryn and he hit the floor in a heap, gasping, wheezing. Soldier crouched beside him.

"Tell me."

Khedryn rolled onto his backside and sat up.

"Happenstance," he said, and Runner growled. "That's the truth. We returned to Fhost from the frozen moon, heard about the attack on the medical facility, and put two and two together."

Soldier seemed to consider this. "Then they are not following us now?"

Khedryn answered truthfully. "I don't know. I don't see how."

"Bah!" said Runner, and returned to his seat.

Soldier studied Khedryn's face for a moment. "I believe you," he said, and stood.

As Soldier turned away, Khedryn said, "How can you be him? Jaden? This . . . doesn't make any sense."

Soldier turned back and looked down on him. "Jaden? That is the Jedi's name?"

Khedryn nodded, wondering if he'd said too much.

"I'm not him," Soldier said. "I'm Soldier."

Khedryn looked away, looked over to the little girl, but she was gone. He did not see her anywhere in the cockpit.

"What are you going to do with me?" he asked Soldier.

Soldier stared down at him with Jaden's intense eyes. The clone cocked his head as if asking himself the same question. He looked to the bald woman, then to Runner.

"This ship has an escape pod," he said to them. "We can put him in it and eject him into space. Maybe someone will find him."

Runner spun in his seat. "Why waste an escape pod? We should space him."

Khedryn's heart beat faster. Sweat formed on his brow, and he despised himself for it.

"Or maybe just kill him right now," Runner said. He lurched to his feet, took his lightsaber hilt in hand, and advanced on Khedryn.

Soldier stepped between them.

"Wait."

"He shot at me," Runner spat, still trying to push through Soldier. "And he travels with the Jedi who tried to kill us both."

Soldier looked back at Khedryn. Khedryn found it unnerving to see such coldness in that face, Jaden's face. He knew his life hung on Soldier's next words.

"It's just an escape pod," Soldier said.

"Seer?" asked Runner of the woman. "What do you say?"

Seer, the bald clone, did not turn from the viewport.

She stared out at the black as if it held some answer she sought. "Mother has no need of him. And neither do we. He should be killed."

Runner grinned and moved toward Khedryn. Soldier hesitated for only a moment before he stepped out of the way, his shoulders slumped. He turned and looked into Khedryn's face. There was no apology in Soldier's expression, but neither was there pleasure.

"There's no reason to kill me," Khedryn said, pleased that his voice remained steady.

"There's no reason to keep you alive," Runner said, and ignited his lightsaber.

"You're murderers, then," Khedryn said. "Typical Sith."

"We're not Sith," Soldier said.

"Might as well be," Khedryn said. He stared the big clone in the face and used the wall to scramble to his feet. His burgeoning fear vanished in the face of the inevitable. He would not die afraid. He stuck out his chin.

"Not with a lightsaber, you Sith bastard. I'm a spacer. You put me out the damned airlock. At least give me that." He'd always figured he'd die in a vacuum somehow. He looked past Runner. "Soldier, give me that."

Soldier looked to Seer, who gave no indication she'd heard Khedryn's plea. Soldier turned to Runner.

"Space him," he said to Runner.

The two clones glared at one another, Runner's blade spitting sparks.

"Do it," Soldier said.

Runner grinned darkly and deactivated his weapon.

"Doesn't matter to me. Dead is dead."

He grabbed Khedryn by the collar and dragged him out of the cockpit, toward the back of the ship, toward the airlock. Khedryn looked back, trying to see the little girl for some reason, but she was nowhere to be found.

*   *   *

Nyss prowled the corridors of the supply ship. He moved in silence, the darkness clinging to him while he familiarized himself with the ship's layout. The clones, four adults and the child, congregated in the cockpit, where they held Khedryn. He set about preparing things.

He found a power transfer, cracked it open to reveal a nest of wires and conduits. Most of them were labeled with small tags. He found the power lines that fed the main lights in the cargo bay and the rear of the ship and cut them with his vibroblade.

All around him, the main overhead lights failed. Emergency lights flared to life, small and dim, creating an environment rich in shadows. He felt right at home.

Khedryn and Runner passed out of the forward section to find that the main lights in the middle section of the ship had failed. Emergency lights cast the corridors and rooms in a dim glow. Runner slammed his palm against the activation switches, but the main lights stayed out.

Runner pushed Khedryn before him through the dark corridors. It barely occurred to Khedryn to resist, maybe take Runner by surprise. It would be futile. His hands were bound and he had no weapon. Besides, if he resisted, Runner would kill him with a lightsaber, and Khedryn did not want to die on the end of a mad clone's blade. He'd take the vacuum every time.

As they walked, Khedryn felt as if he were moving into a tunnel, a womb, not from out of which he would be born, but in which he would die. Chaotic thoughts swirled through his mind, a rush of memories: his time as a child in the ruins of Outbound Flight, the face of his mother, his friends, his enemies, men and women he'd known, his life bouncing off theirs, all of them helping to make him who he was.

People are not equations, he heard Marr say in his mind.

No, he thought, and smiled. People were the sum total of their interactions with other people, the choices they made. He'd made some bad ones in his life, but also many good ones.

Words and arrows painted on the bulkhead pointed the way to the airlock, directions to Khedryn's execution chamber.

"Keep moving," Runner growled.

Khedryn had not realized that he'd slowed. His legs felt weak under him. His breath came rapidly, trying to keep pace with the demands of his racing heart. The corridors seemed too narrow; the walls were closing in on him. He tried to calm himself, determined to die with dignity.

Runner squeezed his arm and pulled him to a stop. The hum and sizzle of the clone's lightsaber split the dimness of the dark corridor. Khedryn fought to keep himself upright.

"The airlock," he said, his voice steadier than he had supposed it would be. "Not like this. We had an agreement, clone."

"Shut up," Runner said, his expression tense, wild, but not focused on Khedryn at all. He looked down the corridor in one direction, spun and looked down another. Khedryn saw nothing but darkness down the corridor in all directions.

Runner's breathing came almost as fast as Khedryn's. Khedryn tried to make sense of what was happening.

The madness, he supposed. Runner was having some kind of episode.

Or maybe . . .

Runner voiced a low, dangerous growl. His hand squeezed Khedryn's bicep so hard it made Khedryn wince.

The darkness before them seemed to swirl and deepen. Runner leaned forward, eyeing it warily, his blade held before him. The sizzle of his lightsaber grew less pronounced; the blade began to sputter. Runner held it before his eyes, staring, as the blade shrank.

"What is—" Khedryn started to ask.

The blade flickered and fizzled out altogether, the puff of smoke from the hilt like a leftover ghost.

A hiss sounded from the corridor before them and Runner jerked to the side and snatched at something in the air. By the time Khedryn registered what had happened it was already over.

Runner held the shaft of a crossbow quarrel. He'd snatched it right out of the air. The silver tines of the tip looked like razors.

A susurration sounded within the darkness of the hallway, the sigh of a soft boot on the floor, or the rustle of a cloak. Runner dropped the quarrel but held on to Khedryn.

The darkness in the hall thickened, rolled toward them, a pale form at its head closing fast. For a moment, Khedryn, his mind still stuck on his pending execution, thought it an apparition of death.

But it wasn't. It was an Umbaran.

Runner shoved Khedryn against the wall so hard it knocked the wind from him and sent him to the floor. Khedryn caught the flash of blades in the pale form's hand. And then the Umbaran and Runner were engaged, their movements so fast that Khedryn could scarcely follow them.

The Umbaran stabbed at Runner's abdomen. Runner sidestepped the stab and punched for the Umbaran's temple with his lightsaber hilt. The Umbaran ducked under the blow, slapped Runner's arm out wide, and stabbed at the clone's chest with his other blade. Before the knife could connect, Runner caught the Umbaran's wrist, planted his feet, spun, and whipped the Umbaran against the wall so hard the pale man's breath blew out of him in an audible whoosh.

Runner charged him and feinted with his off hand while he loosed an overhand slam at the Umbaran's head with the hilt of his lightsaber. The Umbaran ducked and the hilt slammed hard into the bulkhead. A leg sweep put Runner on the ground and the Umbaran leapt after him, his blades stabbing downward.

Runner rolled to the side, away from one stab, away from another, and unleashed a prone kick to the Umbaran's chest that drove the pale man back enough for Runner to regain his feet. He was breathing heavily. The Umbaran, unwinded, held his blades a little away from his body and studied the clone's defenses, looking for openings. They circled, a meter apart. The Umbaran feinted lunges to draw Runner out.

Impatient with the games, Runner charged. The Umbaran drove his blades at Runner's chest but the clone caught him by the wrists, held the knives out wide, and used his greater weight to drive the Umbaran against the bulkhead. There, he slammed one of the Umbaran's hands against the wall until the Umbaran gasped with pain and dropped one of the knives.

The Umbaran shifted his stance and drove his left knee into Runner's abdomen, once, twice—both blows landing solidly—before Runner could position his body too close for knees to do any damage. The Umbaran continued to try and snake his hands free of Runner's grasp, but he could not loose himself from the clone's grip.

Runner grunted, pressed the Umbaran against the bulkhead. A head butt from the Umbaran into the side of Runner's face elicited a grunt of pain from the clone. Snarling with pain and rage, Runner heaved the Umbaran up the wall, off the ground.

The Umbaran did not resist, but used the opportunity to attack, flinging his legs up and scissoring them around Runner's throat. The clone gasped, grunted, his eyes wide as the Umbaran's legs pinched off his carotid. The clone pivoted away from the wall and ran at the far bulkhead, slamming the Umbaran against it.

The impact jarred the Umbaran. He loosed Runner's neck from the grip of his legs but quickly unleashed a straight kick that caught the clone's jaw flush. The blow staggered Runner, and he lost his grip on the Umbaran's right wrist. The Umbaran twisted, put his feet on the floor, and drove his blade into Runner's chest. Runner staggered toward him, his mouth already filling with blood, and the Umbaran drove the blade home again, then again.

Runner's mouth moved as if he were chewing on his final thoughts. He gagged, gurgled, and then collapsed to the floor, dead.

Staring at the Umbaran, Khedryn realized that he should have fled ten seconds earlier. He clambered to his feet and ran off into the dark corridor as fast as he could.

The first turn he came to, he took. The second, he took. The third, he took. He was hopelessly lost and did not care. He slammed himself into a cul-de-sac, a power-exchange port. He tried to control his breathing while listening behind him.

He heard nothing but the gong of his own heartbeat. He tried to process events. Had the Umbaran been aboard the whole time? What did he want? Was he a potential ally? And most important, was the Umbaran following him?

The hallway darkened, or so Khedryn thought, but that didn't make any sense.

He struggled against his restraints, which did nothing but cause them to cut deeper into his flesh. He bit his lip against the pain and stuck his head out, looking back the way he had come. He needed to find a way to get his hands free, then find a weapon—

Something sharp pressed lightly against the side of his throat.

"Hello," said a soft voice that set his heart to racing. "Please do nothing rash. Otherwise, I will have to harm you."

Khedryn swallowed and turned his head toward the speaker. The Umbaran took a step back, the loaded crossbow still pointed at Khedryn's face.

"Move," the Umbaran said, and prodded him with the crossbow.

Khedryn did, and the Umbaran walked him along the corridor until they came to an intersection that had a long safety bar attached to the bulkhead.

The Umbaran slipped his blade—a vibroblade— through Khedryn's restraints. Keeping the crossbow aimed at Khedryn all the while, he removed a set of flex- cuffs from his cloak.

"Around your right hand, then around that safety bar on the wall."

He tossed the flexcuffs to Khedryn.

"Do it quickly, or I'll shoot you in the face."

Khedryn wrapped the flexcuffs around his right wrist, then around the safety bar.

"Tightly," said the Umbaran, and Khedryn obeyed.

"Now sit."

Khedryn did, and his arm, attached to the safety bar, stuck up over his head. He must have looked like a stu- dent with a question.

Sweat soaked his clothing. Blood seeped out of his wrist from where the clone's cuffs had cut into his skin. "What do you want with me?"

"I don't want you at all," the Umbaran said, his voice a sibilant whisper. "I'll be back for you."

"Wait! Who are you? Do you work for the Jedi?"

At that, the Umbaran scoffed and sped off down the corridor. Khedryn marveled at the Umbaran's ability to move in near silence. By the time the Umbaran was a few meters down the corridor, Khedryn had lost sight of him. He seemed to fade into the shadows.

chapter eight

"WE MUST HURRY," SEER SAID TO SOLDIER, HER VOICE far away, her distant gaze on the infinite black outside the ship. "Mother wants us home."

Soldier looked at her and saw the slight pulsing beneath her skin. He glanced behind him to Hunter, sitting in one of the crew seats. She gazed back at him, her green eyes still slightly dazed. He wondered if she recognized him, if she remembered what she had said to him when they had left the moon. He doubted it.

He took Seer by the arm. She hissed at his touch, and he felt the movement under her skin.

"You need meds," he said. He should have brought more to the cockpit from the cargo bay. He hadn't thought they would need more so soon.

"I need to go home," she said, and grinned.

Soldier saw madness in the expression.

"I'm finalizing the course inputs," he said cautiously, and released her arm. "We are going home, Seer. But you have to have meds. All right?"

She said nothing, and he chose to interpret her silence as agreement.

He steered Seer to the copilot's seat, sat her down, and turned to Hunter.

"I need you to go back to the cargo bay and bring back the meds."

Hunter's eyes focused on him, more alert than he'd seen them in days. "Where are they?"

"Forward in the cargo bay. I left the container open. Bring as much as you can carry. Hypos, too. I can mix it here."

Hunter nodded, stood.

He looked around the cockpit for Grace, under the seats, didn't see her.

"Where's Grace?" he asked.

Hunter shrugged and started to head off.

"Find her," he said. "She shouldn't be wandering the ship. And tell Runner to get back here, too."

Soldier would need a copilot. Seer was of no use to him.

Khedryn sat on the floor, head and heart pounding. He pulled against the restraints on his wrist. He winced as they cut into his flesh, as a seep of warm blood made his hand sticky and ran down his forearm.

He tried to make sense of what was happening.

Who was the Umbaran? How had he killed Runner so easily, even deactivating his lightsaber? If he did not work for the Jedi, whom did he work for? And why had he left Khedryn alive?

Khedryn glanced around the dark corridor, looking for anything he could use to free himself. He saw nothing. He struggled again, but the pain put a stop to things almost right away. He cursed with frustration.

A sound to his right gave him a start.

"Who's there?" he asked.

The little girl from the cockpit crept out of the darkness, as skittish as a fawn. She stared at Khedryn, and at the flexcuffs, her eyes as wide as plates.

"Where is Runner?" she asked.

"I don't know," Khedryn said softly. "What's your name?"

"I'm glad he didn't hurt you," she said, and started to back away.

"Wait, don't go," he said. "I need your help."

He did not know if she heard him. She turned and ran back down the corridor without a second look, her movement almost as furtive and silent as that of the Umbaran.

Khedryn cursed under his breath. She was gone.

He sat there, alone with himself, trying hard not to think about what would happen next. His breathing sounded loud in his ears.

A sound startled him, metal sliding on metal—a utility knife slid toward him along the floor from the right. The girl emerged out of the darkness. Her shy smile gave way to a look of terror as the illness afflicting the clones distorted her features. Her cheeks bulged, roiled. She screamed, reached up to touch her face, and Khedryn saw that the skin of her hands and arms looked the same. It was as if an army of insects was crawling under her flesh. Her terrified eyes met Khedryn's.

"Stay there," he said, stretching for the knife. "I'll help you."

But she did not stay. She turned, already weeping, and ran.

Khedryn got the knife, slid its blade out, and cut himself free of the cuffs. He massaged his wrist and thought about what to do. He could make a run for an escape pod, hoping the Umbaran and the clones were too occupied with one another to worry about his escape. After all, the Umbaran said he was not after Khedryn.

But then there was the little girl.

She'd freed him.

He could try to find her, maybe take her with him, but to where? Besides, she was sick and he did not know how to treat her.

Maybe the clones did. He thought of the hypos that

littered the floor of the cockpit. They had medicine there.

To help the girl, he would have to make sure the Umbaran didn't kill the clones. Or he'd have to at least get some of the meds.

The idea ran counter to his instincts, and the last time he hadn't run when he should have, he had ended up with an Anzat assassin sticking a feeding appendage into his braincase.

But there was the girl to consider.

And he was nothing if not stubborn.

He simply could not abandon the little girl. It wasn't in him. He'd been a vulnerable child once, back in the ruins of the Redoubt. Skywalker and Mara Jade could have abandoned him and the others, but they hadn't. They had rescued them all. He wouldn't abandon the girl. Whatever the Umbaran intended for Khedryn, for the clones, it wasn't good. He'd have been happy to leave the other clones to their fate, but not the little girl.

Damned Jedi were rubbing off on him.

Sweat slicked his grip on the utility knife. He tried to control his breathing as he moved as quietly as he could through the ship's dark corridors. He listened from time to time, but heard nothing. In truth, he did not expect to. The Umbaran moved in silence and melded with the shadows as well as someone in an adaptive suit.

He needed to get lucky.

He pulled his last piece of chewstim from his trouser pocket, unwrapped it, and popped it in his mouth.

He'd been unlucky his whole life.

He blew a bubble with the chewstim, popped it quietly.

But he was nothing if not stubborn.

The medicine had brought Hunter back to herself. She remembered almost nothing since leaving the frozen moon. She'd awakened to herself in the cockpit of another stolen ship, the stars wide and dark and deep.

Power surged and ebbed in her, like bursts of electrical current. Her emotions vacillated between controlled ecstasy and contained anger. Her connection to the Force felt deeper, more profound than it ever had in the past. She assumed it was the result of her closer connection to Mother. She'd never felt such potential within herself.

She wished that Alpha had survived, but she understood why he had not—he had failed Mother's test, had fallen to the Jedi.

So said Seer, and Seer spoke truth.

And Seer had said that they would soon meet Mother. Hunter looked forward to that moment.

She moved through the supply ship's forward section and took a turbolift down to the belly. The doors opened onto a long corridor lit only by overhead emergency lights. She hit the comlink on the lift and said, "The lighting is out down here."

No signal. The comm, too, was out.

"Grace," she called. No response.

She stepped into the hallway and the lift doors closed behind her. Immediately she felt something amiss, a pressure in the air, a tension. She'd been bred by the doctors to stalk prey and she'd learned to trust her instincts.

Excitement caused power to crackle on the end of her fingertips. She put the slim, curved hilt of her lightsaber into her palm but did not activate the blade. Quieting her breathing, she listened but heard nothing.

"Runner?" she called.

She let her eyes adjust to the darkness, then moved to one side of the corridor, where she could keep a wall on her flank, and started off. She walked in silence, a hunter stalking unknown prey. With each step she took, she felt more certain that something had happened to Runner.

Did they have a stowaway? Had the Jedi from the moon gotten aboard somehow?

With her genetically engineered senses, she caught the faint coppery tang of blood in the air. She followed it, moving slowly, alert to any sound other than the ordinary hum of the ship's engines.

Ahead, a form lay crumpled in the corridor. She eyed it for several seconds, wary.

No movement. No sound but her own steady breathing.

The darkness made it difficult to see, but the body was too big to be Grace. As she neared it, she noted the long ragged cloak favored by Runner, the boots.

"Runner," she said in a whisper. The body did not move.

She made up her mind, darted forward, and knelt beside it.

Congealing blood covered the floor near Runner, soaked the soles of her boots. She turned his body over. His face was purpled from blows. The hole in his chest had been opened by something sharp and nonenergized, certainly not a lightsaber.

She ran her hands over Runner's eyes to close them and stood. An object on the floor caught her eye. She picked it up—a crossbow quarrel with a tip like a razor.

Running her thumb over it, she glanced down the corridor to her left, then to her right. She licked her lips, feeling exposed. A sound from down the corridor to her right caught her attention, the whisper of a boot on the floor. She could see nothing. The dim overhead lights barely illuminated the corridor, made the hallway a play of shadows.

A strange feeling struck her. At first she mistook it as the normal ebb and flow of the power within her. She thought that the medicine was diminishing her connection to the Force to prevent the illness from progressing too rapidly. But the feeling did not abate. She felt as if she were circling a drain, falling into a hole, and the rate at which she was falling was accelerating.

The darkness around her deepened. To her left and right, the light in the corridor dimmed to sparks.

She backed against the wall and ignited her blade. The familiar red line comforted her, and in its light she sought her foe. She let her anger build, her anxiety, and used it to connect her more deeply to the Force. But the connection felt loose, attenuated, and getting weaker.

"I know you're out there," she said.

She reached out through the Force as best she could, hoping to feel the presence of her opponent.

She felt nothing, just another hole, another vacancy in her perception.

Her calm slipped, replaced by alarm, by burgeoning fear. She bared her teeth and hissed.

Her eyes fell on Runner and she dropped the quarrel. Her blade began to flicker. Fear put down roots in her stomach and spread to the rest of her. She watched, wide-eyed, as the line of her weapon thinned, sizzled, and went out.

Darkness.

She felt entirely separated from the Force, a feeling she had never before experienced, a striking solitude that made her mouth go dry. She was breathing too heavily, betraying her position. She slid along the wall, as quiet as a shadow, her hand sweating around the hilt of her lightsaber, dead metal in her fist.

She needed to get back to the lift, back to Soldier and Seer and Grace. Feeling the wall with one hand, she slowly made her way back the way she'd come.

By the time her mind had processed the sound—the hiss of a fired quarrel—a painful, powerful impact in the side of her chest drove the breath from her lungs and knocked her to the floor.

She wanted to scream from the pain, but she could not

seem to fill her burning lungs with air. She climbed to all fours, tried to lift herself up, couldn't. She saw the shaft of the quarrel sticking out of her rib cage. Blood poured out of her side.

Two feet appeared on the floor before her.

She grabbed at the legs, the movement causing her to hiss with pain, but they stepped out of reach and she skittered on the floor, slick with her own blood, and ended up flat on her stomach. She was dying, alone, separated from the Force, separated from her daughter, her community.

The feet stood before her again.

A supreme effort allowed her to heave her body over. She stared at the ceiling, her breath becoming ever shallower, the pain diminishing as she died.

Her killer took shape in her vision, his silhouette emerging from the darkness as if part of it. Pale hands pulled back a hood to reveal a bald head and a pale face devoid of emotion. His dark eyes looked like holes, the pits into which Hunter's connection to the Force had drained away.

She tried to speak, to ask him how he had done what he'd done, who he was, why he had killed her, but she could not draw enough breath to speak. Something heavy seemed to be on her chest, preventing her lungs from working. Sparks started to appear in her vision, motes of orange and red that announced a brain receiving too little oxygen.

The apparition of death removed something from under his cloak. A crossbow.

While Hunter fought for breath, for a few more seconds of life, he methodically cocked the crossbow, laid another quarrel atop it, and took aim at her chest. He stared into her face as he pulled the trigger. She felt the impact dully, with no additional pain and then felt nothing more, ever again.

*   *   *

The darkness on the cargo deck made navigating the ship slow work. Khedryn could not remember the way Runner had brought him; stress had erased it from his memory, and his hurried flight from the Umbaran had further foiled his sense of the ship's layout. He picked his way along as best he could, following the occasional signs painted on walls. He needed to find the turbolifts, he knew that.

He rounded a corner and froze. Ahead, he saw two bodies. He flattened himself against the wall and watched for a time, listening. He heard nothing.

He approached the bodies at an oblique angle, cautiously, as he might a dangerous animal. He feared he would see the little girl there, her small form broken and bloody on the deck.

He sighed with relief when he saw that one of the dead was Runner and the other an adult female. Two of the Umbaran's crossbow quarrels stuck out of the female's chest. Blood pooled on the deck.

The clones' lightsabers lay near their bodies. With a shrug, he took them and latched them to his belt, even though he had no idea how to operate them. And even if he had, he wouldn't use it. He'd be more likely to hurt himself with it than an enemy.

He checked the clones for any mundane weapons but found none.

The Umbaran had killed at least two of the clones already. The small utility knife Khedryn bore felt entirely inadequate in his hands.

He rose, looked down the hall. He knew how to get to the turbolifts from here. The Umbaran had probably headed to the cockpit.

Khedryn looked back the way he had come, wondering if the little girl was still on the cargo level. He hoped so, but he had no way to know. He toyed again with the idea of turning around and finding an escape pod. If he took a lift up to the crew deck, he knew, he'd be committed. He'd either succeed or die.

He made up his mind and walked the corridors back to the turbolifts. He hit the button and waited for one to come down. Knowing that the door could open to reveal the Umbaran or one of the clones, he stood to one side, coiled, sweaty fingers wrapped around the hilt of his knife.

The door slid open. The lights were out and he saw movement within. A form emerged and he lunged, the knife held ready for an overhand stab.

Having eliminated two of the clones, Nyss had only to contend with Soldier, the child, and the other female adult, Seer. He needed to move fast to take them down before they noted the absence of Runner and the female.

Merged with the darkness, he hurried to one of the turbolift banks and took a lift up to the crew deck. He flattened himself against the wall as the doors slid open. Hearing nothing, he slid out into hallway.

Ahead maybe fifteen meters was the cockpit. The door stood open. He heard voices within: Soldier; Seer. He heard no alarm in them, so he presumed they had not yet grown concerned about the absence of the other two clones.

Hugging the wall, he glided forward, a vibroblade in one hand, his mind keeping a tight hold on his suppressive field. He lingered in the corridor outside the cockpit. His gear included two stun grenades. He took one from his satchel, pressed the button to activate it, and readied himself.

"The course is set, Seer," said Soldier.

"Mother is waiting," replied Seer. "You have done well, Soldier."

"We'll see," Soldier answered.

Nyss loosed his grip on his suppressive field. The lights in the hallway and cockpit dimmed slightly as he extended his power which always manifested in a cloud of dark air, like a black fog.

"Did the lights just dim?" Soldier asked.

Seer made no answer that Nyss could hear.

Nyss intensified the field slowly, incrementally separating the clones from the Force. If he was lucky, they would notice only when it was too late.

The hole in which he existed extended outward from him, deepened, darkened. He felt Seer slipping into it, her connection to the rest of the universe slowly draining away. Soldier, too, fell into it, but only partially. Soldier lingered around the rim, and Nyss was unable to fully sever his connection to the Force.

Odd. Nyss had never before felt resistance to his power.

Perhaps Thrawn actually *had* cloned a breakthrough Force user.

"Are you all right?" Soldier asked Seer. Nyss heard growing suspicion in his tone.

"Something . . . is wrong," Seer said.

Nyss heard a gasp, a muffled thump. He imagined Seer falling to the floor.

"I don't feel Mother," Seer said, her voice soft, despondent.

A high-pitched scream from right behind Nyss made him spin around. The girl, her wild red hair haloing a terrified expression, stared wide-eyed at him, one hand raised to her mouth.

How had she sneaked up on him?

He raised his vibroblade for a throw, but the girl turned and ran before he could loose it.

"Grace!" he heard Soldier shout from the cockpit. The hum and sizzle of an activating lightsaber broke the quiet.

Nyss cursed, whirled, and flung the stun grenade blindly, just as Soldier pelted through the cockpit door, red blade and red anger going before him.

Nyss looked away and covered his ears as the grenade exploded with a bright flash and a bang loud enough to almost shatter eardrums. The moment it went off, he drew his other blade and assumed a fighting posture.

Soldier, caught in the tail end of the grenade's effect, staggered from the blast, wincing.

Nyss bounded toward him and shouldered him into the bulkhead. While Soldier grunted from the impact, Nyss stabbed his vibroblade into the clone's right forearm. He kept the cut clean and avoided slicing through bone. He did not want Soldier dead, just manageable.

Soldier's grunt turned to a shout of pain, blood poured from the wound, and he dropped his lightsaber, as Nyss had intended.

Still pressing his body against Soldier's, Nyss kicked the weapon away. He thought the fight was over, but the clone, only partially affected by Nyss's power, unleashed a Force-augmented punch to the side of Nyss's face.

Instinct and training saved Nyss. He rolled with the blow, which otherwise would have shattered his jaw. Instead, it merely staggered him, knocking him back two steps and loosening a couple teeth.

"If you've hurt Grace . . ." Soldier said, shaking his head as if to clear it. Blood poured from the cut on his arm. Rage poured from everywhere else.

Nyss had never before fought a Force user who actually could use the Force in his presence. He knew that surprise was the sole reason he had the upper hand at the moment.

Knowing he could not let up, he took a chance, putting his head down and charging the clone. The Prime braced himself, then slammed a fist down on Nyss's back, the power in the blow cracking Nyss's ribs.

Nyss endured the pain, grabbed the clone around his legs, and heaved him to the floor. They hit the deck in a tangled heap, punching and clawing at each other. The clone's blood smeared Nyss's face, turned the grapple into a slick, sticky mess.

Nyss struggled to keep his suppressive field in effect, to intensify it, but instead of him pulling Soldier into the hole, Soldier, fueled by his anger, seemed to be pulling Nyss out of it, dragging his existence into the light. Nyss had lived in his hole so long, his existence separate from all but his sister, that the thought of a forced connection to others nearly caused him to panic.

His terror met Soldier's anger and each held the other in balance, Soldier's powers weakened but not entirely suppressed, Nyss's solitary existence threatened but preserved.

Nyss clawed at Soldier's eyes, and Soldier turned his head to the side. Nyss slammed his head into Soldier's face—once, a second time. He felt Soldier's nose give way, felt the spray of blood as the nose exploded.

But Soldier did not lose consciousness. With his good hand, he clawed at Nyss's eye, got a finger into the socket. Panicked, Nyss whipped his head to the side, dislodged the finger, and slammed his head down into the clone's face. The blow caused Nyss to see sparks but fully shattered the Prime's already broken nose. Bone crunched. More blood sprayed. The clone, momentarily stunned, went limp.

Nyss snaked an arm free of the clone's grasp, reversed his grip on his vibroblade, and slammed the hilt into the side of Soldier's head.

The Prime groaned and went still. Nyss collapsed on top of him, breathing heavily. The adrenaline drained out of him, and its absence left him with nothing but pain.

Blood from Soldier's arm continued to leak from the wound. Cursing, Nyss sat up, wincing at the pain in his ribs. Rising to his knees, he tore a strip of cloth from his cloak. With it, he made a makeshift tourniquet and tied it around Soldier's arm to stop the bleeding. He'd need to find a medkit and a tube of Newskin as soon as possible.

He stood, and the corridor spun. He blinked, stayed still until the sensation passed, then staggered into the cockpit. Seer lay on the ground, unconscious. She had a bruise on one side of her face. She must have struck an instrument panel when she fell. He considered killing her, but figured the One Sith could find some use for her.

He checked the various lockers in the cockpit and found a medkit and a roll of deckstrip. He took the tube of Newskin from the medkit, filled Soldier's wound with it, then covered it with gauze. With the deckstrip, he bound the hands and ankles of Soldier and Seer and heaved them against the rear wall of the cockpit.

When he was done, he raised Syll on the comlink. "I have control of the ship, the Prime, and Jaden Korr's ally, the spacer."

"Are you all right?" Syll asked. She must have heard the strain in his voice.

"Yes," Nyss said. "The Prime is not fully susceptible to our power. So it was . . . more difficult than I expected."

He checked the instruments, saw the coordinates that Soldier had input into the navicomp. He did not recognize the system, but then he did not know the Unknown Regions very well.

The clones would never make it to their destination, whatever it might have been, but Wyyrlok or the Master might find it useful to know where they had gone.

"I'm sending you some coordinates," he said to Syll. "Record them for later." After he'd sent them, he said, "I'll hail Jaden Korr. Be ready."

Behind him, Soldier moaned. He would awaken soon.

* * *

Khedryn halted in mid-attack, the knife held high.

The form in the lift was the little girl.

She froze with fear and they stared at each other, both of them wide-eyed.

She took a step backward into the lift. Her skin bubbled and bulged, and he knew her sickness was worsening.

He quickly lowered the blade and tried to make himself look harmless. "No, it's okay. I'm sorry."

She took another step back into the lift, skittish, and looked like she might bolt, though she had nowhere to go. He put the knife in his pocket and spoke in a calm voice.

"I didn't know it was you, sweetie. I thought—"

The lift door started to close. He lunged forward, caught it with his hand, and held it open.

At his sudden motion, she let out a little peep of fear.

"Never mind what I thought," he said. He knelt down to look her in the eyes and make himself look smaller. She seemed to be calming now that he'd put the knife away. "I won't hurt you. You know that, right?"

She nodded.

"But there's another man on board. He might hurt you and your . . . friend. He's bald, with—"

She was already nodding.

"Do you know where he is?" Khedryn asked.

"Up there," she said, pointing back at the lift. She brushed her ratty red hair out of her eyes. "He was . . . fighting Soldier. Soldier was bleeding."

Khedryn needed to get to the crew deck.

"Is your medicine up there?" he asked.

She nodded.

"All right. Go hide in the cargo area. Wait until someone comes for you. Either me or . . . someone else."

She eased past him and started to go.

"Wait," he called, and she turned. "Do you know how to launch one of the escape pods?"

She looked at him as if he were speaking another language.

"All right. Never mind. Just go hide. Everything will be fine. Okay? Okay? I'm going to make sure that your . . . people can take care of you."

She nodded.

"What's your name?" he asked.

"Grace," she said, and looked at the ground, shy. She behaved like any little girl anywhere in the galaxy.

"Figures," he said, smiling.

He took a deep breath, turned, and boarded the lift. Inside, he hit the button that would take him to the crew deck, to the Umbaran, to the clones.

He could not justify to himself what he was about to do, not rationally. He just felt as if he could not let Grace down.

The doors started to close and she was still standing there, her head tilted to the side, looking at him. Her expression unnerved him. He caught the doors with his hand before they closed all the way.

"What is it?"

She hemmed and hawed, shifting from foot to foot.

"What is it, Grace?"

She looked up at him, a shy smile on her face. "Why are your eyes like that?"

The question was so surprising under the circumstances that Khedryn was truly stunned into silence. He took his hand from the door to run his palm over his hair and the doors started to close.

Grace stood there, waiting, as the doors formed a wall between them.

"They got this way because they've looked at too many weird things." He smiled and made a silly face.

She giggled.

"Now, go," he said, and the doors closed. He chuck-led all the way up to the crew deck. By the time the lift doors opened, however, his mirth was gone. An empty corridor stretched before him, a long, dim tunnel. The Umbaran had probably disabled the lights.

Soldier's mind clawed back to awareness. His head throbbed with each beat of his heart. Blood congealed in his beard, his hair. He groaned, blinked away the grog-giness, and realized that his hands were bound behind his back. His ankles, too, were bound with deckstrip. He was seated on the floor, still in the cockpit of the sup-ply ship. The overhead lights had been turned off. The dim glow of instrumentation provided the only illumi-nation.

His first thought was of Grace, her scream, and a rush of adrenaline cleared his mind. Sitting up, he glanced around, alarmed. Seer sat next to him, propped against the wall, her head tilted to the side, still unconscious. A vicious bruise, already turning purple, marred the sym-metry of her features. She had smashed her face into the instrument panel when she fell, when she and Soldier had both felt the odd sensation of falling away from the Force.

He twisted his head around and did not see Grace. She might have gotten away, or . . . something else might have happened to her.

The thought of harm coming to her—the only one of the Community's surviving children—caused a surge of anger. As his anger grew, so did his power. He pushed the power into his body, used it to augment his strength, and tested the bindings on his wrists.

They bit like teeth into his flesh. Ignoring the pain, he tried to muscle them apart. But he could not. He could not draw fully on the Force: something was interfering with the connection.

A sibilant voice from the front of the cockpit said, "You won't be able to break the bindings. There's no need to struggle. I have no intention of harming you."

"I can't say the same," Soldier said. He tried again to break them, failed. "What did you do to me? To us?"

"You feel separate from the Force?" the Umbaran asked.

"How did you do it?" was all Soldier asked.

The Umbaran chuckled. "By pushing a bit of my world out into yours."

Soldier did not understand. He imagined he never would. He could see the Umbaran only in silhouette, standing with his back to Soldier and Seer as he studied something on the ship's instrumentation.

"Who are you?" Soldier asked. "What do you want?"

"I want you," the Umbaran said. "You're of interest to the Master."

You're of interest. Soldier had often heard phrases like that from the doctors in the cloning facility. It always heralded something unpleasant.

"Why?" he asked. "I'm no one."

"That's not true at all," said the Umbaran.

"Then take me. Let Seer and Grace go."

"I'm afraid I can't do that. Quiet now," the Umbaran said. "I've got a call to make."

Junker emerged from hyperspace in the outer reaches of the system. The light of a distant red dwarf cast the cockpit in crimson. Marr set to work on the scanners.

"System has two gas giants and a thick asteroid belt. Nothing else."

"Where's the supply ship?"

"Searching," Marr said, keying in a broad sensor sweep. "I have it. It's on the other side of the asteroid belt. Our silhouette is so small that I doubt they've detected us this far out."

"Agreed," Jaden said. He engaged the ion engines and streaked toward the asteroid belt. In an effort to avoid detection, he kept *Junker* on the same plane as the bulk of the asteroids, trying to use them as cover. His mind raced along with *Junker*. He needed to come up with a way to board the supply ship.

Before they reached the asteroid belt, the ship-to-ship communicator pinged. Jaden and Marr both stared at it in surprise.

"That's an open hail," said Jaden.

"From the supply ship," Marr said, and they shared a glance.

"Maybe Khedryn has gotten free and is trying to raise us," Jaden said. He opened the channel.

A soft, sibilant voice carried over the comm and destroyed whatever hope he'd had for Khedryn's escape.

"I know that you can hear this, Jaden Korr. Listen carefully to what I am about to say. My name is Nyss and I have taken control of the medical supply ship out of Fhost. The clones you were after are dead or captured. Khedryn Faal is now in my custody."

"The clones are dead?" Marr asked, incredulous.

Jaden stared at the comm, trying to make sense of the sudden turn of events. He pushed the transmit button. "You are to turn Khedryn Faal over to us immediately."

Nyss's voice answered, his soft tone turned hard. "You give exactly no orders here, Jedi. Do you understand? You will do exactly what I say and only what I say."

Jaden's fist clenched in frustration. "Who are you? What do you want?"

"I will explain that in person, Jedi."

The request puzzled Jaden. "You want to meet?"

"I want to trade. Khedryn Faal for you. Otherwise, I'll kill him."

Jaden cut off the transmission and looked over at Marr. Lines furrowed the Cerean's brow.

"Thoughts?" Jaden asked.

"He is probably lying. How could he have gotten aboard? How could he have killed all the clones? He could *be* one of the clones. All of this could be a ploy to get at you."

"A lot of unknowns," Jaden said, nodding.

"Too many," Marr said.

Nyss's voice carried over the comm "You have sixty seconds. After that, I will kill Khedryn Faal."

Jaden slammed a fist on the transmit button. "Harm him and I'll hunt you across the galaxy."

"Fifty-eight seconds."

Frustration almost pulled a curse from Jaden. It did pull a curse from Marr.

"What do we do, Master?" the Cerean asked.

Jaden could feel his worry for Khedryn. He made up his mind.

"We trade. He wants me for some reason. He can have me. But I plan to be more than he can handle. The important thing is to get Khedryn to safety. Agreed?"

Ambivalence twisted Marr's face into a landscape of worry.

"Forty seconds," Nyss said.

"Agreed," Marr said reluctantly. "I don't see any other option."

Khedryn slid out of the lift, his fingers white around the hilt of the knife. Voices from ahead sent his heart spinning and froze him to the floor. He heard the sibilant whisper of the Umbaran and . . .

Jaden's voice?

Or was it Soldier's?

He crept forward, hunched, hugging the wall, trying to merge with the darkness. He winced at the soft sound of his shoes on the deck. The corridor offered almost no cover at all, so he tried to move rapidly, hoping speed would do where stealth was not possible. The last thing he wanted was the Umbaran and his crossbow to catch him at a distance, without cover. Khedryn had never missed a blaster more in his life.

The cockpit doors were open, the cockpit dark beyond, lit only by the dull glow of instrumentation. Staying close to the wall, Khedryn moved closer.

The voices fell silent. Fearing he'd been heard, Khedryn froze. His breathing sounded like a bellows in his ears. He expected the Umbaran to appear in the cockpit doorway at any moment, crossbow cocked.

More voices from inside the cockpit. Khedryn heard no alarm in them and assumed he had not been heard.

Hoping the conversation would mask the sound of his final approach, he hurried to the doorway, crouching low, and peeked his head around the doorjamb.

The Umbaran sat in the pilot's seat facing away from Khedryn. The comm chirped with an incoming message, and Jaden's voice carried over the speaker.

Jaden hit the transmit button to speak to Nyss. "Done. A trade, then. Me for Khedryn."

"Very good," Nyss answered. "That is a spacer's freighter. Get into a hardsuit and exit your ship."

"A hardsuit?" Marr exclaimed, off comm.

"Fly toward the supply ship in the suit," Nyss continued. "When you are near enough, I will release Khedryn Faal in an escape pod."

Jaden's mind began to move through possibilities, tactics.

"You have five minutes to exit your ship," Nyss said. "I'll be watching."

The connection closed.

* * *

The sound of Jaden's voice summoned a fierce grin from Khedryn. The realization that Jaden and Marr had somehow trailed him filled him with a rush of emotion. He looked past the Umbaran through the cockpit, hoping to catch a glimpse of *Junker,* but saw only the black. No matter. They were out there.

He understood what had happened and why the Umbaran had let him live—he wanted to trade him for Jaden. Jaden, of course, had accepted.

Blasted Jedi were easy to play.

Once again Khedryn considered making a run for an escape pod. With *Junker* out there somewhere, all he needed to do was get into the black and they could reel him in. Jaden would not have to put himself at risk. Khedryn had seen what the Umbaran could do to Force users, suppressing their power somehow. He had to warn Jaden, or get off the supply ship somehow.

But there was still the little girl to consider. He had no doubt that the Umbaran would kill her or simply let her die of her disease. Khedryn could not abandon her. He would not be able to look Jaden or Marr in the face if he did.

The Umbaran sat in the pilot's seat, staring at the comm.

Khedryn eased into the cockpit, hunched low, knife ready.

A stirring to his right drew his attention.

Soldier sat on the deck against the wall, his hands and ankles bound with deckstrip. The female clone, Seer, lay beside him, her eyes closed, either dead or unconscious.

Soldier's eyes fixed on Khedryn, flashed first with surprise, then suspicion. Khedryn knew what he had to do. He put a finger to his lips for silence.

"I don't like this," Marr said, shaking his head. "I don't like this at all."

Behind them, R-6 beeped agreement. Jaden had almost forgotten that the droid was in the cockpit.

"Keep monitoring that ship and let me know of anything unusual," Jaden said to R-6. To Marr, he said, "Where are the hardsuits?"

As they jogged through the corridors, Marr said, "He could shoot you out of space the moment you leave *Junker*."

"He could try," Jaden said, and put his hand on his lightsaber hilt. "Though that supply ship has little in the way of armament."

"He could ram you, Master. There's any number of ways. A single leak in the suit and it's over."

"He's gone to a lot of trouble to just kill me, don't you think? He wants me alive for some reason."

A tilt of Marr's enormous head conceded the point. "Presumably not for a reason you'll like. None of this makes sense."

"I agree," Jaden said, and they started walking again. "But do you have a better idea?"

Marr's eyes found the floor and he shook his large head. "No."

"The supply ship has a weak tractor beam. He'll try to reel me in once I'm out of *Junker*. Don't let that happen unless Khedryn is clear. Listen, Marr. The critical thing is to get Khedryn to safety. Understand? Get *Junker*'s tractor beam on his pod as soon as he's out. After he's secure, we'll improvise something."

"Improvise something?"

"Trust me when I tell you that's the life," Jaden said with a smile. "Nothing ever goes according to plan. Half the time I'm just making it up as I go. Get used to it, eh?"

Marr smiled, then nodded at one of the lockers near the airlock. "Right there," he said. He opened the locker to reveal three hardsuits, one with a helmet suitable for a Cerean. "You know how to put it on?"

"Been a while, but yeah."

Jaden handed Marr his lightsaber and then, piece by piece, donned the hardsuit. He felt like he was donning the archaic armor of the Clone Wars. He checked each joint seal as he went. When he missed something, Marr corrected it. Soon, Jaden was armored against outer space. He hooked his lightsaber to the outside of the suit.

"Helmet on," Marr said. "Test the seal."

Jaden pulled on the helmet, activated the electromagnetic seal. His breathing sounded loud in the dome of the helmet. The HUD on the faceplate showed a good seal at the neck and everywhere else.

Marr tapped the helmet. "Comlink," he said.

Jaden tested it and found it worked fine.

"You know how to operate the thruster controls?" Marr asked.

Jaden nodded. A simple joystick array built into the right wrist provided propulsion control. He could control it with his thumb.

Marr once more double-checked the suit's joint seals.

"I said it's been a while," Jaden said, "but I've done this a time or two. The joints are good."

"You've done it a time or two, but I've done it dozens of times. A seal can show green but be weak. That can pops a leak in the black, you'll be dead before I can help."

"Right," Jaden said, sobered. "We stay on live comm. Tell me right away when Khedryn is off the supply ship. Then tell me when he's aboard *Junker.*"

"Will do." Marr thumped the suit on the shoulder. "You're good."

Jaden turned, but Marr's curse pulled him around.

"One more thing," Marr said, grabbing something out of his pocket. He unsealed Jaden's helmet, removed it, and offered him a piece of chewstim.

"For luck," the Cerean said. "It's tradition on this ship."

Jaden took it and popped it into his mouth.

Marr put the helmet back on and resealed it, then circled Jaden, eyeing the suit. "You're all green, Master."

"Then let's do it."

Jaden moved to the airlock, the boots of the hardsuit thumping on *Junker*'s deck. Marr opened the interior airlock door and Jaden stepped inside. Marr closed the door behind Jaden and then his voice sounded over the suit's comlink, reverberating in the helmet.

"I'll be in the cockpit. May the Force be with you, Master."

Jaden activated the decompression sequence and prepared to open the outer door.

"And with you, Marr."

As Khedryn watched, the Umbaran shifted in his chair and activated the comm. A female voice answered his hail. Khedryn used the opportunity to crawl over to Soldier. He said nothing, merely brandished his small knife. Soldier's gaze hardened, but Khedryn shook his head to indicate that he intended no harm. He slit the tape around the clone's ankles.

"How close are you?" the Umbaran asked.

"Nearly in-system," the female voice answered.

Khedryn put his mouth to the clone's ear and said, "For Grace."

Soldier noticeably tensed at the mention of the little girl's name. Khedryn wondered if the girl was Soldier's daughter. Soldier turned so that Khedryn could get at the tape that bound his wrists.

"What are you planning?" the female asked over the comm.

"I'm planning to get Jaden Korr aboard the ship, then we take—"

Khedryn slit the binding on the clone's wrist, and when he did, the tip of his knife tapped the metal of the deck.

The Umbaran spun in his seat and leapt to his feet, twin vibroblades appearing in his hands as if by magic.

Khedryn clambered to his feet, his own inadequate knife in hand, and started to slide for the cockpit doors.

"You!" the Umbaran said, and moved toward Khedryn.

When Soldier stood, free of his bonds, the Umbaran stopped and his eyes widened. Khedryn almost grinned.

"Umbaran," Soldier said, his voice heavy with a promise of violence.

For a moment, all three stood there, Khedryn in the door, the Umbaran a few paces away, Soldier along the wall.

The Umbaran's eyes narrowed. The darkness around him deepened.

An idea hit Khedryn.

"Here!" he said, and tossed to Soldier one of the lightsabers he'd taken from the dead clones.

Soldier snatched it out of midair and ignited the blade, bathing the cockpit in red light. "Hunter's blade," he said.

The Umbaran shifted on his feet and the cockpit grew darker. Khedryn imagined energies he could not see swirling around him. The Umbaran stared at Soldier, at the blade Soldier held, and it began to thin, to sputter.

"Not this time," Soldier said between gritted teeth.

The blade thickened, thinned, thickened, flickered, grew solid once more.

Khedryn was bearing witness to a battle of wills that he did not understand.

"Go," Soldier said to Khedryn.

"We take him together," Khedryn said, holding the pathetic knife in his hand.

Soldier's lips curled with rage—not at Khedryn, but at the Umbaran. "Who are you to me, spacer? If Seer tells me to kill you after I kill the Umbaran, I will do exactly that. Go. Get off the ship. And do not follow us. Tell the Jedi I said that. Tell him not to follow us."

Khedryn understood none of that. "I freed you, Soldier—"

"Go!"

"Neither of you are getting off this ship," the Umbaran said. The vibroblades in his hands began to hum, an answer to the hum of Soldier's lightsaber.

Khedryn looked at Soldier, at the Umbaran, out at the black.

Junker was out there—Marr, Jaden.

He turned and ran back the way he had come. Soldier would kill the Umbaran and care for Grace. Khedryn would convince Jaden to leave the clones alone, and they would return to Fhost to gamble and drink.

Or not, if he knew Jaden.

He reached the lift in moments, the clash of energized blades loud behind him. He did not slow. The doors opened; he piled in, hit the button for the cargo deck, and started down. The lift moved far slower than he would have liked. He did not know the layout of the ship, but he figured he could access the escape pods from the cargo deck. He just needed to find them.

chapter nine

JUNKER'S AIRLOCK VENTED, THE EXTERIOR DOOR OPENED, and Jaden faced the void. He put his thumb on the thruster control stick and propelled himself into space. A single burst set him in motion and inertia did the rest. In moments he was floating free, hundreds of meters from *Junker*. The freighter looked tiny against the vast background of stars.

"I'm clear," he said.

"I have you," Marr answered.

"Khedryn?"

"Not yet," Marr said.

"Hail the supply ship. Tell him I'm aborting if Khedryn isn't released immediately."

Jaden used the thrusters to stop his movement and hold his position. The supply ship hung in space, small at ten kilometers' distance. The asteroid belt in the system looked like dark clouds floating between Jaden and the system's orange star. He felt pensive, as if something were about to happen.

"Is something odd going on, Marr?"

"Not that I can tell, Master."

Nyss felt Soldier fighting against his power, the clone's anger a match for his emptiness. Eyeing the red line of Soldier's lightsaber, its glow a direct affront to his ability, Nyss knew that he had to escape. Perhaps he and Syll together could completely cut Soldier off from the Force, but Nyss could not do it alone.

At Soldier's feet, Seer stirred, groaned. Soldier looked down and Nyss seized the opportunity, pelting out of the cockpit. Soldier roared and gave chase.

Ten strides down the hallway, Nyss hit the button to summon the lift and spun around to face Soldier's onslaught. Soldier unleashed two-handed overhand slashes that Nyss parried with his blades. The cortosis coating his blades not only allowed them to withstand the slash of a lightsaber—at least for a few passes—they also caused Soldier's weapon to spark wildly. Contact with cortosis for a long enough time could temporarily short out a lightsaber, but Soldier's blade moved so quickly that the contact between the weapons was momentary at best. But eventually, Soldier's lightsaber would destroy Nyss's blades.

Nyss dropped to the floor and swept a kick at Soldier's legs, but the clone anticipated the attack, leapt over the sweep, and slashed downward at Nyss's leg.

Nyss pulled his leg close—the lightsaber put a gash in the deck, showering the corridor in sparks—rolled aside, and rode the momentum to his feet. The clone growled and lunged at Nyss, his blade a whistling red line of slashes, stabs, and cuts. Sweating, panting, Nyss positioned his vibroblades to form a wall, answering every blow of the clone with a parry. He did not even try to counterattack. He was trying to hold his ground and play for time.

The door to the lift opened behind him.

Bursting into motion, Nyss unleashed a desperate series of stabs, blocking the clone's lightsaber out wide with one vibroblade and stabbing at his chest with the other. The clone flipped backward, temporarily disengaging, and Nyss ran for the lift. When he got inside, he slammed his hand against the button to close the doors.

Soldier roared, bounding after him.

The doors started to close, but too damned slowly.

Desperate, Nyss flung one of his blades through the shrinking opening between the doors. Soldier, unprepared for the throw, pulled up short and deflected the vibroblade with his lightsaber.

The doors closed and the turbolift started downward.

The red line of Soldier's blade shot through the metal of the doors. As the lift descended, the weapon cut a sparking vertical gash in the side—but in a few seconds, the lift had moved out of reach.

Nyss did not let himself relax. He paced the lift as it descended to the cargo bay. The supply ship had four escape pods, and he knew where he needed to go to get access to them.

The lift reached the cargo deck and the doors parted.

An impact on the roof of the turbolift caused the entire car to vibrate.

Soldier.

Nyss crouched low as the red line of a lightsaber scythed out of the ceiling and began to cut a circular hole in the roof. Sparks and slagged metal rained down.

"You are not getting away from me!" Soldier shouted. "And if you've harmed Grace . . ."

He left the threat unspoken, but Nyss understood it well enough. He bolted out of the lift and headed for the escape pods.

Khedryn doubled back for the second time. Sweat dripped into his eyes. His breathing was coming too fast. He had to be going in the right direction this time, didn't he? The darkness made it hard to know whether he was retracing the same path. The cargo compartments and the corridors connecting them all looked the same.

He saw writing on the wall ahead, got close enough to read it in the dim glow of the emergency lights. Stenciled letters pointed him to the emergency escape pods. He breathed a sigh of relief and ran, following the arrows. He reached an intersection and turned.

On the far end of a long compartment, a metal stairway descended ten meters into a bay lined with four doors—the escape pods. He hurried for the stairs. He'd be aboard *Junker* in moments.

Something whistled past his ear, pinged into the bulkhead, and ricocheted to the floor. He froze and looked down to see what it was: a crossbow quarrel.

He whirled, cursing, and saw the Umbaran running toward him.

Khedryn turned and ran, hunching to make himself small. Another shot pinged off the bulkhead. The Umbaran must have had some kind of repeating mechanism on the crossbow. He darted across the large compartment. The distance might as well have been a parsec. He didn't figure there was any way he could make it.

He zigzagged as he ran, wincing at the expectation that he'd be shot from behind at any moment.

A shout and growl sounded from over his shoulder and he looked back. Soldier barreled around the corner behind the Umbaran, his lightsaber lighting the way before him.

The Umbaran saw Soldier, too. He slung his crossbow and ran for the escape pods.

Khedryn reached the stairs, pelted down them, and hit the first escape pod door. It opened and he ran in. He heard the Umbaran tearing down the stairs behind him. Khedryn wished he could have launched all the pods, leaving the Umbaran there to face Soldier, but there was no time.

The pod door hissed shut. Khedryn stared through the tiny viewport in the thick door and made an obscene gesture at the Umbaran as he ran by.

Afterward he strapped himself into one of the four seats, activated the pod's systems, and hit the emergency launch button.

"Three, two, one," said the computerized voice, and the pod shot out of the belly of the supply ship like a blaster shot.

It galled Nyss to flee, but he was at a disadvantage fighting Soldier. Not only could Soldier use the Force to resist his power, but Nyss couldn't just kill Soldier—he had to keep him alive.

Nyss would need his sister to capture the clone. They could regroup aboard the scout flyer, develop a new plan. He punched the button to open one of the escape pods and the doors hissed open.

Soldier's heavy tread thumped down the stairs after him, the hum of his lightsaber the harbinger of his wrath.

Nyss hurried into the pod, closed the door, and started the emergency launch sequence. He focused his mind on the hole of his existence, the emptiness, and let it spread from him.

Soldier appeared on the other side of the door, his bearded face filled with rage. He raised his flickering lightsaber for a stab into the pod's door, a blow that would render the pod unspaceworthy, would force Nyss to face him.

The hole Nyss projected deepened. He strained to make it as dark a void as he had ever before managed.

Soldier stabbed the blade into the viewport, but only the hilt slammed into the transparisteel. For a moment, surprise supplanted rage.

Nyss's power had suppressed the blade's crystal.

Soldier slammed a fist into the viewport, his mouth open in a snarl.

Nyss turned away and sagged against the door as the pod shot away from the supply ship, from Soldier.

The velocity of the spherical craft pinned Nyss to the wall for a moment. Breathing heavily, he activated his comlink.

"The clones have retaken the ship. I'm in a pod. Fix on my signal and pick me up. Quickly. Weapons hot."

"On my way," said Syll. "Weapons hot."

Jaden floated in the space between *Junker* and the supply ship.

"No response, Master," Marr said. "He's not answering our hail."

Jaden stared at the supply ship as if he could see through its walls and see what was happening within.

"Something is going on," he said.

"Maybe you should return to *Junker*. We can take the ship's boat, force a dock with the supply ship, and get aboard that way." Marr's voice hitched. "Wait. . . ."

Motion drew Jaden's eye as the bubble of an escape pod—its metal glinting in the light of the star—launched from the supply ship's starboard side.

"Marr—"

A second pod shot from the belly of the supply ship.

"Master, two escape pods just—"

"I see them."

Static barked in Jaden's ear as a signal cut into their frequency. Khedryn's voice echoed in Jaden's helmet, carried across kilometers of space.

"Jaden? Marr?"

"Khedryn!" Marr said.

Khedryn said, "The clones are back in control of the supply ship! I'm in the escape pod."

"How?" Marr asked.

"Which pod?" Jaden asked.

"Which pod? There's another?" Khedryn asked. "The Umbaran must be in it. He fled the ship, too, when the clones took back control."

"You're in the pod that launched first," Jaden said.

"I don't know. I've got thruster control. I'll jig for you."

One of the pods, the one that had launched first, did a jig in space.

"Got it," Marr said. "Do you see us?"

"Coming at you," Khedryn said. The pod's thrusters flared and the metal ball darted toward *Junker* and Jaden.

Behind Jaden, *Junker*'s ion engines flared to life.

"I'm coming to get you both," Marr said.

"Both? Where are you, Jaden?" Khedryn asked.

"I'm in a hardsuit," Jaden said.

"Stang, man. I'm gone awhile and you start thinking you're a spacer! Marr, you let him go floating in the black?"

"He was insistent," Marr said.

Another streak of motion drew Jaden's eye and wiped the growing grin from his face. A ship bounced out of hyperspace not far from the other escape pod.

"Master, another ship just entered the system." A pause then, "Its weapons are live."

Nyss saw the sleek lines of the scout flyer emerge from hyperspace. He engaged the pod's thrusters, the scout flyer's ion engines flared, and the distance between the two ships shrank rapidly. The pod lurched.

"Tractor is on you," Syll said over the comlink. "Pulling you in."

"There is a second escape pod."

"I see it."

"Is the Jedi outside their freighter?"

A moment passed while Syll consulted scanners. "He is."

"Destroy the pod and the freighter. We'll pluck the Jedi out of space after that."

They'd still have to figure out what to do about the Prime, but at least they'd have Korr.

The pod slammed hard into the scout flyer and metal groaned.

"Have you," Syll said.

"On my way," Nyss said. He slipped from his seat as the docking rings mated.

Jaden watched the second escape pod attach itself to some kind of small craft, a scout ship, maybe, saw the scout ship wheel in their direction, and understood right away what was happening. Marr's voice over the comlink only confirmed it.

"That ship is coming right at us. Weapon's locking onto *Junker*."

"Get the deflectors up!" Jaden said to Marr.

Before the words had cleared his mouth, the scout ship's wing-mounted weapons lit up. Lines of red plasma stretched across the black gulf. The freighter, its deflector array inactive, took the blast in its port side. Flames exploded outward into space, the silence of it making it surreal. Explosive decompression ejected bits of metal and mundane debris into space. The ship listed, spitting flames and smoke.

"Marr!" Khedryn and Jaden shouted.

They could hear the Cerean's stressed breathing over the comlink. His voice, however, was calm. "We're all right. Ar-Six, seal off the compromised compartments. Deflectors are live. Engines are functional."

Jaden eyed the scout, which was now wheeling toward Khedryn's pod. A single shot against the pod would vaporize it. Jaden needed to buy a few moments.

"Khedryn, hard to port! As much as the thrusters can give you! Now!"

Khedryn must have heard the urgency, and he did not question the order. The pod's thrusters fired, and it cut a hard turn to port.

Jaden estimated its velocity and the distance, and fired the thrusters of his hardsuit, taking a trajectory that would put him near the pod—or so he hoped.

Unprepared for the abrupt turn of the pod, the scout ship wheeled again to follow. Jaden cut through space toward the pod. So, too, did the scout ship.

"Faster, Khedryn," he muttered.

"That's all it's got, Jedi. Where are they?"

"Right behind you," Jaden said.

Khedryn cursed, his breathing loud over the comm.

The scout leveled off, put itself on a firing line to the pod. Jaden had to do something, and do it now!

He fell into the Force as the scout ship's wings flared and the weapons fired. To him, events seemed to slow. The lines of the ship's lasers extended outward from its guns, slowly reaching across space, crayon lines drawn by an invisible child.

Power filled Jaden, and with it he reached out for Khedryn's pod, roped it with his mind, and yanked it hard toward him. Despite his use of the Force, the differential mass between his body and the escape pod did not allow for a clean pull. His movement toward the pod increased even as the pod sped more rapidly toward him.

Still, it was enough. Though the proximity of the shot caused the pod to lurch hard, the red lines stretched through space behind it. Jaden grunted with the effort to maintain his mental hold on the small craft.

"What just happened?" Khedryn shouted.

"You were almost hit," Jaden said, as he blazed through space toward the pod.

"Let's try to avoid that."

"Let's," Jaden said, smiling. But now the distance between him and the pod was closing rapidly, too rapidly. If he hit it too hard, he'd lose a seal on his suit and that would be that.

Meanwhile, behind it, the scout ship cut hard toward the pod, reestablishing a firing line.

Jaden put their distance apart at three hundred meters . . . two hundred . . . one hundred. The scout was in position. But so was Jaden. He ignited his lightsaber. The hardsuit would restrict his mobility, but he'd have to make due. He'd received his training in zero-G a long time ago. He'd use the Force to steady himself in space, otherwise any action in zero-G would precipitate an equal and opposite reaction that would make precision movement almost impossible.

Twenty meters.

"Thrusters hard to starboard," he said to Khedryn, and fired the suit's thrusters.

The pod's port thrusters fired, angling the vessel to starboard. The scout jigged to stay on it.

Jaden, still holding the pod with the Force, slammed hard into it feetfirst. He grabbed at a protuberance—a comm antenna—with his free hand just as the scout ship fired.

Still enmeshed in the Force, he sensed the trajectory of the blasts, the line of their approach. His lightsaber spun through space, the Force-augmented motion stressing the hardsuit. The shots slammed into the yellow line of his blade, and he deflected them back at the ship's cockpit. They split the space between them and knifed into the cockpit, which exploded into flame. The scout ship, bleeding smoke, streaked toward the pod.

"Port, Khedryn! Port!" Jaden shouted, watching the scout get closer and closer. The ship would slam into them both.

Straddling the pod, Jaden pushed with the Force against the oncoming ship, the pressure assisting the pod's thrusters. He crouched low as the scout ship wheeled over and past them, so close he could have touched it with his fingertips. The ship continued its trajectory and velocity, not turning around, heading into the deep system. Perhaps the blasters had damaged its controls. Or perhaps killed the pilot.

"Khedryn," Jaden said. "Are you all right?"

"Good," Khedryn said. "I think."

"Get us aboard, Marr," Jaden said to the Cerean.

"Tractor beam has the pod," Marr answered.

An alarm rang in Jaden's suit, the sound surprisingly subdued given the urgency of its warning.

"I'm leaking," he said.

"What?" Khedryn asked. "What did you say?"

Khedryn's face appeared in the tiny viewport of the escape pod, his misaligned eyes fixing on Jaden's faceplate. Worry twisted his bruised, bloody expression. He hit a button to activate the comm.

"Did you say you're leaking?"

"Affirmative," Jaden said.

Khedryn cursed.

"On my way," Marr said.

Jaden deactivated his lightsaber and held out his arms, examining the hardsuit. It was venting air through a pinhole in the ankle seam and at the right elbow.

"I see them," Khedryn said. "Two holes."

Jaden did not comment. He wanted to preserve oxygen. His HUD told him he had twenty-nine seconds before the tanks emptied. Twenty-eight.

"I have twenty-seven seconds," he said. "Twenty-six."

"Hang in, Jaden," Khedryn said. He put his palm on the glass of the viewport. "Hang in."

Jaden nodded in his suit. He steadied heart and mind,

trying to consume as little air as possible while watching *Junker* turn and blast toward him. Twenty seconds. Nineteen.

He was getting dizzy as his oxygen depleted. *Junker's* tractor beam pulled the pod through space at a breakneck pace, even while Marr piloted the freighter toward them.

"I'm at twelve seconds," Jaden said.

"Where the hell are you, Marr?" Khedryn asked.

"Ar-Six has the helm, Khedryn."

"What?" Khedryn asked, indignant. "A droid is flying my ship?"

Spots formed before Jaden's eyes. "Almost out," he tried to say, but the words sounded garbled.

Marr's voice echoed in his helmet. "Do you see the airlock, Master?"

Jaden tried to focus on *Junker* as it spun its side to the pod to show the hole of an open airlock. A form hovered there in the lighted box of the compartment: Marr in a hardsuit. His thruster flared and he shot toward Jaden. Jaden's vision went in and out. He heard Khedryn's voice in his head, but the words seemed far away, whispers he could not quite comprehend.

Marr appeared before him, his concerned face visible through the lit faceplate of the hardsuit. Jaden tried to speak but could not. Marr's words cut through the clutter of his fading consciousness.

"I have you, Master."

And then they were moving back toward *Junker.* Jaden stared at the open airlock, like a mouth in the side of the ship.

"It's hungry," he tried to say, smiling, but his lips would form neither words nor a smile, and a part of him recognized the ridiculousness of the observation.

Khedryn was barking over the comlink, but Jaden could not understand him, could not hold his eyes open.

* * *

The scout flyer shivered from an impact. An alarm screeched. In moments, Nyss smelled smoke.

"What happened?" he asked. "Syll, what happened?"

His sister did not respond. He hurried through the dim, close corridors of the flyer, the smell of smoke getting more acute. When he reached the cockpit and tried to push the door open, he found that something was blocking the door.

"Syll," he called. "Syll!"

Nothing.

He muscled open the door and saw that it was his sister's form that had obstructed it. Panic seized him; it sent his heart racing and stole his breath. He knelt at her side and turned her over so that he could see her face. Blood, warm and sticky, made her hair glisten. He probed her scalp for the wound, felt the indentation in her skull, and drew back as if she were hot.

"Syll," he said.

She said nothing. Her eyes stared at him, empty, glassy, and he knew she was dead. She must have struck her head on something when the ship lurched.

The hole he lived in, the sanctuary in which he existed, separate from other living things, yawned under him. Staring at Syll's face, he felt himself spiraling around the edge of the void. The darkness in the cockpit intensified as he plummeted.

But as he continued to look at Syll's face, grief stopped his descent. Anger filled the void and halted his fall.

He was alone in the universe, forever alone.

He ground his teeth and clenched his fist and shouted aloud.

Someone would pay for his loss, his solitude.

He would kill the Jedi's allies, kill the clones, kill them all, kill *everything*.

He spared a glance out the cockpit and saw nothing

but a field of stars. There was no sign of the escape pod or *Junker* or the supply ship. The scout flyer was hurtling into the deep system, away from the star.

He triggered the autopilot to avoid a collision and realized his hands were shaking. He calmed himself and gently lifted Syll from the floor. Feeling numbed by his anger, he set her into her usual copilot's chair and strapped her in.

"It's beautiful, Syll," he said, nodding out at the deep system. "The dark, I mean."

He'd never felt such pain in his life.

Soldier's anger began to diminish the moment the Umbaran's pod shot out of the ship. He stood there for a time, chest heaving, rage abating, staring at the empty escape pod sockets. Bleeding from the wound in his arm, Soldier turned and staggered through the cargo bay. He deactivated his blade.

"Grace!" he called. "Grace!"

He did not think of Seer or Hunter or Runner. He thought only of Grace. For a reason he could not understand, her survival meant everything to him.

"Grace! Grace!"

His voice echoed off the walls, resounded through the bay. The alchemy of his emotional state transformed his concern for Grace into power. The Force filled him. He threw his head back and shouted his frustration into the air in a prolonged howl of pain and fear.

"Grace!"

He gestured with his left hand and flung a shipping container halfway across the cargo bay. It slammed into a stack of other containers as metal crumpled and medical equipment spilled out onto the floor. He gestured with his right hand, and another container flew out of his way, his rage opening a path before him. He clenched his fist and a third container began to crumple in on itself, his power squeezing it down to half its size, a quarter.

Grief filled him, lodged in the mental space his anger had abandoned. He fell to his knees and his eyes welled. He did not wipe the tears as they fell.

He had failed Grace, failed all of them. His life had mattered to no one.

"Soldier?" said a small, diffident voice behind him.

He whirled, the smile already wide on his face.

Grace stood three meters from him, her red hair hanging lankly before her pale face. For the first time, her thinness struck him. She was not eating enough.

He held out his arms and she ran to him. He wrapped her up, feeling the horrific movement beneath her skin. She already needed another hypo. He held her close, weeping.

"Come with me," he finally said. "You need meds."

"Are you okay?" she asked, and he could only laugh and nod.

She did not resist as he took her hand and led her toward the cockpit.

"Is my . . . mother dead?"

Soldier squeezed her hand. Hunter's lightsaber hilt hung from his belt. "I think so, yes. I'm sorry, Grace."

Grace said nothing. Soldier felt her grief, but it was dulled, distant. She'd seen so much already in her life that tragedy moved her little. He hated that, hated the scientists who'd made them and condemned them all to a wretched life and forced them to kill for their freedom, hated that they could not simply live, find enjoyment in what they would. Grace would have that, even if the rest of them had not.

"What about the man?" Grace asked.

"What man?"

"The man with the funny eyes."

She meant their captive, the spacer, the ally of the Jedi. "I don't know for certain. But I think he is off the ship."

"I think so, too," she said, and squeezed Soldier's hand. "I hope he is. He was nice."

Jaden heard voices, opened his eyes. Marr's enormous head hovered over his face, forehead creased by worry lines.

"Master, can you hear me?"

From somewhere off to the side, R-6 made a sympathetic whistle.

"I can hear you," Jaden said, blinking to clear his blurred vision.

Relief filled Marr's eyes. He kept a hand pressed against Jaden's chest, as if to prevent him from trying to sit up.

Jaden was aboard *Junker,* in the corridor outside the airlock. His hardsuit helmet lay beside him on the deck. He had been running out of air. . . .

"How did you—"

"We got you aboard, pressurized the airlock, and dragged you in here," Marr said. "You weren't entirely without air for more than a few seconds. Your blood oxygen is probably quite low, though. Just relax. Breathe. Let your head clear."

There was the sound of running footsteps on the deck, then Khedryn's voice. "Is he all right?"

"He's fine," Marr said.

"I'm fine," Jaden said, staring at the ceiling, not quite ready to try and sit up. "How are *you*?"

Marr turned to look at Khedryn and swore. It was the first time Jaden had ever heard the Cerean curse.

Khedryn's trousers showed a long rip in the thigh. One side of his face was purple and swelling, making the mismatch of his eyes all the more pronounced. Blood stained his shirt here and there. His hair stuck out at wild angles. His nose looked as crooked as a Hutt.

He waved a hand to dismiss their concern. "I'm fine. Just keep getting uglier. I blame you two." He stood beside Marr and stared down at Jaden, not with concern, but . . . something else.

"Help me up, will you?" Jaden asked.

Marr assisted him until he was seated upright. Dizziness assailed him, and he put his hands down on the deck to steady himself. R-6 made a concerned beep.

"I'm fine, Ar-Six."

Khedryn, Marr, and R-6 crowded around him. Khedryn took one side, Marr the other, and they helped him to his feet.

"Where's the supply ship?" Jaden asked.

Khedryn and Marr glanced at each other. R-6 beeped the droid equivalent of a shrug.

"We just got aboard, Master," Marr said. "No one is on the scanners."

"It's good to have you back aboard," Jaden said to Khedryn.

"Good to be back," he said.

Marr put a hand on Khedryn's shoulder in welcome.

"Let's get to the cockpit," Jaden said. He shed pieces of the hardsuit as he went. When they reached it, they could see the supply ship through the canopy, moving away from them. They could not see the scout flyer. Marr bent over the scanners.

"The supply ship is under ion-engine power, heading to a jump point. We can't catch it."

"No," Jaden said. "But we can follow it. We've still got the beacon aboard."

"A beacon," Khedryn said. "That's how you tracked me?"

"Took one of your signal beacons from the hold," Jaden explained.

Marr, still eyeing the scanner, said, "The scout flyer is headed away into the deep system. The second escape pod docked with it."

"Then the Umbaran is aboard it," Khedryn said.

"An Umbaran?" Jaden asked. "The person who called himself Nyss?"

"Yeah, he's Umbaran. And he . . . did something to the clones, Jaden. Cut them off from the Force somehow."

Jaden shook his head. "That's not possible."

Khedryn ran a hand over his jaw, testing it as if it hurt. "I'm only telling you what I saw. When the clones fought him, they couldn't use the Force. Even their lightsabers were nonfunctional. They were working and then they weren't."

"You've never heard of anything like that, Master?" Marr asked.

"Never. You're sure?" Jaden asked Khedryn. "Maybe it was a device of some kind."

"Some kind of neurological scrambler, perhaps," Marr offered. "Or maybe something unique to the clones, a vulnerability attributable to their illness."

Khedryn shook his head. "I don't think so. It seemed to be the Umbaran himself. Look, I don't pretend to understand it. But that's how it seemed to me. He cut the clones off from the Force. Well, all but one."

"What do you mean?" Jaden asked. "Which one?"

Khedryn swallowed and would not meet Jaden's eyes. "Soldier, he called himself. I helped him get free of the Umbaran so I could . . ." He trailed off, then said, "One of the clones is a little girl. I couldn't leave her to the Umbaran."

Jaden understood completely. "I would have done the same thing."

Jaden's words caused Khedryn to puff a little with pride. "Well, yes. Right."

"So why did he want you, Master?" Marr asked. "And what's his interest in this?"

Jaden shook his head. Matters remained muddled. He had no clear insight into events. Khedryn seemed to want to say something.

"Khedryn?" Jaden asked. "What else?"

Khedryn cleared his throat, then looked away. "Jaden, I don't know how to tell you this. . . ."

All at once, Jaden understood. "I know already. One of them is a clone of me."

R-6 whistled in surprise.

Khedryn looked up, his swollen eye nearly bugging out of his head. "How did you know?"

"I fought him back on Fhost."

Khedryn looked appalled. "And you—Well, that must have felt . . . weird."

Jaden shrugged. "Which one is it? Soldier?"

"Yes," Khedryn said. "And, Jaden, he was . . . different from the other clones."

"What do you mean?" Marr asked.

"Different how?" asked Jaden.

"Not as sick as the others, maybe not sick at all. They seemed crazy, but he just seemed . . . confused. Angry, but not crazy. When they wanted to kill me, he tried to stop them. There's something about him. . . ." He looked up. "He's got your eyes. You know what I mean? He's looking for something."

Jaden did not know what to say.

"He's more like you than in just looks," Khedryn said thoughtfully. "And he seemed able to at least partially resist the Umbaran's power. Maybe you can, too?"

"Maybe," Jaden said, oddly troubled to hear that he and the clone shared a temperament.

People are not equations, Marr had said. Jaden wondered.

"We need to get after them," he said.

"The Umbaran or the clones?" Marr asked.

"The clones."

Khedryn cleared his throat. "He said not to follow. Soldier said that. Why follow? There's only three left. One is a child."

"I would never hurt a child, Khedryn," Jaden said.

"I know that."

"But that clone killed people on Fhost. They're dangerous still."

Khedryn sighed. "Jedi, I just want to catch my breath for a moment. You know?"

"I do," Jaden said, nodding. "But there's no time."

chapter ten

SOLDIER SCOOPED GRACE UP AND CARRIED HER TO THE cockpit. Seer awaited them there, conscious, standing before the copilot's chair, staring out the transparisteel. She did not look at them when she spoke.

"There are only we three now."

"What happened to your face?" Grace asked her, eyeing the bruise on her cheek.

"Shh," Soldier said, and placed her in one of the crew chairs. He buckled her in, tousled her hair. "Everything is all right now," he said, and smiled.

She did not smile back, and he felt the seed of grief within her. She was trying not to let it grow roots, but he suspected it would. She'd lost her mother—and everyone else in the Community except him and Seer.

He found a loaded hypo and injected Grace. She didn't make a sound. He hoped the medicine would work fast. He turned and put his hands on Seer's shoulders and eased her into the copilot's chair. She did not resist, and he felt her skin roil under his touch. She, too, was failing. Everyone was, except him.

"You need meds, Seer," he said.

"I told you no more, Soldier," she said. "We're soon to see Mother. No more meds. Mother will heal us all."

"I'm not sick," he said.

"Not in body," she said, still staring out into the black. Soldier wondered what she saw there.

He decided not to argue. Grace had her meds and that was what mattered. He took the pilot's seat and looked at the navicomp. The coordinates were still on the screen, a numerical code that, if Seer was right, would lead them to Mother.

"Are you ready now, Soldier?" Seer asked, finally looking at him. "Now, after all of this, are you ready?"

He looked out the canopy, back to Grace, and nodded.

"Let's go to Mother," he said, and engaged the hyperdrive.

Mother felt the connection to Seer grow stronger. She sensed loss through the connection. Something had happened to Seer and the others she journeyed with.

I will make it all worthwhile, she projected to Seer. *Come home. Come home, now.* Soon, Mother would be free.

Nyss scrolled through the coordinates in the scout flyer's navicomp for the coordinates he had uploaded from the supply ship. He knew where the clones were going, and he knew that Jaden Korr would follow them there.

The coordinates targeted a system deep in the Unknown Regions. Very little data about it existed. The system's star was a pulsar, and the system itself exhibited extraordinarily high levels of radiation. Calculations based on astronomical observations confirmed the presence of two planets and an asteroid belt, but no planetary survey showed up in the records.

"You did well recording the course," he said to his sister's corpse. He tried not to notice that her chin was on her chest. He left her beside him because he could not bear to part with her, because he could not bear to be alone in their ship, because he wanted a reminder to keep his pain fresh.

But he knew he would not be able to face Soldier and Jaden without help.

"I'm going to awaken the Iteration," he said to Syll. "It's time."

But first he needed to put some distance between himself, the Prime, and the Jedi. He input into the navicomp a short hyperspace jump into a neighboring uninhabited system and engaged the hyperdrive. The ship dashed into the blue tunnel of hyperspace.

When it came out, he would awaken the Iteration. Then he would track down the Jedi and the Prime. He would do what he had been sent by Wyyrlok to do. Then he would kill everyone else.

Marr, on a scanner, said, "The Umbaran's ship is jumping out of the system."

Khedryn cursed.

Jaden put a hand on his shoulder. "There's little we could have done from *Junker*."

Khedryn nodded. "Let's hope he's gone for good."

R-6 appeared, his mechanical arms bearing medical supplies. He offered them to Khedryn. Khedryn considered them, took them, and stuffed gauze into his nostrils.

"You're all right, droid," he said.

Jaden looked at him with a surprised smile.

"People change, Jedi. Otherwise we're just droids of flesh. Isn't that what you said?"

"So I did," Jaden said.

Marr said, "The supply ship's hyperdrive is spooling up, too."

As one, they all looked out the canopy. The supply ship vanished in a blink, jumping out of the system.

"Let's get a lock on our tracking beacon and follow them," Jaden said.

"They're looking for someone or something they call 'Mother.' To me, it sounded like a religious thing." Khedryn fixed Jaden with a meaningful stare. "I said he had your eyes, yeah? Maybe he had a Force Vision, too?"

Jaden looked out into the black, pondering.

"Go get me some caf, droid," Khedryn said. "You've got to earn your keep on this tub, and med supplies don't do it. We run on caf out here."

R-6 made a long-suffering series of whistles and beeps and wheeled off for the galley.

Across the void, through the Power, Mother felt Seer and the others getting closer, felt the comforting connection of their minds, so welcome to her after eons of solitude.

Mother was calling them to her, and they were answering.

And when they arrived, they would free her. Seer would be the one who would provide Mother the flesh she has craved for millennia.

She hoped for this, allowed herself to believe that it would be so.

She knew that Seer hoped for things, too, and that Seer allowed herself to believe they would be so.

In that way, Mother learned how to lie.

She'd used others in the past, the shells of beings that littered her prison, but all of them had crumpled under her embrace, their form unable to bear her touch.

Matters would be different this time.

So she hoped. So she believed.

Perhaps she had begun to lie to herself? How would she know?

She'd been alone so long, adrift in nothingness, existing at the bottom of a deep hole from which she could look out and up at the universe but never experience any of it. Her cage condemned her to life alone, as an observer, never as a participant.

She wished to end her solitude, to experience the universe she'd felt indirectly through the millennia. She wished to express the rage she had harbored for so long.

Seer would provide her a way.

Soldier's hands shook on the stick as the supply ship started to come out of hyperspace. He tried to hide the shaking from Seer. He hoped for, even secretly expected, beauty, the light of revelation, Mother, and *meaning*. After all, Seer had been right about everything up to then, and her visions had led them there.

And his purpose, he thought—*he believed*—had been to bring them.

The cockpit was silent as the blue swirl gave way to the black of ordinary space. Soldier held his breath, hopeful, pensive, desperate.

An alarm began to wail the moment they entered normal space. The sudden burst of sound startled him and it took a moment for him to respond. The readout showed a system bathed in radiation.

Grace covered her ears, whimpering and rocking in her seat. Seer seemed barely to notice the sound. She simply stared out at the system as if its dark expanse held truth.

Soldier quickly adjusted the deflectors to account for radiation in-system. The alarms went quiet. He checked the sensors.

"The dose was small," he said. "No damage."

Seer nodded absently. She was sweating, flush, her dark eyes sunk deep in the pits of their sockets.

"It'll be all right," Soldier said over his shoulder to Grace. "It's all right."

At the sound of his voice, she opened her eyes and stopped whimpering. She looked tiny in her seat, fragile. He was pleased to see that her skin no longer crawled. The meds had done their work, for now.

He turned back to the instruments. They had emerged from hyperspace at the edge of the system. Through the cockpit's transparisteel, he could see the distant pulsar, a dark ball resting in the middle of a network of colorful arcs and whorls that stretched out from the pulsar in beautiful curtains hundreds of thousands of kilometers on a side. He presumed the light show was caused by the interaction of the pulsar's electromagnetic field with some ambient energy in the system. He'd never seen anything like it in simulations.

They'd found beauty, at least. Now they needed revelation.

"Pretty," Grace said, standing up in her seat.

Soldier nodded, pleased to hear the wonder in her voice.

A thick belt of asteroids ringed the pulsar, visible as an irregular black line against the background glow of the inner system. Sensors showed many of them to be metallic, an odd alloy that the scanner could not identify. He tried to refine the scan, but the metal defied identification.

Two small planets, barren and rocky, orbited the pulsar in the deep system, not far from the supply ship. Both were in tidal lock. Neither could possibly be inhabited.

He checked and rechecked the scanner, looked for something he might have missed. He found nothing, so he went over the readings again, his hands moving more rapidly across the control pad, his frustration building.

How could there be nothing?

They had come so far, done so much, done *too much* for there to be nothing. Emptiness yawned in him, despair, a feeling similar to the emptiness he'd felt when the Umbaran had almost disconnected him from the Force. Except now he'd been disconnected from hope.

"Seer," he said, his voice dull. He could not believe it. They had sacrificed everything to see an interstellar light show. Seer had been wrong.

She gave no indication she'd heard. Concentration creased her brow.

He was already sick of her feigned religiosity. Her trances were nothing more than the fevered imaginings of an ill mind. For Grace, he tried to keep the disappointment from his voice.

"Seer, there's nothing here. We need to leave."

"There," Seer said, nodding at the larger, nearer planet. "Go there, Soldier."

Her refusal to acknowledge how wrong she'd been caused anger to bubble in him, to put a sharp edge on his voice. His knuckles whitened around the stick.

"There's nothing there, Seer. It's a dead planet. The whole system is dead."

She turned in her seat to face him. There was no doubt in her eyes and her lack of it drove him to distraction. "Go, I said."

His anger boiled in the face of her ridiculous conviction. Unable to stop himself, he leapt from his seat, took her by the shoulders, and shook her, the power of the dark side filling him. Words burst from him.

"Did you hear me, woman?! There's nothing here! It was all a mistake, lies! Everything was for nothing! Do you understand? For *nothing*!"

She did not resist him; she only smiled, and he found the expression so oddly inappropriate that the anger went out of him in a rush. Breathing heavily, he let her go.

Grace stared at him wide-eyed, her legs pulled to her chest, cowering in her seat. He felt ashamed of himself.

"It's all right, Grace. Everything is okay. I just . . . forgot myself for a moment."

Seer put a fever-heated hand to his face. He recoiled at her touch, suddenly disgusted by the feel of her, but she did not lower her hand.

"Your belief has always been so fragile, Soldier. Mine is not so easily eroded. Do as I say. Take us to the larger planet, around to the dark side."

He searched her eyes for a lie, for doubt, but saw none. Her certainty took him aback.

"There's nothing there," he said, his tone doubtful.

"The scanners cannot reach that side," she said.

"The system is full of radiation," he said. "Nothing could survive there."

"Mother is there," Seer said. She smiled and her flesh pulsed, a bubble that caused her cheek to swell and turned her smile into a leer. "You were to bring us here. Do so."

Hearing her state the purpose he had set for himself made the hairs on his neck stand up. Moving as if on autopilot, he took his seat, put his hands on the stick, and angled the ship toward the large, black rock.

"Around to the dark side," she said. "We are almost there."

Grace crept out of her seat and stood at the arm of Soldier's chair, staring expectantly out the canopy. The planet grew larger as they neared it. Soldier's heart beat faster with every ten thousand kilometers they covered. He realized he was holding his breath, daring to hope even when reason told him that hope was foolish.

Beside him, Grace was doing the same. He swung the ship around to the dark side of the planet, the side that had been shielded from his scans.

And when they saw, Soldier and Grace gasped as one. Seer only smiled.

* * *

Jaden, Marr, and Khedryn studied the minimal data available on the system to which the clones had jumped.

"Maybe they had a misjump?" Khedryn said, scratching his head. He finished the last of the caf in his mug.

R-6, standing behind the trio, hummed as he offered Khedryn the pot of caf the droid carried. Khedryn held out his mug and R-6 filled it. Khedryn thanked him and the droid whistled with pleasure.

"Possible," Marr said. "That system is bathed in radiation. Why would they want to go there?"

"*Junker*'s deflectors will keep us clean of the rads," Khedryn said. "Their deflectors could do the same."

"Agreed," Marr said with a tilt of his head. "But there can't be anything in that system but rocks."

"Two planets," Jaden said, looking over the math and long-range observational data. "An asteroid belt, maybe."

"In a sterile system," Khedryn said. "Like I said, a misjump. Or a waystop. Could be they had a mechanical issue and needed to get out of hyperspace for a repair."

"I don't think so," Jaden said, running his hand over his goatee. "There has to be something there."

"One sure way to find out," Khedryn said, crossing his arms over his chest. "Who's got the chewstim? I'm out and we don't jump until I have some."

Marr felt around in his pockets, came up empty. Jaden had none. Khedryn's face fell.

R-6 beeped excitedly and extended a thin appendage from the cylinder of his body. In it, the droid held a piece of chewstim. Khedryn smiled, unwrapped it, and popped it in his mouth.

"Now we're ready. Well done, droid."

In moments, Marr had the jump coordinates and course in the navicomp.

Khedryn activated the hyperdrive and they leapt into the blue.

The immensity of the station, the disquieting lines of its form, humbled Soldier. He had doubted Seer, had thought they were on a course to nowhere, but in the end Seer had been right. Again.

He felt her looking at him, measuring his response, judging him.

"Do you believe now, Soldier?" she asked.

He hesitated, then nodded.

The huge station, built of some smooth, greenish substance that did not appear to be metal, floated above the planet in geosynchronous orbit. A shaft of some kind descended from one end of the ovoid station all the way down to the surface of the planet.

"Move the ship close to the station," Seer said. She had risen halfway out of her seat, as if buoyed up by her belief.

Soldier flew the supply ship in closer. Even the large ship seemed tiny compared with the station's bulk. Its green surface featured the irregular bumps and curves of something organic rather than made. As he watched, a portion of the station's hull lurched out.

Soldier exclaimed in alarm and started to pull up on the stick and engage the engines. Seer's calm voice stopped him.

"It's all right, Soldier."

He stared at her, at the station, and took his hands from the stick.

The bulge in the station expanded into a tube, a docking terminal that reached for one of the docking rings on the supply ship. As ship and station connected, more appendages extended outward from the station to grasp the underside of the ship and hold it in place.

Soldier stared at it all in wide-eyed wonder.

"You can power down," Seer said, her voice distant. "We're going aboard."

Soldier powered down the supply ship and he and Grace followed Seer to the airlock. When it opened, a loamy, organic smell filled the air. Seer breathed deeply.

Grace plugged her nose. "Stinky. What is this place?"

Seer seemed to be listening not only to Grace but to some other voice only she could hear. "This place is home."

Her skin roiled, rippled, but she seemed not to notice.

They walked into the docking tube. It felt warm beneath their feet, spongy, inviting. It opened onto a large, arched corridor that extended left and right. Forms lay all along the corridor, skeletons of beings that had died there long before. Hundreds of them.

"Those are bodies," Soldier said.

Seer seemed not to care. She walked into the corridor and turned right, as if she knew exactly where she was going. Soldier pulled Grace close to him.

"Don't look," he said to her, as they picked their way through the skeletal remains.

Rotted clothes, mere tatters of fabric, clung to the mummified bodies. Soldier noted the remains of humans and nonhuman sentients, their skin pulled taught against bones to show teeth and tendons and muscle. He could not tell how they died.

"Where is Mother?" Soldier asked. He spoke in a low tone, as if afraid of waking someone. The station appeared to be abandoned, a vast emptiness, a tomb for the mummified dead.

Seer held out her arms and turned a circle, dancing among the dead. "She's all around us, Soldier. But she wants us to see her face. Come. Come."

She hurried down the large corridor. Soldier and Grace struggled to keep up.

"We must go down," Seer said. "To the planet. There we'll commune with Mother in person."

Soldier thought of the shaft that connected the orbital station to the planet. The idea of descending it alarmed him.

"How will we get down there?" he asked. "Maybe we should go back to the ship and take it down."

Seer shook her head, the smile she'd been wearing since walking into the station seemingly plastered to her face. "Mother will show us the way."

Soldier did not argue the point. He was finished arguing with Seer. She had, after all, brought them to Mother.

He put a comforting hand on Grace and followed Seer.

Nyss stood before the Iteration's stasis chamber. The small window in the upright chamber's lid afforded him a view of the Iteration's face, Soldier's face, Jaden Korr's face even down to the goatee. He hated that face, the face that had taken his sister from him.

But he would need the Iteration if he was to succeed in the task Wyyrlok had set for him.

He punched the open sequence into the stasis chamber's control panel. He had replaced his lost weapon, and the cool hilt of a vibroblade filled each of his fists. The Iteration had been forced into stasis. He could awaken . . . displeased.

Nyss let the hole of his suppressive field stretch out to engulf the Iteration. He thought the field more powerful since the loss of Syll. The hole of his existence had grown darker, the depth of his solitude deeper. He seemed to live in his own pocket, isolated from everything and everyone else.

Strange, he thought, that his sister had been a limit to

his power over the years. He had long considered her an amplifier.

Still, he wondered if his newfound power would allow the field to function fully against the Iteration. It had worked only partially on Soldier. Would it function against Jaden Korr?

The chamber hissed as it vented frozen gas and slowly raised the body temperature of the Iteration. Nyss watched the bio-readouts as the Iteration climbed his way back to consciousness. His brain waves spiked and his gray eyes opened, fixed on Nyss.

Nyss hit the speaker button. "Can you hear me?"

The Iteration nodded. "Something is wrong, I cannot . . ."

". . . feel the Force?"

"Yes."

"That is my doing," Nyss said, pleased. He pulled the field back to himself so that it no longer affected the Iteration.

"Do you remember who you are?" he asked.

"I'm an iteration of Jaden Korr."

"You're *the* Iteration, at least for now. And I need your assistance."

The stasis chamber door clicked and slowly opened. The Iteration began detaching himself from the tubes that connected him to the chamber's life-support system.

"Assistance with what?"

"With murder," Nyss answered.

One dead, one taken—that was Nyss's mission.

"Whose?" the Iteration asked.

Nyss ignored the question. "We need to move quickly."

He spoke the coded phrase that turned the Iteration into an automaton.

The clone's eyes went blank and staring, his body slack. He started to fall, but Nyss caught him before his face slammed into the deck, then spoke the phrase that brought the Iteration back to full consciousness.

"What happened?" the Iteration asked, pulling free of Nyss.

A test, Nyss almost said, but instead he replied, "Probably just an aftereffect of the stasis. You'll be fine. Follow me."

In the cockpit, the Iteration eyed Syll's body, looked at Nyss with a question on his face, but said nothing.

"My sister," Nyss said. "Stay here."

He lifted Syll from the seat. She was cold and limp in his arms.

"I can help," the Iteration said.

"No! Never touch her! Never!"

Glaring at the Iteration, he left the cockpit and carried Syll back through the ship to the stasis chamber. He placed her within the chamber, closed and sealed the door, and set the temperature within to a bit above freezing.

She'd stay with him just as she was—present but not present, there but not there, dead but preserved.

Hadn't he always wondered if they were really dead? Now he knew.

When he returned to the cockpit, he found the Iteration in the copilot's seat, checking coordinates in the navicomp.

"Is that where we're going?" the Iteration asked, indicating the coordinates Nyss had pulled from the clone's navicomp.

"Yes," said Nyss. "And we're going right now."

Marr fine-tuned *Junker*'s deflector as the ship came out of hyperspace. The distant pulsar and its corona bathed the cockpit in color. From their distance and angle of observation, the system's asteroid belt looked as if a huge hand had sketched a line across the system, dividing top from bottom.

"Deflectors are blocking the radiation," Khedryn said, eyeing the scanner. "Nice work, Marr."

Two planets floated through the space of the system, separated in their orbits by millions of miles.

Jaden felt a faint ache in the back of his skull, a ping against his Force sensitivity.

"What is that?" he said slowly, staring out at the system.

"What is what?" Khedryn asked. He followed Jaden's gaze out the canopy. "I don't see anything, but then I'm the one with the funny eyes. What is it?"

Marr leaned back in his chair. "I feel it, too."

"The dark side," Jaden said.

"The clones?" Marr asked.

Jaden shook his head. "Something else."

Khedryn rolled his eyes. "You've got to be kidding me. Some other mysterious dark-side thing?"

"Where is it coming from?" Marr asked. He was already running a more comprehensive scan of the system.

"I don't see the clone's ship on the scanner," Marr said. "Both of the system's planets are in tidal lock, so there's an area of each I can't scan from here. We'll need to move in closer."

"Why would they put down on one of those planets?" Khedryn asked. "They're rocks."

Marr shook his head. "Could just be in geosynchronous orbit in a blind spot. We need to get closer to see."

Khedryn fired the ion engines and *Junker* started devouring the distance in ten-thousand-kilometer bites.

"Odd," Marr said. "That asteroid belt . . ."

Jaden went over to the Cerean's station, reviewed the data over his shoulder.

"What's that metal?" he asked.

"Scan can't identify the metal," Marr said to Jaden. "But there's a lot of it. It's . . . hmm."

"What?"

Marr refined the scan further, focused not on the asteroid belt but on a few of the metallic asteroids in particular. He looked up from his scanner, the wheels of his mind visibly turning behind his brown eyes. "Some of it shows structure."

"Structure?"

"Did the supply ship hit an asteroid and blow?" Khedryn asked. Jaden could hear the concern in his voice, concern for the clone child.

"No," Marr said. He stared out into the gulf. "But those asteroids aren't naturally occurring rock. They are a destroyed structure of some kind."

"That's impossible," Jaden said, but he could not dispute the readings on the scans. "It would have been massive. No one has that kind of technology."

"Not anymore," Marr said.

Jaden took Marr's point at once. "Are you saying what I think you're saying?"

"I'm only offering a possibility."

"It's that old?"

Marr raised his eyebrows, shrugged. "I can't say for sure, but it's old. It could be that old."

Khedryn leaned back in his seat. "Someone want to fill me in? What are we talking about here?"

Jaden leaned back in his chair. "Marr is suggesting that the asteroids, the destroyed structure, could be Celestial in origin."

"Or Rakatan," Marr said. "Or another civilization from that time of which we have no record."

Jaden knew little about the Celestials—no one did— and only a little more about the Rakatans. Vague references from his history classes as an apprentice in the Academy bubbled up from the depths of his memory.

The Celestials had been an ancient race of unknown appearance but possessed of incredible knowledge.

Their technology was said to be able to move entire star systems.

The Rakatans and their so-called Infinite Empire had arisen after the Celestials vanished from the cosmic stage. They used technology powered by the dark side of the Force, technology almost on a par with that of the Celestials, to conquer sector after sector. Their war with the Gree and the Kwa had torn the galaxy apart. Some aftereffect of their technology could have accounted for Jaden's faint perception of the dark side in the system.

But like the Celestials, the Rakatans had faded from the galaxy millennia ago, their entire civilization the victim of some catastrophe or war. Today, the few scant ruins of their civilization still scattered about the galaxy provided tantalizing fodder for archaeologists and historians, but nothing more.

"You think this is plausible?" Khedryn said, to no one in particular. He popped a bubble with his chewstim. "I thought half of that stuff was a myth. I mean, the *Rakatans*?"

"It's not a myth," Jaden said. "At least not all of it."

Khedryn looked from Jaden, to Marr, to Jaden. "Next thing you'll be telling me they turned the star into a pulsar during one of their wars to destroy whatever that asteroid belt had been."

Jaden said nothing, his mind turning.

"You aren't saying that!" Khedryn said. "Come on! I need some caf. Droid!"

Marr said, "From what little we know, that would almost certainly have been within their power."

Khedryn turned back to the stick, shaking his head. "This is crazy. Completely crazy."

R-6 filled Khedryn's mug and Jaden put a hand on R-6's dome. "Ar-Six, bundle what little we know into a packet and send it via subspace back to the Grand Master. I don't want this information to go unreported."

R-6 beeped agreement and plugged into one of *Junker*'s network sockets.

"That ought to make for good reading," Khedryn said, as *Junker* approached the nearest of the system's two planets. "Coming around to the dark side of the planet."

Junker chased the horizon line of the barren, blasted surface of the rocky planet. As they came around to the far side, Jaden and Marr leaned forward in their seats, R-6 beeped a question, and Khedryn gave their thoughts voice.

"What is *that*?"

Mother felt Seer and two others when they approached in their vessel. Instinct she could not control caused her cage to cradle their ship, to connect her body to it. She shivered with delight when she felt the tread of their feet upon her cage.

I am here, Seer, she projected, and reveled in the connection to Seer that close proximity allowed. *I wish to look upon you and for you to look upon me.*

She felt Seer's glee at her mental touch, an offering of happiness that Mother gladly received. She projected directions into Seer's limited consciousness.

This is the path, she sent, and Seer heard and heeded.

Mother tracked their progress as they approached. She could scarcely contain her excitement. She would be embodied, at last reified in something other than the prison of the station.

But then Mother felt a disturbance in nearby space, emotions contrary to her will. She removed her attention from Seer and her companions and reached out into the void around the prison.

There, she felt the presence of other minds, hostile of intent, and they were coming.

She could not stop them, not yet, but she could delay them.

She reached out with her power to the ancient remains that lingered with her in the station, filled them with sparks of her power. She'd burned most of them out long before, but what little remained could serve her purpose for a time.

She felt them as they rose, felt the shambling tread of their feet on her cage.

Hurry, Seer, she projected. *Hurry.*

chapter eleven

A CYLINDER AS LARGE AS A STAR CRUISER HUNG IN GEO-synchronous orbit over the rocky face of the dark side of the planet. The cylinder tapered to a point at one end, fattened to a rounded end on the other. In form, it reminded Jaden of a kind of shell. Its surface, the deep greenish black of ocean depths, was smooth, without any visible viewports or docking stations.

The narrow end of the cylinder faced away from the planet, toward the system's star, while the wide end faced the planet's surface. A thick tether of the same green material extended from the wide end, reached all the way to the planet's surface, and vanished in a dimple of the rocky crust.

"Looks like the damned planet has a tail," Khedryn said, and Jaden agreed.

The entire structure emitted dark-side power, a breeze of evil wafting into space, polluting the entire system. This power felt different, though, a flavor of the dark side that Jaden had never before encountered.

"I feel it, too," Marr said, blinking as if against a stiff wind. "It feels angry, but also . . . there is sadness, despair."

Marr had put his finger on it. Ordinarily the dark side felt to Jaden like manifest rage, its touch a storm of anger, but this felt more subdued, an anger mellowed by disappointment and suffering. He'd felt something akin to it from Soldier.

"Strange," Jaden said, thoughtful. He erected a mental shield to block it out.

"Neither the cylinder nor the tether are made of metal or any identifiable composite," Marr said, scanning both.

Jaden eyed the structure, unable to shake the image of the planet as an egg, the cylinder and tether the tail of a beast breaking its way out of the planetary shell, a world birthing a monster into a universe.

"It is organic," Marr said, sounding surprised.

Jaden's flesh goose-pimpled.

"Well, *maybe* it's organic," Marr said.

"What do you mean?" Jaden asked.

Marr pored over the data the scanners fed to his monitor. "It shows characteristics of being organic, but there are organized power lines within it. Even power nodes and relays. But they're like veins and arteries as much as conduits. And the whole thing is hollow, filled with openings that look like corridors and rooms. I think that tether is a lift or . . . some kind of pathway down to the surface."

"Stang," Khedryn said. "It's a ship of some kind?"

Marr shook his head. "More like a station, I'd say. But I don't see how it could have been built this way. Everything is sealed and there are no . . . seams or welds or anything like that."

"So what are you saying?" Khedryn asked.

Marr looked up from his monitor. "I think it was grown."

R-6 let out a long whoop of surprise.

"Grown!" Khedryn exclaimed. "How could it have been grown?"

"Like a tree," Marr said.

"That's a big kriffin' tree," Khedryn said.

"I think it's Rakatan," Jaden said, voicing his thoughts. From what little information the Jedi archives contained, he knew the Rakatans had used mechano-organic technology infused with the dark side, at least during some of their reign. It seemed to fit.

"There's no way to know for certain," Marr said.

Khedryn pointed out the canopy. "Look! There's the clones' ship."

The arrow of the ship hung in space beside the cylinder. A docking port extended from the cylinder, connecting to one of the ship's airlocks; tendrils stretched from the cylinder to cradle the underside of the ship. It reminded Jaden of a fly trapped in a web.

"I don't see another docking station," Khedryn said. "There's nowhere to put in."

"Keep *Junker* at a safe distance. Marr and I will take *Flotsam* in close," Jaden said, referring to *Junker*'s boat. "We'll find a way in."

Khedryn turned in his seat and fixed Jaden with his asymmetrical gaze. "I'm not staying behind."

"Khedryn," Jaden said, but Khedryn held up a hand to cut him off.

"You don't give orders on this ship, Jaden. Besides, you two left me behind back on Fhost and look where that got us."

The rebuke stung Jaden, and it must have showed.

"I didn't mean it that way," Khedryn said.

"It's all right," Jaden said. "But listen. The clones are powerful Force users and this station was built using the power of the dark side. I don't want you to take this wrong, but I don't think this is a situation where you can be of much help to us."

At Khedryn's hurt expression, he added, "This time *I* didn't mean it that way."

"Of course you did," Khedryn said. "And you might be right. But Marr ain't exactly a Jedi Master." He turned in his seat and reached out a hand to Marr. "No offense."

Marr shrugged it off. "None taken. You're right. I'm . . . new."

Jaden put a hand on Khedryn's shoulder. "But Marr's better equipped to deal with what we're going to face there, Khedryn. The clones came here looking for something."

"Mother," Khedryn said.

"Right. And . . . I think it's best if you stay aboard, at least for now."

Khedryn shook Jaden's hand loose. "You're trying to manage me. I don't like it. You can't shield me from danger, Jedi. I've been living on the edge my whole life."

Jaden smiled, trying to use levity to diffuse the situation. "Seen a lot of organic space stations made by the Rakatans with dark-side technology, have you?"

Khedryn smiled sheepishly at that. "Point taken."

"Look, you know I respect you and your capabilities. But this is something Marr and I should do alone. Besides, like before—well, I mean, like I intended before—we need a pilot to remain on *Junker* in case we need a rapid evacuation. We know the clones are aboard, but that's all we know. We might need to leave in a hurry."

"The droid can fly her," Khedryn said.

"A *real* pilot," Jaden said, and R-6 chirped indignantly. "No offense, Ar-Six."

"Now he's insulting you, too, droid," Khedryn said. "Well, it's been a real good few minutes in this cockpit, hasn't it." He turned to Marr. "You agree with this?"

Marr kept his face expressionless. "I do."

Khedryn blew a heavy sigh. "Stang, but things are changing around here. Looks like it's you and me then, droid."

R-6 hummed sympathetically.

"All right," Jaden said. "Let's go, Marr."

As they left the cockpit, he said to Marr, "He'll be all right."

"He will. You know, I'm in over my head here, too, Master."

Jaden grinned. "That makes three of us, then. But let's see if we can't swim awhile anyway."

They took position in *Flotsam*'s cockpit, ran a quick diagnostic, and got on the comm with Khedryn. The ship's boat detached from *Junker* and floated free in space. Jaden engaged the engines and the small craft darted toward the enormous station.

"I'm curious as to what that tether connects to below the surface," Marr said.

"As am I," Jaden answered, imagining a hollow planet filled with Rakatan technology.

"I'll swing *Junker* into the fringe of the asteroid belt," Khedryn said. "Just to stay out of sight."

Jaden heard R-6 beep and whistle indignantly.

"Right. *The droid* and I will take *Junker* into the belt."

"Good thought," Jaden said. The Umbaran or his allies could still find them somehow, though that seemed unlikely. Still, there was no reason to leave *Junker* exposed in open space.

Flotsam closed the distance to the station.

"I think we can assume the clones are not in their ship," Marr said.

"Agreed. This is what they were looking for. They're inside somewhere."

"There has to be another docking port," Marr said, studying the readouts of the station. "The station is too large for just the one."

"Also agreed. Let's get closer."

Beside them, *Junker*'s engines flared and carried the freighter toward the black line of the asteroid belt. Jaden took *Flotsam* in close.

The nearness of the station caused the wash of dark-side energy to intensify. Jaden walled it off and kept it at bay. He eyed Marr. "Are you all right?"

Marr nodded. "I am. It feels unfocused."

Jaden was impressed. Marr's sensitivity was acute. "It does."

Had the source of the power been a sentient being, Jaden would have assumed its attention to be elsewhere. As it was, he figured the technology used to build the station just emitted low-intensity dark-side energy in all directions.

"We're nearing the belt," Khedryn said. "Listen, should I say 'Good luck' or 'May the Force be with you'? I'm confused now, what with all the changes. . . ."

Jaden and Marr both laughed.

" 'Good luck' will do," Jaden said.

"Good luck, then," Khedryn said, then more seriously, "And may the Force be with you both."

"And with you," Marr answered.

"We'll be listening on this frequency," Khedryn said.

Flotsam closed on the enormous Rakatan cylinder. Jaden piloted the boat in close, studying the smooth, glistening surface of the cylinder through the cockpit's canopy. As they flew over it, the surface rippled and bulged, not unlike the skin of the sick clones.

"What was that?" Jaden asked.

Marr studied his monitors.

Jaden braced, imagined the cylinder forming a giant appendage and swatting the boat into space. But it didn't, and the bulge in the cylinder rode along its surface as might a wave, matching vectors with *Flotsam*. Thin lines of white light glowed within it.

Realization struck. It must have hit Marr similarly.

"Slow down, Master," Marr said, but Jaden was already disengaging the engines and stopping their forward momentum with the thrusters. The bulge in the cylinder's surface stopped when *Flotsam* stopped. It grew larger, and an appendage extended outward from the station toward the ship.

"There's our docking port," said Jaden.

"Amazing technology," Marr said.

Jaden maneuvered *Flotsam* with thrusters until its docking ring faced the station. He moved the boat closer and the bulge expanded, reached across the short distance, formed itself into a tube, and connected to *Flotsam*'s docking ring. More bulges formed in the cylindrical station, stretched into tendrils, and extended under *Flotsam*, holding it in place. The boat settled softly into the station's grasp.

Jaden and Marr shared a look, unstrapped themselves, checked their gear, and headed back to the docking ring. The hatch twisted open.

A blast of warm, humid air from the station struck them. It carried the faint, sickly-sweet smell of organic decay.

Hair-thin filaments of light lined the tube, like veins. They flashed at intervals. Marr studied them, and Jaden imagined him measuring the frequency of the flashes, trying to find meaning in the pattern.

"The filaments are clearly a means of transmitting power, and probably information," the Cerean mused.

They stepped into the tube. The surface gave somewhat under Jaden's boots, like soft rubber. Marr put a hand on the wall, and a spiderweb of filaments glowed in the wall at the point where his hand touched it.

"It's warm and sensitive to touch," he said. He removed his hand and the glow from the filaments ended. "Those filaments are everywhere, integrated into the structure. It's possible the entire structure is nothing but the filaments, so fine and closely knit that the walls appear to be a coherent solid."

Jaden felt the dark-side energies growing more focused. He held his lightsaber hilt in his hand. "The Order's scientists can study this later, Marr. Right now, let's find the clones."

"Right, Master."

They moved through the docking tube and into the station proper. A vast, high-ceilinged corridor extended to their left and right. The glowing filaments meshed into small clusters above them, lighting the corridor in a dim, greenish glow.

Jaden let the Force fill him, closed his eyes, and reached out with his consciousness for the clones. He did not perceive them, felt only the inchoate, dispersed dark-side power contained in the station. The amount of the power was striking, but it was diffuse, like soft rainfall, like air, something all around them but only barely noticeable. Were it concentrated, it would have been a tsunami, a cyclone.

"Come on," he said, and started in the direction of the tether. Perhaps the clones had gone down to the planet.

Before they'd moved thirty meters, cysts formed in the walls, hundreds of them, before and behind them, on both sides of the corridors.

"What are those?" Marr asked.

Thin slits formed in the cysts, split open, and expelled the mucus-covered, mummified remains of hundreds of sentient beings. They stood unevenly on bony legs as their empty eye sockets fixed on Jaden and Marr.

"Back to back," Jaden said.

The clawed hands of the dead extended toward them and, as one, the feet of hundreds of the ancient dead lurched and plodded toward them.

Nyss and the Iteration said nothing as the scout flyer emerged from hyperspace. Immediately Nyss engaged the ship's baffles. Most scanners would pass directly over the ship without noting it. A soft alarm indicated a radiation danger, so Nyss adjusted the deflector to filter out the harmful rays.

"I can feel the dark side of the Force," the Iteration said. "It's faint, but present."

Nyss grunted acknowledgment. He cared little for what the Iteration felt.

"You don't speak much," the Iteration said.

Nyss did not look at the Iteration when he replied. "You are not someone to whom I wish to speak. In a standard hour you'll be someone else." He looked over at the clone and grinned harshly. "We'll speak then."

The Iteration shifted in his seat and said nothing, but Nyss could sense his discomfort. He supposed the Iteration lived in his own kind of hole. He'd been "alive" for mere hours and was, in effect, to let himself die soon. Had he not been appropriately programmed by the One Sith's scientists, Nyss might have worried about him balking.

He scanned the system and picked up a ship, the freighter flown by the Jedi and the spacers. It hung on the fringe of the system's asteroid belt.

Nyss engaged the ion engines and sped toward it. As they neared, the Iteration said, "The Jedi is not aboard that ship. If he was, I would sense him."

"Then we're free to blow it from space," Nyss said.

He approached from an angle above the freighter and brought his weapons online.

An explosion caused *Junker* to lurch forward. R-6 whooped in alarm, and Khedryn grabbed at the stick as he nearly slammed his head into the instrument panel.

"What the hell was that?" he shouted.

The force of the explosion caused the ship to hurtle toward a nearby asteroid. The oblong ball of rock filled his field of vision, the details of its cratered surface looming larger and larger in his sight. Khedryn cursed and engaged the reverse thrusters.

Another explosion rocked the ship, and the red line of a laser cut the space beside them, slammed into an asteroid, and blew it to pieces. Shards of rock rained against *Junker*'s hull, pelting it with metal and stone. Khedryn had probably saved the ship through pure luck, reversing the thrusters at just the right moment.

"Someone is shooting at us!" he said, and R-6 whooped again. He directed deflector power to the rear and fired up the engines as an alarm began to blare in the cockpit. His instruments showed him a fire in the engine room.

"Get that fire out, droid," he said to R-6.

He engaged the engines as another shot skinned *Junker* along the top. A boom sounded and for a fleeting, terrifying moment the entire instrument panel lost power, but backup brought it online fast. Khedryn shoved the stick forward and accelerated the ship deeper into the asteroid belt.

He checked the scanner as he flew, trying to get the signature of their attacker. He had it in a moment—the scout ship.

"The Umbaran," he said.

The Umbaran had followed them somehow and his ship, like the creature himself, must have had some kind of cloaking or baffling technology. Khedryn had not even noticed him coming out of hyperspace. *Junker* had no weapons and Khedryn had no crew. He had to get out of there.

Hunching in his seat, he weaved his way through the asteroid field. His caf cup clattered to the deck and spilled its contents. He cursed and pulled the stick about wildly—spinning, speeding up, slowing down, diving, climbing. He remembered Jaden doing something similar, at full speed, and never touching an asteroid. But

Khedryn did not have the Force to help him. He had only his instincts and his training. Sweat soaked him already.

R-6's beeps and hoots of distress made for a distracting sound track to the breakneck maneuvering. More red lines cut space beside them, and another asteroid exploded into bits. The blast wave sent *Junker* sidelong into another asteroid, and the impact jarred Khedryn's teeth. The metal of the hull shrieked. Khedryn cursed again and again.

"I have a damned droid aboard but no weapons installed. Got that exactly backward, didn't I? If we live through this, I'm fixing that at our next port of call."

R-6 beeped agreement. Khedryn saw that the droid had remotely extinguished the fire in the engine room.

Another impact shook the freighter, another. Khedryn could not tell if the lasers were hitting him or if he was bumping into asteroids.

To R-6, he said, "Raise Jaden and Marr. Tell them the Umbaran is in the system."

R-6 let loose with a frantic barrage of droidspeak that Khedryn did not understand, though he could tell the droid was either frustrated or alarmed. He checked the instrument panel and immediately saw why. The Umbaran's attack had knocked out their transceiver. They could not communicate with Jaden and Marr. *Junker* was mute. And without the ship's transceiver to amplify the transmission, their personal comlinks would not work except at very close range.

More laser blasts cut through space, caused *Junker* to veer, and sent them pelting toward a large asteroid. R-6 gave a long, high-pitched, distressed whoop while Khedryn pulled back on the stick and got *Junker*'s stern up. The belly of the ship skimmed the top of the asteroid, probably losing a layer of hull. Khedryn cursed again and, with nothing else for it, accelerated *Junker* to full.

* * *

Nyss focused on the glow of the freighter's engines before him, following the YT's movements as the two ships danced through the asteroid field. The YT's pilot was good and the freighter maneuvered more easily without its ship's boat. Nyss's firing computer could not get a lock. The lasers had grazed the ship a couple times, had had a couple of near misses, but the confines of the asteroid belt made it difficult to establish a firing line.

"Scan to find the ship's boat," Nyss said to the Iteration, and the clone bent over the scanner console.

The YT dove and Nyss pushed the stick forward to follow. A huge asteroid floated before him and he pulled up rapidly, dragging the belly of the scout flyer across its surface and causing him to veer to starboard. He righted the ship, wheeled back to port, and tried to get a fix on the YT. He saw its engines below him, deeper in the asteroid field, and started to head down.

"Wait," the Iteration said. "I found it. And something else."

The Iteration's tone caused Nyss to pull up and slow the ship. At that speed, he maneuvered easily through the slow-moving asteroids of the field, but the freighter vanished from sight, lost amid the floating rocks.

"There, above the nearest planet," the Iteration said.

"I don't see it," Nyss said, looking out the cockpit.

"Get above the belt."

Nyss saw the scan readout in his HUD, which indicated a huge structure in geosynchronous orbit above the rocky surface of a desolate planet. He pulled the flyer above the plane of the asteroid belt and caused the image in the transparisteel canopy to magnify.

There, he saw it clearly—an enormous, greenish lozenge floating above the planet, connected to the surface by a miles-long shaft. He did not need further scans to know that the station was a mechano-organic construct. He recognized the telltale signs of Rakatan technology, the same technology reflected in the mindspears he carried.

"What is that?" the Iteration asked.

"A Rakatan station," Nyss said.

The Iteration did not respond. Perhaps his memory implants did not include anything about the Rakatan Infinite Empire.

Nyss saw two ships docked to the station: the medical supply ship hijacked by the clones, and the small ship's boat that had been attached to the YT freighter.

Jaden Korr and the Prime were both aboard the station, it seemed.

He gave one last look back for the YT, saw nothing, fired the engines to full, and shot across space toward the station.

Jaden ignited his yellow blade and Marr activated his purple one. Among the walking dead Jaden noted humans, Rodians, Kaleesh, and a dozen other species, many of which he did not recognize. Thin lines glowed under their flesh, the same glowing filaments that lined the walls. Somehow they were connected to the station, or the station was connected to them.

"Let the Force flow through you," Jaden said to Marr.

The dead picked up speed, their shambling stride giving way to a faster walk. Their mouths were open but no sound emerged. They were an army of clawed hands and teeth.

Jaden fell into the Force as they approached. He unleashed a blast of power that struck the leading corpses and they exploded in a shower of bone and dried flesh. Marr did the same, managing to knock several to the ground.

Again Jaden unleased a blast, again destroying corpses by the dozens. And then the dead were upon them:

empty eyes, clawed fingers, teeth, and the swirl of dark-side energy that animated them.

Jaden whirled among them, his yellow blade a scythe harvesting the dead. He kept one eye on Marr as he slew, watching his apprentice slash with his blade, fire his blaster, slash, stab, and fire. Jaden decapitated a corpse and loosed a blast of energy that exploded another five. His weapon rose and fell, rose and fell. He lost count of how many he felled, how many Marr felled, how long they'd been fighting. The animated corpses were slow, mindless, more annoyance than threat.

After a time, he and Marr stood alone in the corridor amid the dried remains of hundreds of dead. One of the bodies stirred at Jaden's foot. He crushed its skull under his boot and deactivated his blade.

"Are you all right?" he asked Marr.

Marr deactivated his blade but did not holster his blaster. "Fine, Master."

"That was a delaying tactic," Jaden said. "The clones passed unmolested."

"But who is trying to delay us?" Marr asked.

"Let's go find out," Jaden said, and they sprinted down the corridor.

Sweat made Khedryn's hands slick on the controls. He had no choice but to keep flying at speed, to risk *Junker* getting pulverized against an asteroid to avoid its destruction by the Umbaran's lasers. Spinning *Junker* ninety degrees, he shot through a narrow gap between two asteroids about to collide. He slammed the stick down, cutting under a third large asteroid, then pulled it up and nearly scraped the surface of another. If he'd been standing on *Junker*'s exterior, he could have reached out and touched one of the huge rocks.

R-6 beeped a question, and it took a moment for Khedryn to realize its import.

Where was the laser fire? He checked the scanner, but the asteroids clouded the readings so severely that it was hard to know if the Umbaran was still in pursuit. He slowed a bit, wheeled around a large asteroid, dived below a smaller one.

No fire.

"Did we lose him?" he asked aloud.

R-6 beeped uncertainly.

Khedryn dived, spinning, until *Junker* broke free of the asteroid belt into open space. He pulled up on the stick, ready to dart back into the cover of the field should his scanners pick up the Umbaran's ship.

They didn't.

He patted *Junker*'s instrument panel and allowed himself a relieved breath. He hoped the Umbaran had blown himself up in the asteroid belt, but a scan of the area showed otherwise.

The scout ship was headed fast toward the Rakatan station on the dark side of the planet.

Khedryn cursed—he seemed to do more of that without Marr around—and ordered R-6 to get the transceiver operational as soon as possible. He had to warn Jaden and Marr.

"I'm going aboard the station," he said to R-6. "They're going to need help."

The droid beeped with concern.

Nyss did not appreciate the size of the Rakatan station until they closed with it. It was larger than a star cruiser. It dwarfed the scout ship, and that was only the orbital portion of the station. He maneuvered along the side of the station, right behind the medical supply ship, and, as he had anticipated, a docking appendage extended outward and connected ship to station. More appendages extended underneath the ship, cradling it, holding it steady.

"What is this place?" the Iteration asked.

"This is where you'll be reborn," Nyss answered, standing. He gathered his gear: knives, crossbow, quarrels, the mindspears. "Use the Force. Tell me if you sense the Jedi."

The Iteration closed his gray eyes and concentrated for a moment. He opened them and said, "I don't, but he could be too far away."

"Follow me," Nyss said.

He opened the ship and entered the dark, moist tunnel of the docking tube. The moment he stepped on the warm, slightly giving surface of the station, filaments in the walls and floor began to glow.

"This way," he said, and headed in the direction of the shaft that connected the orbital station to the larger station built into the planet's crust. "You're going to take me to the Prime."

The Iteration fell in behind him, his lightsaber hilt in his hand.

Jaden imagined that the clones had gone down the tether that connected the station to the planet. Leaving a heap of ancient corpses in their wake, he and Marr headed in that direction. Jaden kept a wary eye open for any more animated remains emerging from side rooms.

There were no doors as such, just thin seams in the wall that parted at their approach. Finned squares in the ceiling might have been vents, or speakers, or both.

"I think this must have been a prison, or maybe a lab," Marr said. "That's the only thing that makes sense. It also accounts for all the bodies."

They moved quickly and quietly through corridors and chambers of no discernible purpose. Whatever equipment had once been in the rooms had been removed long before. Some could have been cells, as Marr speculated, though they might just as easily have been a barracks for ancient soldiers.

Thin lines of light blinked in the walls from time to time, and the touch of their boots on the floor elicited little sunbursts of light around the contact. Jaden had the odd sensation that the station was noting their passage. Static squawked from his comlink, as if the connection to Junker had just been severed. He pinched it to activate it.

"Khedryn, do you copy? Khedryn?"

More static.

Marr tried his comlink and had the same result.

"Could be the walls," he offered.

"Could be," Jaden said, and they kept going.

Dark, rectangular touchpad panels were attached to the wall at intervals. Jaden put a finger on one, and colored patterns of light—but no text—moved across the screen. He did not touch anything more on the pad and it powered down. Here and there they noted small, irregularly shaped apertures in the walls. Hair-thin filaments hung from the edges.

"The technology is unlike anything I've seen," Marr said, reaching out a hand to one of the filaments.

Jaden grabbed his wrist to stop him. The filaments came to life, writhing in response to the proximity of Marr's hand. The hole twisted partially closed with a wet, mushy sound.

"I think these are some kind of power sockets," Marr said. "Or a communication port. The filaments are probably the link. They're laced all through the walls."

"Let's keep moving," Jaden said.

They continued to pick their way through the ancient station until they reached the large, domed, circular chamber that connected to the tether. Seeing it, Marr blew out a whistle.

Holes about a meter in diameter dotted the floor at intervals. Jaden and Marr approached them, looked down, and saw that the holes opened onto shafts that fell away into darkness, presumably descending miles to the surface of the planet below. Damp air redolent with organic decay wafted up the shafts. More of the ancient dead, maybe. An upright touch panel stood beside each hole.

Marr touched one of the control pads and it ignited with light. A beam from the panel shot out at him, flashing over his body.

Jaden moved to shove the Cerean out of the beam, but Marr held up his hands.

"It's all right," he said, as the beam bounced across him.

He nodded at the control panel, where a silhouette of his body had appeared on the screen. Orderly flashes of color blinked in the margins of the screen, communicating information Jaden could not understand. When the light show stopped, the shaft at Marr's feet narrowed a bit, as if sizing itself to fit to his body, and lines of glowing filament lit in its walls, illuminating its downward length for kilometers.

Marr glanced at Jaden, eyebrows raised. "I thought the tether was a lift system of some kind. It appears I was right."

Jaden eyed the shaft. "Do we just slide in?"

"It looks that way."

The thought of taking a ride down a kilometers-long mechano-organic shaft into an unknown environment held little appeal for Jaden. But there was nothing else for it, so he touched his hand to the nearest control panel and it scanned his body as the other had done with Marr. The scan felt like a soft breeze on his skin, and when it was done, the shaft at his feet twisted closed a bit to accommodate his form. Lines of glowing filament lit it up. They looked like they went on forever. Jaden assumed the shafts all had to let out at the same place, though he could not be sure.

"If we end up separated, you stay put and I'll find you," he said. "Ready?"

Marr nodded, and they each sat at the edge of their respective hole and began to lower themselves into the shaft. The moment Jaden's legs entered the shaft, the walls bulged out from the sides, took his legs in a warm, gentle grip, and started to pull him in, a sensation that felt disquietingly like being swallowed. He did not resist it.

"Marr," he called, as the shaft pulled him the rest of the way in. "Are you all right?"

His last word stretched out into a shout of surprise as the bulges holding him in the shaft rippled down its length, taking him with it, descending so fast he might as well have been falling. He gritted his teeth and tried to keep his stomach from rushing up his throat. He was engulfed in the warmth of the walls, the glow of the lines of light.

He fell a long while before the descent began to slow, then finally, to stop. The shaft released its grip on him when he felt firm floor under his boots.

The shaft had deposited him in a large circular chamber, a mirror of the one above, but with tubes descending from the ceiling rather than holes opening in the floor. Control panels for each of the tubes stood at intervals around the room.

The stink of decay, much stronger now, filled the air. His sensation of the dark side felt more concentrated, too. The soft rainfall of power had become a downpour. Jaden tried to filter it out while he nested himself in the Force and reached out with his mind for the clones.

The intense, uncomfortable feedback of contact with a dark-side user pulled at his consciousness. They were not far.

Beside him, the nearest tube bulged like a serpent's belly and disgorged Marr. The Cerean stood for a moment with his hands on his hips, staring back up the way he'd come.

"Remarkable," he said, then turned to face Jaden, his head cocked in a question. "Do you feel that? The dark side is . . ."

". . . stronger," Jaden finished for him.

Marr nodded. "If the station is Rakatan, and is powered in part with dark-side energy, we could be sensing the power center of the station."

"We'll soon know," Jaden said, and led Marr in the direction he'd felt the clones. A vertical seam in the wall slipped wetly open to reveal a corridor beyond. Filaments glowed like veins in the walls.

They walked through, the dark side growing stronger with each step.

Having watched Jaden and Marr in *Flotsam,* Khedryn knew the Rakatan station would dock with *Junker* when he got close. He flew the ship in, maneuvered it near and watched in wonder as the station birthed a docking tube and reached out for *Junker.* Once the ship was settled, Khedryn unstrapped himself from his seat and patted R-6 on the dome.

"Keep the engines hot, little man. And keep working on that transceiver."

R-6 whistled an affirmative.

Khedryn took a blaster from the cockpit weapons locker and stuffed it into his hip holster. He started to head off, thought better of it, and took a second blaster from the locker and put it in a thigh holster.

"Can't have too many," he said to R-6. "Lock the ship down when I'm clear. And contact me immediately when you have the transceiver up."

Again R-6 whistled an affirmative.

Khedryn hurried to the airlock and opened it. The warm, organic stink of the Rakatan station wafted into the ship, and . . . something else, something that caused his hair to stand on end.

"Maybe I'm getting sensitive to the dark side," he muttered, and stepped off *Junker*.

He barely noticed the filaments that formed a dense, glowing matrix in the walls and floor. Explosions of light ignited under his feet as he ran over the smooth, warm floor. He tried not to think too hard about the technology. The docking tube opened onto a large corridor. He headed right, toward the tether, remembering that Marr had thought it might be a lift of some kind. He tried to raise Jaden and Marr on his comlink as he went, but he received only a blast of static in response. Perhaps the energy of the station further restricted the already limited range in which the comlinks would operate without *Junker*'s transceiver.

He stopped when he came to a pile of bodies—sentients of all kinds, crushed, dismembered. There was no blood at all, just the remains of ancient, dried-out corpses. A cursory look told him that Jaden and Marr were not among the dead. Probably the bodies had been there for centuries.

"Jaden!" he shouted, and went from a walk, to a jog, to a run. It was a risk to shout—the Umbaran could be near and Khedryn would never spot the stealthy bastard. But he did not care. He had to warn them. "Marr!"

The filaments in the walls responded to his shouts, flaring red and green in answer to his voice. He clutched a blaster in each hand, eyeing every shadow and dark corner suspiciously.

Ahead, he thought a wall blocked his path, but as he

approached, a vertical seam in the wall split wetly and opened into another chamber.

"Stang," he said, and hurried through.

The door squeezed closed behind him. He'd never felt more isolated in his life.

chapter twelve

THE MOMENT SOLDIER OPENED THE DOOR, A BLAST OF dark-side energy blew outward in a gust, as if it had been pent up for centuries. Soldier tucked Grace behind him and leaned into it as he might a strong wind.

"We're here," Seer said, quiet awe in her tone.

A large oval chamber stretched out before them, its high ceiling lost in the darkness. Filaments glowed in the walls and floor: white, green, red, and yellow, the lines of color packed so densely that the entire surface seemed aflame. The lines all converged on a cylindrical mound that sat in the center of the chamber. It stood twice as tall as Soldier and expanded and shrank at regular intervals, like a lung. Glowing filaments, these as thick as ropes, coiled around it and sank into the floor. Soldier felt the intelligence in it, and the reality of the situation hit him all at once.

Mother was not a person or thing in the station. Mother *was* the station. And they were staring at her heart.

"Do you feel her?" Seer said, grinning wildly. "Do you feel her, Soldier?"

Seer's flesh, her sick, afflicted flesh, pulsed in answer to the heaves of the cylinder. So, too, did Grace's. Soldier put a protective hand on the girl. He put his other hand on his lightsaber.

Soldier did not feel Mother, but Seer's ecstatic rush of emotion pushed against his mind, threatening to catch him up in it. He resisted, as much out of habit as will.

Still, he realized that they had made it. After all they had endured, they had made it. Seer had been right. Mother would heal Seer and Grace, would give Soldier purpose. His eyes welled.

"We made it," he said to Seer.

She looked over at him, smiling, her eyes, too, filled with tears of joy. "We did."

"Can she . . . heal us?" he asked.

She touched his cheek, then turned and moved into the chamber. Soldier held his ground with Grace, feeling unworthy to enter.

"What is it, Soldier?" Grace asked.

"It's Mother," Soldier answered.

In response to Seer's approach, the filaments in the walls glowed in organized curtains of red, white, green, and yellow, cascading down the walls and across the floor.

Soldier found them hypnotic.

Grace gasped in wonder. "So pretty."

Soldier felt Grace's awe, her wonder, and was pleased he had been able to bring her to Mother. If nothing else, he had done *that,* and it was of worth.

With each step Seer took, a splash of color formed under feet, so that she walked to Mother on circles of light. The ropelike filaments around the cylinder squirmed like serpents as Seer drew near.

Seer fell to her knees before Mother's heart and bowed her head.

"We heard your call and traveled far to reach you, Mother."

The filaments in the walls and floor answered with starbursts of red, green, and yellow. Seer looked around, exaltation in her eyes.

"It's beautiful, Soldier! Beautiful!"

The flesh of her face formed lumps, appeared to bubble, made her expression a grotesque distortion of a smile.

Grace pulled back from Soldier. "I don't like this, Soldier," she said.

"It's all right," he said. He could feel her flesh moving under his touch.

Power gathered in the chamber. The lights in the walls flared and flashed wildly.

"Heal them, Mother," Soldier said. "Please."

The floor around Seer formed lines and cleaved open. She knelt on a circle of the floor, an island. Thin filaments emerged from the opening that surrounded her. They waved in the air, glowing red and green. Seer looked at them, smiling, rapturous.

Soldier, too, was smiling. The filaments would heal Seer, then Grace.

The filaments extended upward until they towered over Seer, until she was surrounded by them.

"I feel it, Soldier," she said. "It's happening!"

All at once the filaments descended toward Seer, covering her in a gentle wave. Lights flashed along their length. Seer laughed, held up her arms. The filaments twisted around her arms, her torso, her legs. Her laughter suddenly took on a questioning tone.

The filaments flared red, twisted tightly around her, snaked up her neck, and covered her face. Her laughter died.

"Mother!" she said. "Mother!"

In moments, Seer was cocooned in the filaments, her form squirming desperately in their grasp. The filaments turned from red to green to yellow, the light pulsing. Seer's body spasmed, and Soldier realized that the filaments were pumping something into her. Her body swelled and roiled until it was barely recognizable as human. Pustules formed on her skin, burst, bleeding sparks.

"What is happening?" Grace cried.

Soldier had no idea, but it clearly was not what Seer had expected. He activated his lightsaber and advanced toward her. The walls and floor flared angry red, bolts of energy shot from all directions, and a blast of power lifted Soldier from his feet and blew him from the room. He slammed into the wall of the corridor outside, his breath knocked from him in a whoosh. Grace ran to his side, her eyes filled with fear.

"Soldier!" Seer screamed, pawing at the filaments that covered her mouth . . . that went into her mouth and down her throat. "Soldier!"

More filaments squirmed out of the floor and covered her, wrapped her entirely, except for one eye and her open, screaming mouth. They glowed red, green, yellow, the current of light pulsing as more and more energy poured into her form. They pulled her down into the hole in the floor, and Grace screamed.

Halfway under, Seer reached a hand in Soldier's direction, terror in her visible eye. Her lips, engorged with power, fumbled over the words, but Soldier recognized them nevertheless.

"Help me! Help!"

He used the Force to pull his lightsaber hilt to his hand and ignited it. Fear for Seer, anger at Mother's betrayal—both gave him power. The dark side surged in him.

As he stood, the door to Mother's chamber closed like a curtain, with not even a seam visible. He could hear Seer's muffled, panicked screams coming from within. He could cut his way through. He took his blade in a two-handed grip.

"Soldier," Grace said, her tone surprisingly calm.

Her voice cut through his anger, his fear, cut through all the clutter in his mind. He looked at her, his breath coming hard. Her flesh sagged in places, bulged in others. He could barely recognize her. Only her eyes remained unaffected, and they pleaded with him for help.

"I want to go home," she said.

"We don't have a home," he spat, and hated himself for the despair he heard in his voice. He had spent himself, all his hopes, on Seer's dream. And Seer had been wrong, her faith a lie, his belief in her a fool's errand.

"Please, Soldier," Grace said.

Before he could answer, a sound carried from deep in the station, a visceral scream that sent shock waves throughout the floors, walls, and ceiling. The filaments flared so bright he had to cover his eyes. Searing energy seeped from the walls, leaving blackened gashes behind. Touch panels exploded out from the wall and hung loose on dimly glowing filaments that looked like entrails. Smoke leaked into the air. An alarm began to sound and everything went dark.

"Soldier, I'm scared," Grace said.

Soldier ignited his lightsaber and used its red light to find her. She huddled against one of the walls, her eyes wide, fearful. He knelt, hugged her, decided that he still had at least one purpose. He lifted her to her feet.

"Stay close to me," he said. "I'm going to take you home."

A door parted before Khedryn like a curtain of flesh, to reveal a large circular chamber beyond. Holes dotted the floor. Control panels of a kind he'd never seen before stood beside each of the holes. He approached them warily, holstering one blaster and trading it for a glow-rod. Shining the beam down one of the holes, he saw that its smooth sides descended as far as he could see, presumably to the planet's surface. His stomach fluttered at the thought of sliding down one of those tubes for several kilometers. But it appeared he'd have to do exactly that if he was to locate Jaden and Marr or the Umbaran.

"Stang," he said.

He moved to one of the control panels, having no idea how to operate it. He touched the featureless plastic rectangle and it lit up. Lines of color spread across its surface, presumably communicating some kind of information, though he had no idea what.

A beam of white light shot from the panel and played over his body, raising the hairs on his arms. He flinched, but it did no harm and a silhouette of his body showed up on the screen. The hole at his feet shrank, the sound moist, grotesque, and then was still, a mouth waiting to devour him.

Desperate for something that would allow him to avoid stepping into the shaft, he clicked his comlink, clicked it again, again. Nothing.

"Damned droid," he said.

He got down on the floor and lowered himself into the shaft. Its walls closed in on his legs, seized him, started pulling him in. He cursed as the shaft pulled him in farther. Claustrophobia threatened as the shaft closed on his stomach, his chest, his neck, his face.

He swore, the sound muffled, as he felt himself pelting down the shaft, cradled in the station's grip. He fell for time indeterminable, unable to see anything but the lines of light glowing deep in the walls of the station's malleable walls.

Abruptly the lines flared red, the flash so bright it left him seeing spots. He heard a deep vibration that sounded from somewhere far off, the reverberations causing the shaft to shake.

And then the lights went out all around him. His downward motion stopped.

He was stuck somewhere in the shaft, in darkness, gripped by the walls.

The power had gone out.

Panic set his heart to racing, stole his breath, turned his mouth dry. He tried to fight it, holding on to hope that a backup system would activate and allow him to finish his descent, but long seconds turned to a minute and still he was stuck. He could hear his heart pounding in his ears, his breath loud and hot and damp on the walls. He tried to reach for his comlink, managed to elbow out enough space and give it a squeeze.

"Ar-Six?" He disliked the fear he heard in his voice, but he could not dispel it. "Ar-Six."

Nothing, of course.

He was stuck in the belly of an ancient station. No one knew where he was. And even if they did, how could they get him out?

He let fly with a string of expletives, and the outburst helped steady him. He had managed to elbow out some room to click his comlink. Maybe he could maneuver himself out of the station's grip and slide the rest of the way down.

But what if he was still a kilometer up? He had no way to know how far he had descended. He'd been going fast, but . . .

"To hell with it," he said, and started to squirm. He could not sit idle.

Grunting and straining, he pressed against the walls with his body and they began to loosen. His legs came free, dangling loosely beneath him, and for a moment he almost lost his nerve. But he'd be damned if he'd die in the gullet of some ancient space station. He worked until he got the opening under him wide enough to slip his shoulders through. Awkwardly, he reached for his glowrod and tried to maneuver his body out of his way so that he could look down the length of the shaft and see how much of a fall remained.

He aimed the glowrod down, dropped it, and cursed. His hands lost their purchase and he fell through the hole he'd made.

The sickening plummet into darkness put his stomach in his throat. He screamed as he fell, scrabbling at the smooth walls, unable to find any purchase to slow him, tearing his fingernails from their beds.

He knew he was going to die. He would fall for a kilometer and finally slam into a floor somewhere, pulverizing himself.

Even as he imagined his demise, he hit the ground hard, but after only a few seconds of sliding. The impact sent pain shooting up his feet, ankles, knees. He crumpled. His backside slammed to the ground and his head thumped into the floor. Lights exploded in his sight as everything went dark.

Nyss prowled the corridors of the station, attentive to every sound in his search for the Prime and Jaden. Now and again he saw a corpse, some ancient, mummified remains of this or that species, some of which had not been seen in the galaxy for thousands of years.

Under his vest, he carried one of the unused mindspears. The Iteration, lagging behind him, carried another. Perhaps the Iteration kept his distance because he felt Nyss's power and it made him uncomfortable.

The lighted filaments in the walls led him onward. Shadows painted the corridors and rooms. He moved in silence, invisible. He left the Iteration farther and farther behind and did not care. He wished to face both the Prime and Jaden alone, to cause both of them pain for what they had done to Syll. Then he would annihilate who they had been and make them into what the One Sith wished.

Nyss halted. Ahead, he caught motion in the dim light of the corridor. He heard the sound of soft voices. He recognized Jaden Korr's.

Using his comlink, he said to the Iteration, "Remain where you are. I've found them."

He pulled his power close about him, melded with the darkness, and crept forward. All he needed was an opportunity.

The station shook, as if with a distant explosion or impact. The lights blinked out. Darkness like ink shrouded the corridor. The alarms fell silent and quiet settled on the corridor, as if the station were drawing breath for a scream. The dark-side power that suffused the air, the walls, the floor began to recede, the aftereffect of some event Jaden did not understand.

"Master?" Marr asked, and Jaden heard the nervousness in his tone.

"Be calm," Jaden said softly. "Feel the Force."

He activated his lightsaber, and its yellow light reared shadows at the edge of his vision. He felt as if he had just made himself a target.

Marr spaced himself a pace from Jaden and activated his blade. Purple joined yellow.

"What just happened?" the Cerean asked in a whisper.

Jaden shook his head. The dark-side power invested in the station had diminished, as if it had moved or concentrated itself somewhere outside of his immediate perception. He fell into the Force and extended his perception beyond the visual.

Immediately he thought he felt . . . something, but he could not lock his senses on it. It was as if his perception had encountered a hole. He'd never experienced anything like it. It was not one of the clones, but something else.

All at once he remembered Khedryn's words about the Umbaran's ability to disconnect the clones from the Force.

"We are not alone here," Marr said, perhaps picking up the same thread.

"No," Jaden said, squinting into the darkness. "We're not."

Screams knifed the silence and put Jaden on edge—the alarm reactivating. Overhead emergency lights came on, dim and flickering. The glowing filaments in the wall put on their patterned light show, but it was slower now, as if they'd lost the animus that had powered them previously.

Jaden caught movement at the edge of his field of vision. He spun, blade ready.

Nothing.

"What is it?" Marr asked, his voice a hiss.

"We need to move."

"Agreed." Marr spoke into his comlink. "Khedryn, do you copy?"

Still nothing but static.

"He knows how to take care of himself," Jaden said. "Come on."

They started down the hall, leading with their blades. Jaden felt as if they were walking down the throat of a beast. The slow flashing of the emergency lights made it impossible for his eyes to adjust to the darkness. Marr tried his comlink again.

"Khedryn, do you copy?"

Still nothing.

As they advanced, the lights grew dimmer. Jaden did not know whether to attribute it to system failure or . . . something else. The scuff of a boot on the floor turned him around. He saw nothing but darkness alternating with a play of shadows from the flashing lights.

"Against the wall," he said to Marr, and they backed up. Before they reached the wall, the darkness around them deepened so that the lights in the ceiling became as faint as distant stars. Jaden could see a few paces, no more.

A feeling started in his stomach, a flutter, as if he were falling from a great height. His connection to the Force slipped from him, drained into some dark hole into which he could not see or reach. He grabbed at it, tried to focus his concentration and hold on to the one certainty of his existence, but it slipped away and left him alone, bereft, hollow.

"What is happening?" Marr asked, his voice an octave higher than usual.

"The Umbaran," Jaden said.

As one their lightsabers winked out.

Marr felt dizzy, vaguely nauseous. He hadn't realized how much he'd come to rely on his connection to the Force. Though he'd only recently become aware of the true nature of the connection, it had been there his whole life, and its absence left him profoundly uneasy. His legs felt weak under him. He gripped his deactivated lightsaber in a sweaty palm and reached behind him for the wall, wanting to steady himself.

Something heavy and metallic slammed into the back of his skull. Sparks exploded before his eyes and pain buckled his knees. His vision went black for a beat and he was falling, falling. He tried to shout a warning to Jaden, but his mouth would not work. He regained enough sense to catch himself on his hands before his face slammed into the floor. He crouched there on all fours, head spinning.

Incongruously, he noticed the smooth texture of the floor, its warmth.

A kick from a booted foot slammed into his side, cracked ribs, and drove him over and flat on his back. He stared up at the ceiling, unable to breathe, unable to think, his broken ribs sending a stab of hot pain through his abdomen.

A face appeared above him, pale, hairless—the Umbaran. His dark eyes were holes; his mouth was an angry slash. The darkness clung to him like mist, and Marr could not quite focus on his outline.

He reached for his blaster but his arm seemed to be moving too slowly.

The Umbaran loomed over him. A vibroblade appeared in his hand.

"Master," Marr tried to say, but it only came out a groan.

Soldier and Grace hurried through the corridors of the station.

"Do you know where we're going?" Grace asked. Her voice sounded so small.

"Yes," he said, but the word was a lie. He had been so awed by the station, by what appeared to be the vindication of Seer's beliefs, that he had not paid close enough attention to the route they had taken to see Mother's face. He had only a general idea of where they were going.

The dimness of the corridors did not help. The overhead emergency lights blinked on and off, as did the glowing filaments in the walls and floor. Every room and corridor looked the same as every other.

"I'm frightened," Grace said.

He knew. He could feel it coming off her. Hoping she could not feel *his* fear, he put his hand on her shoulder as they hurried along, his lightsaber hilt in his hand but not activated.

He looked behind them regularly, terrified that Seer would appear somehow, or that some other manifestation of Mother would come to take him and Grace as it had taken Seer. The floor and walls shook with vibrations from time to time, and they reminded Soldier of Seer's ecstatic shivers when she communed with Mother. The similarity alarmed him.

"Come on, Grace," he said, pulling her along. "We have to hurry."

A door parted before them to reveal a long, dark corridor. From ahead, between the wails of the alarm, Soldier heard a shout, grunts, the sounds of combat. He knelt down and looked Grace in the eyes.

"Stay ten meters behind me and don't make a sound."

Eyes wide, she nodded.

Soldier rose and stalked forward.

Jaden heard Marr's pained groan, saw the Umbaran standing over him with a bare knife. Acting on instinct, he extended a hand, drew on the Force for a blast of power . . . and cursed. He had no power. It seemed the Umbaran could disrupt all connection to the Force: his own and that of his lightsaber crystal.

He reached for his blaster as the Umbaran flung a vibroblade at him.

Used to responding with Force-enhanced reflexes, he found his unenhanced reflexes too slow. The blade struck him in the bicep, slit skin and muscle, and scraped against bone. The pain shocked him, and blood, warm and sticky, poured from the gash.

The Umbaran kicked Marr in the head, causing the Cerean to go limp, and then bounded at Jaden. Jaden pulled the knife from his bicep and readied himself.

The Umbaran came at him in a frenzy, all knees and fists, a swirl of motion and gauzy darkness. Jaden sidestepped a punch for his throat and stabbed at the Umbaran with the vibroblade. The blade nicked the Umbaran's side, but barely, and he spun, locking Jaden's arm under his armpit and wrenching his wrist. Pain ran the length of Jaden's forearm and the vibroblade fell from his hand.

Grunting, the Umbaran threw a reverse elbow and caught Jaden in the cheek. Jaden staggered, but managed to wrest his arm free and loose a wild punch at the Umbaran's jaw.

The Umbaran ducked under it and tripped Jaden with a leg sweep. Jaden hit the ground, rolled into a backflip, and regained his feet, then retreated as the Umbaran loosed a flurry of punches and kicks. Jaden backed up, blocking, ducking, counterattacking where he could.

Blood poured from his arm. He was weakening, slowing, and the Umbaran must have known it. The Umbaran left off his attack and circled, playing for time.

"I wanted to spill your blood," he said. "For my sister I wanted that. But now . . ."

The Umbaran relaxed, then spoke a phrase in a language Jaden did not understand. He eyed Jaden as if expecting the words to have some effect on him, as if they were a magic incantation. The Umbaran's eyes widened when Jaden apparently did not respond as he expected.

"How can—"

Seeing an opportunity, Jaden charged, leading with a series of spinning kicks that the Umbaran blocked but which allowed Jaden to take the initiative. Unleashing a spinning back punch, he caught the Umbaran on the cheek, staggering him. Jaden ducked under the Umbaran's wild counterpunch, and launched an uppercut into his midsection. The blow doubled the Umbaran over and Jaden put a knee into his face.

The Umbaran crumpled to the ground on his backside, but his dazed eyes remained open and he held his hands awkwardly before him in a defensive posture. Jaden did not hesitate. He leapt atop the Umbaran and squirmed around him until he had him straddled from behind. There, he closed his forearms around the Umbaran's throat and began to squeeze.

The Umbaran clawed at Jaden's hands, flailed his legs, but to no avail. He died in seconds.

Jaden tried to stand, managed to get up on wobbly legs. He looked down. Blood drained from his slit arm, peppered the floor. The room spun. He was going to fall. A blurry form materialized before him, his height. He thought it might be Marr.

His vision went dark and he fell.

Marr opened his eyes. He lay flat on his back, his body a slab of meat that felt only pain. When he inhaled he felt as if someone had slipped a knife between his ribs. His head throbbed. Blood pooled under his head, warm and sticky. He inhaled, then winced at the pain it caused.

Alarms screamed from overhead. Dim emergency lights in the ceiling flashed on and off, a confusing strobe that made it hard to focus. His thoughts coalesced, memories connected, allowing him to think clearly. Something was in his fist, a cold cylinder of hard metal.

The hilt of his lightsaber.

Little good it had done him.

It takes decades to master the weapon, Marr, his Master had told him. *But you are making excellent strides.*

He remembered where he was, what had happened. He remembered something hitting him in the back of the head, a kick that staved in his ribs, the Umbaran's face.

"Master," he said.

Adrenaline fueled by concern for Jaden allowed him to move, to support himself on his elbow.

Two meters away from him a figure knelt over Jaden. The figure held a lightsaber in his right hand, the red blade bathing Jaden's still form in crimson.

Jaden's voice again sounded in his mind. *The point to*

remember is that wielding the weapon is not a test of your physicality. It is fed by your relationship to the Force.

When Marr's eyes focused clearly on the person standing over Jaden, he gasped.

It was Jaden. Or rather, another clone of Jaden. Not the clone from the frozen moon, but another, a perfect simulacrum of Marr's Master. He wore modern clothing, and his hair and beard were neatly trimmed. For a time, Marr could do nothing but watch, sickly fascinated, his mind moving through various possibilities, trying to figure out how there could be two clones of his Master, one born in a Thrawn-era cloning lab, and one born . . . somewhere else.

As Marr watched, the clone took a device, a metal handle with a thin spike attached to it, and plunged it into Jaden's temple. Jaden's back arched and his body went rigid. His lips peeled back from his teeth in a grimace of pain. Lines of white blinked along the filaments that composed the base of the spike, similar to the lights in the wall of the station, and in that moment Marr realized that the device, too, was Rakatan in origin.

"No!" he shouted, and climbed to his feet.

The Jaden clone turned, eyes hooded. His red blade cut the air, reflecting in his eyes.

Marr's heart rate accelerated. He reached for the Force and, to his surprise, felt it all around him. His eyes fell on another form not far from Jaden and barely visible in the dim light—the Umbaran. Jaden must have killed him.

Jaden screamed, an awful, animal sound so filled with pain and despair that it made Marr's eyes well. The device, buried to its handle in his skull, blinked ever faster.

The clone looked down at Jaden, then back at Marr. His eyes—not Jaden's eyes despite their physical similarity—bored into Marr.

"Who are you, Cerean?"

The question, asked in Jaden's voice, unnerved Marr. He scrambled to his feet, fighting off a bout of dizziness. "I'm his friend."

The clone smirked, the expression alien to Marr despite being on what seemed Jaden's face. "Then I suppose it's well that I won't remember that I killed you."

The clone strode toward him, blade held low, his expression a promise of violence.

Marr reached for his blaster with his off hand, drew it, and fired again, again, again. The clone deflected each shot as he closed, his expression one of contempt. Marr backed away, still firing, but the clone closed the distance. His face, like but unlike Jaden's, wore murderous intent with comfort.

Marr thumped into the wall. Its pulsing warmth penetrated his cloak. The clone extended a hand and used the Force to pull Marr's blaster from his hand.

Behind the clone, Jaden screamed again, louder. His hands curled into claws. A network of veins became visible in his face and forehead. His eyes opened, staring, empty, then closed, and his body fell back.

"No!" Marr said.

"Don't worry," the clone said, and raised his blade. "He'll live on. In me. The device takes his memories, his life, and gives them to me."

The red line descended for Marr's head. Marr ignited his blade—Jaden's blade, the line purple and steady—and parried the clone's blow.

The clone's eyes widened. The crossed blades sizzled.

"I'm more than just his friend," Marr said through the X of their blades. "I'm also his apprentice."

Marr augmented his strength with the Force and slammed his fist into the clone's abdomen. The clone staggered back a step, wheezing, and Marr followed up with a decapitating slash.

The clone's blade flashed, intercepted Marr's, twisted, and sent the purple-bladed lightsaber flying across the chamber. The clone looked up, smiling, and Marr saw that he was not wheezing. He was laughing.

"You aren't much of an apprentice," he said.

Marr took a step back, his confidence rattled. The clone sneered and advanced after him.

Fear, hungry and blinding, rose in Marr. His heart accelerated, and for a moment he thought only of running. But over the clone's shoulder he saw the body of Jaden, the Master who had trained him, who had taught him so much in so short a time.

Strength comes from your relationship to the Force.

"And from your relationship to others," Marr said, and sought the Keep. He found it, inhabited it.

The clone advanced, blood in his eyes.

Marr's fear fell away, replaced by calm.

The clone raised his blade.

Marr sank deeper into the Force and held his ground, unarmed but not defenseless.

The red line of the clone's blade descended in a glittering arc.

For Marr, events slowed. The blade moved down toward his head in slow motion. His mind did not so much process as feel the arc of its approach, the speed of its descent, the energy the blade generated—had to generate—in order to stay coherent, all of it numbers, equations, formulae.

Do not think. Feel.

At peace and without fear, he felt the Force fill him with more power than he'd experienced before. He overflowed with it, could barely contain it. He funneled all of it, everything in him, into his arm and hand, and as if of its own accord, his arm rose to intercept the blade.

He did not wince as his fist closed around the angry red gash of the clone's blade. He felt heat, was distantly cognizant of pain, of his flesh sizzling, peeling under the blade's onslaught.

But he also felt the blade in his hand, a thin slit of hate around which he wrapped his fist, channeled his power, and held on for all he was worth.

The clone's eyes widened, his mouth opened to speak, but before he could utter a sound, Marr made a knife of his free hand and drove his fingertips into the clone's exposed throat.

All at once time and motion returned to normal speed.

Taken by surprise, the clone dropped his blade and staggered backward, gasping for breath.

Still deeply connected to the Force, Marr extended a hand and unleashed a blast of energy that threw the clone bodily across the corridor and slammed him into the far wall, where he sagged and slid down, his chin on his chest.

"I might not be much of an apprentice," the Cerean said, as much for himself as the clone, "but I'm one hell of a friend."

He took mental hold of his lightsaber hilt, used the Force to pull it to his hand, ignited it, and walked across the corridor toward the clone. His wounded hand screamed with pain. He could feel charred ribbons of flesh dangling from his palm, but he ignored the agony.

The clone did not respond to his approach. Marr stood over him, raised his blade high for the kill, and . . . thought of Jaden.

He looked back at his Master, stared at him for a long moment, hoping to see his chest rise with breath.

Nothing.

Pushing aside his burgeoning grief, Marr pointed his blade at the clone's chest, knelt, and checked to see if the clone still lived. He did.

He'll live on, the clone had said. *In me.*

Marr's mouth went dry when he thought about the course he was considering. He stared at the clone, his face stripped of its anger by unconsciousness. He looked exactly like Jaden.

Almost.

Unwilling to consider it any longer for fear of losing his nerve, Marr simply acted. He tore a strip of cloth from the clone's clothing and wrapped his wounded hand. He refused to look at it; the pain of wrapping it almost made him pass out. When he was done, he took the clone's right hand in his own and severed the last three fingers just below the first knuckle. The clone groaned from the pain, but that was all. The heat from the blade cauterized the wounds and stanched the bleeding to a crimson seep.

Marr rose and walked to Jaden's body. He reached for his Master's throat to check for a pulse, just to be sure, but could not at first bring himself to touch him. Swallowing, he did . . . and felt no pulse.

Grief threatened to overcome his thinking and he almost reconsidered his course, almost walked away, believing that perhaps he should just leave Jaden at peace, one with the Force.

But he could not.

He licked his lips and closed his hand around the handle of the blinking device still buried in Jaden's head. It felt warm in his hand, alive, like the walls of the station.

He steeled himself and jerked the device out of Jaden's head. It came free with a wet sucking sound, and the moment he pulled it loose literally millions of filaments, each a fraction of the diameter of a hair, squirmed in the open air before almost immediately recombining, intertwining to form a single, seemingly solid, spike.

Marr stared at it a long while. It seemed impossible that Jaden was . . . in it. Yet that was what the clone's words had implied. And if any civilization could have mastered consciousness transfer, it would have been the Rakatans.

His mind made up, he carried the device back to the Jaden clone. He had no idea how to operate it, so he had to hope that it would self-activate, like the station's docking mechanism. It seemed alive, so that might be possible.

The clone's eyes opened, fixed on the device, widened.

"It's not ready," he said, and reached for Marr's hands.

Marr swatted the clone's hands away, drove a knee into his chest, and took him by the throat.

"You mean *you're* not ready," he said, and drove the spike into the clone's temple. It penetrated the skull with almost no resistance, and the handle warmed, then began to vibrate in his hand.

The clone's mouth opened wide to match his eyes, but no scream emerged. Tendons corded his neck and his body went rigid. The handle continued to vibrate, and Marr imagined the millions of tendrils squirming into the gray matter of the clone's brain, wiping out who he had been and replacing him with Jaden.

He waited, hoping, while the alarms wailed, the lights flickered, and somewhere deep in the station the dark side gave birth to something he did not understand.

Needing something familiar, desperate for it, he tried his comlink again.

"Khedryn, do you copy? Khedryn?"

Static and no hope. He stared down at the Jaden-clone, hoping he was no longer the Jaden-clone.

If things worked, Marr did not know what he would say to Jaden. Would Jaden remember the clone? Had Jaden even seen the clone? Marr did not know.

More important, Marr did not know if he had done the right thing. After all, the clone had apparently wanted to do exactly what Marr had, had been willing to kill to do it. Hadn't Marr done the clone's work for him? Why had they wanted to . . . replace Jaden?

He pushed the thought from his mind and another one took its place.

What if the device had not worked? What if the mind contained in the body remained that of the clone?

Then Marr would fight him and die. He looked at his wounded hand, the blood seeping into the cloth. He barely felt the pain. The pain in his heart overwhelmed it.

He stood, hurried to Jaden's body, and picked it up. It was limp, already cooling. Trying to keep grief over Jaden's death at bay with hope for a rebirth, he carried it a ways down the corridor, where he stripped it of its blaster, robes, and lightsaber.

He returned to Jaden's new body—he allowed himself to think that way—and felt for a pulse. It was there still, strong. He stripped off the clone's robe, replaced it with Jaden's, put Jaden's lightsaber on the belt. He strapped on the holster with its blaster, took the clone's blade—he took solace in the fact that its hilt was different from Jaden's—and cast it aside along with the Rakatan device.

Then he watched, and waited. Long moments passed. Distant explosions shook the station.

Growing nervous, he withdrew a bit from Jaden and sank into the shadows on the far side of the room. There he watched, as seconds stretched into eternities.

After a time, Jaden stirred. His eyes opened and he put a hand to his head, touched the wound that Marr had put there with the Rakatan spike.

Marr considered calling out, thought better of it, and decided to simply watch. As he did, an arm took him from behind, closed around his throat, and choked off his windpipe.

"Make no sound," someone said in a whisper. "Or you die."

Marr felt the hilt of a lightsaber pressed against his

back. His attacker would need only to activate it and the blade would impale him.

"What did you do to him?" the voice whispered, and the arm let up enough on Marr's throat to allow him speech.

"I don't know," Marr said. It was the truth. "What do you want?"

"I don't know," the voice breathed, his fetid breath hot on Marr's cheek. "To leave here."

Before them, a mere thirty meters, Jaden stood on wobbly legs. His expression looked dazed.

"Who are you?" Marr asked. It had to be one of the escaped clones.

"My name is Soldier." He reached around Marr's waist and took his lightsaber.

Jaden started moving down the corridor, away from Soldier and Marr. After he had moved some distance off, Soldier, still holding Marr about the throat, softly called out, "Grace."

A redheaded girl, maybe nine years old, stepped from the shadows. Her sickness deformed her face, the flesh bulging in one cheek, swollen around one eye.

"It's going to be all right," Soldier said to the girl. "We're getting out of here."

"Just let me go," Marr said. "All I want to do is help Jaden. I won't even tell him I saw you."

"You keep secrets from your Master?" Soldier asked.

Marr nodded, his eyes going to where he had hidden Jaden's "old" body. "If necessary," he said softly.

"Do you know how to get back to the lifts?" Soldier asked. He squeezed Marr's throat. "Don't lie."

"Yes," Marr said. He nodded at Jaden. "He is going in the right direction."

"Then we follow him," Soldier said, and they did, as Jaden stumbled through the hallways of the Rakatan station. Marr watched him from the darkness, wondering if he'd done the right thing.

Eventually Jaden came to a large doorway. Marr felt the presence behind it, the wash of dark-side energy pouring through the vertical slit of the doorway. Jaden must have felt it, too, for he hesitated, and put his hand on the hilt of his lightsaber.

"That is Mother," Soldier said softly. "Talk to him. The Jedi."

Marr swallowed, then uttered a word that he hoped still applied.

"Jaden."

chapter thirteen

THE PRESENT

HIS MASTER TURNED AS MOTHER SHRIEKED BEHIND THE closed door. He did not look like himself, and Marr feared the worst. Jaden's eyes fixed on Marr, on Soldier, his brow furrowed.

"I know you," he said. His lightsaber ignited, making his drawn face look sallow. He wobbled on his legs, put a finger to his temple, and winced as if he were being bombarded by a rush of memories.

Marr wanted to go to him, to help him, but Soldier held him fast and activated his lightsaber. The red blade sizzled and hummed beside Marr's ear.

Jaden recovered himself, held his yellow blade in his hand, regarding Soldier and Marr. Marr saw recognition in his Master's eyes, but not understanding. He looked lost, confused. Marr well knew why.

A shriek from the chamber behind Jaden drew all their eyes. The child crept up behind Soldier and Marr, looking for comfort—or protection.

Marr knew that something awful lurked behind the door.

"Talk to him," Soldier repeated.

"Master," Marr said, and the word felt odd on his lips. "Do you . . . really know me? Master?"

Jaden's brow furrowed. He lowered his lightsaber. "Marr?"

The tension and dread Marr had been carrying drained out of him in a rush. He let himself hope that his actions might have worked, that his Master, whole in mind, stood before him.

"Yes," he said, unable to hold in a smile. "It's me. Yes."

Jaden's expression hardened and fixed on Soldier. "Soldier, isn't it? Let him go."

Soldier's grip tightened on Marr's throat. "I can't. I need to get off this station. You and he are showing me the way."

Something huge moved in the chamber behind Jaden. Footsteps thumped. The floor vibrated under their impact. Marr felt the dark-side power pouring through the vertical slit. It made him nauseous.

"This is not the time for this," Marr said.

"I can't let you leave," Jaden said, as stubborn as ever. "You murdered half a dozen people in the medical facility on Fhost. You're a Sith."

Marr felt Soldier sag under the accusation. "I'm not a Sith. I'm not a Jedi. I'm just . . . a soldier. The others killed the innocents on Fhost. Not me. I'm . . . better now, Jedi. I was lost but . . . not anymore."

Jaden looked unconvinced, his lightsaber a yellow line that he would not allow Soldier to cross.

Soldier's voice was desperate. "We just want to leave, Jedi. We just want to leave and be left alone."

"We?"

"He has a child with him, Master," Marr said.

"Grace," Soldier called over his shoulder.

The child emerged from the darkness behind them. Jaden's expression softened when he saw the girl. His eyes sought Marr's and, with them, he asked a question.

"He could have killed us both already," Marr said. "I was vulnerable. So . . . were you."

"But I didn't," Soldier said.

Another shriek came from the chamber beyond, closer now. The door bulged. A monsoon of dark-side energy squeezed through the door's seal.

"Soldier . . ." the girl said, fear causing her voice to shake. She sagged to the floor and Soldier released Marr and went to her, pulling her close. She buried her face in his chest as he stroked her hair.

"It will be all right. Didn't I say it would be all right?"

Marr saw Jaden's resolve erode.

"He's not a Sith," Marr said, knocking the last bricks out of the wall of Jaden's resistance.

Jaden, staring at Soldier and Grace, deactivated his lightsaber.

Soldier released Marr and Marr went to Jaden, stared into his face, looking for any sign that he wasn't who he should be. He saw nothing of the Jaden-clone's mannerisms or expressions. Jaden appeared to be Jaden. Marr allowed himself to hope.

"It's good to see you," Jaden said. He put his hand to the hole in his temple. "I must have gotten hit on the head."

"You did," Marr said, hoping that Jaden would not probe too deeply into events until Marr had organized his lies. "Do you remember what happened?"

"Everything's blurry right now," Jaden said. He held up his wounded hand, the stumps of his fingers seeping blood. "I reinjured these somehow."

"The fight with the Umbaran, I imagine," Marr said. "We'll figure it out later. For now, we need to get off this station. All of us."

Jaden looked past him to Soldier. "What about the other clones? There were more than just you and Grace."

Soldier stood with his hand on Grace. "We're all that's left."

Jaden stared him in the face, and Marr wondered what it must be like to look upon and interact with a clone of yourself.

People are not equations, Marr had said to his Master. Maybe not. But he hoped people were their choices and their memories. If they were, then Jaden was Jaden. If they weren't, then Jaden was . . . something else.

"That's the way out," Jaden said, nodding at the chamber behind him.

Soldier activated his lightsaber and tossed Marr his. Marr and Jaden ignited their blades. Grace fell in behind them.

The door slid open to reveal horror.

"Seer," Soldier said, the word so profoundly sad it might as well have been a one-word elegy.

Grace whimpered and buried her face in Soldier's cloak. Soldier put his hand on her head, a gesture so loving that it unsettled Jaden.

Jaden recognized the face of the female clone from Fhost. Seer, Soldier had called her. But little else about her remained human.

Her torso and hairless head were pale and bloated, like a drowned corpse's. Veins and arteries stood out so prominently from her skin that they looked as if they might soon burst. They glowed with light the same way the filaments in the walls glowed.

A nest of filaments wrapped her entirely from the waist down. If she still had legs, Jaden could not see them. She looked like a demon, a half-serpent born of the dark side and Rakatan technology.

A cocoon of energy surrounded her body and leaked in blue bolts from her eyes and fingertips. She focused her gaze, and the weight of her regard caused Jaden to take a half-step back. The power she embodied staggered him.

"Seer," Soldier said, his voice thick with despair. "Are you still there, Seer?"

"She's gone," Jaden said, wincing against the power pouring off her.

"But Mother is here," said the form, her voice deep, echoing through the large chamber. "And now you will pay. *Everyone* will pay!"

Jaden knew they had to get through her to get back to the lifts. He did not hesitate.

"Keep the girl safe," he said to Marr, and charged.

Before he had taken three steps, Force lightning, jagged and sparking, flew from Mother's bloated fingers and slammed into him. He interposed the yellow line of his lightsaber and spun it in rapid circles, attempting to wind the lightning up around his blade, but its power was too much. It blasted through his defenses, struck his body, the pain like a dozen stabbing knives, and threw him sidewise five meters. He landed prone and filaments snaked out of the floor and wall, writhing, reaching for him. He slashed them with his lightsaber and bounded to his feet to see Soldier also charging Mother.

A rope of filaments exploded out of the floor, grabbed Soldier by the ankles, lifted him high, and slammed him back into the floor, once, twice. He looked like a rag doll.

"Soldier!" Grace cried.

Marr, with one hand still on Grace, pulled his blaster free and unloaded at Mother. The first shot struck her in the chest and left a black, smoking hole in her bloated, pale flesh. The second did the same and she roared with pain, her body spasming, writhing. Before Marr could fire another shot, Mother held up her hand and Marr's blaster flew from his hand to hers. She crushed the weapon in her fist and gestured at Marr with pinched fingers.

The Cerean rose from the ground, gagging, legs kicking.

"Run," Marr grunted at Grace, but she stood still and stared, transfixed.

Jaden fell fully into the Force, gestured with outstretched arms and two flattened palms at Mother, and unleashed a blast of power. The energy struck her full in the side, blowing her a meter sidewise and causing her to release Marr, who fell to the floor.

Jaden attacked, leaping high toward the ceiling, flipping at the apex of his leap, and taking his lightsaber in a two-handed grip so that he could split Mother in half.

But she'd already recovered from his blast. She turned her dark eyes on him, raised a hand dismissively, and seized him with her power.

He was no match for her. Her power held him against the ceiling and began to press. His breath went out of his lungs in a whoosh. His chest started to collapse. He interposed his own power to offset her, but her push was inexorable.

He watched Marr sprint to Soldier's aid, cut him free of the filaments that bound him, and help him to his feet. Jaden wanted to order them to run, to take the girl and get out of there, but he could not call out, could not do anything but use every ounce of his Force-strength to keep Mother from crushing his ribs and organs.

Marr and Soldier charged Mother. Filaments writhed out of the floor and walls to attack them from all sides. Soldier's blade flashed as he ducked, spun, leapt, and whirled, closing on Mother with every step, leaving a mess of smoking, squirming filaments in his wake. Marr, less graceful but still effective, cut his way through the filaments as he might thick foliage, slashing two-handed, spinning, using the limited techniques Jaden had taught him.

As they neared her body, she roared, and baleful green

Force lightning poured from her in all directions, sheathing her in power. Jaden, on the fringe of it, felt the energy sear his flesh, smelled the stink of burning flesh, opened his mouth in a scream for which he could draw no breath.

Soldier and Marr tried to catch up the lightning in their blades, but it was too much, came at them from too many angles, and both of them fell to the ground, writhing with pain.

With Mother's attention elsewhere, Jaden felt her grip on him lessen. Despite his pain, he drew on the Force and let power explode outward from him. It freed him from her grasp and he flipped as he fell. He hit the floor on his feet, crouched, and exploded into a leap toward her, his lightsaber held high. He reached her before she could swat him aside. His blade hummed as he slashed and opened a gash in her chest.

Energy, dark and cold, exploded outward from the wound, from the walls, the floor. It blew Jaden backward and slammed him into the wall. He cushioned the blow with the Force, and that just barely kept it from cracking his skull.

Mother's eyes widened and she staggered backward, shrieking. She spasmed and raged, a storm of energy filling the room as her fury grew.

They were no match for her. Jaden could see that.

"Run!" he said, climbing to his feet. "Now!"

The four of them sprinted past Mother and toward the slit of the door. It did not open, so all three of them slashed at the wall with their lightsabers. It felt like cutting flesh. Mother screamed behind them, and Jaden felt her shift her girth, felt the regard of her eyes on his back.

"Move!" he said, and pushed Marr, Grace, and Soldier through the hole they'd cut. "Move!"

He slipped through behind them as Force lightning

ripped through the hole, slammed into his back, and drove him face-first across the corridor.

"Master!" Marr said, but Jaden was already on all fours and trying to stand. Dizziness caused him to wobble, but Marr and Soldier kept him standing. Mother's voice boomed from behind them.

"You will not escape me!" she said. "Only I will leave this station."

The door slid open behind them. Mother's form loomed. Jaden loosed a blast of power at her, Soldier did the same, and they all ran for their lives.

The wail of an alarm brought Khedryn back to consciousness. He lay there, blinking at the dim emergency lights glowing in the ceiling above him, unsure of where he was. He'd gotten stuck in the alien lift, and he'd fallen the rest of the way down the shaft. He must have hit his head when he landed.

The power had gone out, but backup seemed to have been restored.

He ran his fingers over his scalp and felt the sore, seeping lump on the back of his skull. His glowrod lay on the ground near him, still working. He rolled over and crawled for it, his legs and back aching with every movement. He might have cracked something in his feet or legs, but he was pretty sure he hadn't broken anything too badly.

He picked up the glowrod and aimed it around the room to give himself a better look. He'd fallen through one of the tubes that extended downward from the ceiling. He crawled underneath one of them and looked up into it. It seemed to extend upward forever.

Control panels like those in the chamber above stood on the floor under the bottom of each tube. He touched one and it did not operate. Cursing, he touched another, but still nothing. How would he ever get back up? He touched a third and it came to life, starting to scan his body as the one above had done.

He stepped out of the light before the scan had finished. His breathing came easier now that he knew the control panel and lift were operational. He would be able to get back up.

But now he needed to figure out where to go. A single vertical slit in the wall looked like the only way out of the chamber. He walked toward it and it slid open with a wet susurration. Before he stepped through, his comlink crackled and he heard a series of questioning beeps from R-6. Alone in the belly of the dark station, he latched onto the sound of the droid as a lifeline. Khedryn resolved in that instant to learn better droid-speak.

"Nice job, Ar-Six. I'll tell you right now that you're welcome on my boat anytime."

The droid whirred with satisfaction.

"Patch me through to Jaden and Marr."

The droid beeped when he made the connection.

"Jaden," Khedryn said. "Do you read? Jaden?"

Mother's screams of rage haunted them as they ran wildly through the station's corridors. Jaden, Marr, and Soldier hacked their way through any doors that did not open at their approach.

"She's getting closer!" Grace cried.

"Move, move, move!" Soldier said.

Jaden's comlink crackled and Khedryn's voice carried over the connection.

"Jaden, do you read? Jaden?"

"Where are you?" Jaden asked, his voice tight, tense as he ran, as Mother shrieked.

"We docked. I'm at the bottom of the lifts. The Umbaran attacked me. He's on the station. Watch yourself."

"He's dead," Jaden said.

"Good, then—"

"Worse is coming," Jaden said.

"Worse? What do you mean?"

"I mean get out of there, Khedryn," Jaden said. "I don't know if we'll make it."

"Listen, Jedi, I'm not leaving you two—"

Suddenly an idea struck Jaden. "Khedryn, get up to the clones' supply ship. Set the engines to overload."

"What?"

"Blow the ship, Khedryn! I want the whole orbital station to go up."

"No," said Soldier. "The meds are on that ship. Grace has to have them."

"It's the only ship big enough to do enough damage," Jaden said. "And we're *all* dead if we don't blow the station. We can't stop Mother. We'll get her meds some other way."

To that, Soldier said nothing.

"That'll kill us all, Jaden," Khedryn said.

"We'll get off before it blows. Or if we don't, you will. Do it, Khedryn."

"Move your butts, then, Jedi."

"Watch out for the bodies," Jaden said. "There could be more up there."

"I saw them already. They're just dead bodies, Jaden."

"They aren't dead," Jaden said. "Mother uses them."

"'Mother' *what?*"

"Just watch yourself."

Khedryn had heard the alarm in Jaden's tone. He'd never before heard anything like it from the Jedi. He stepped up to one of the control panels, activated it, let its light scan his body. The tube above him adjusted in size to accommodate his form, then stretched downward to gulp him. He closed his eyes as the warm flesh surrounded him and held him tight.

He ascended rapidly and breathed a sigh of relief when he reached the top of the lift. The floor vibrated, shaking with some distant impact. He ran back the way he had come, through corridors and rooms dimly lit by glowing filaments that flashed and blinked crazily.

Imagining the relative position of *Junker*'s docking point to that of the supply ship, he turned left and sped down a hall.

He saw the hole of the supply ship's docking tube ahead and raced toward it.

Forms emerged from side corridors, animated corpses with hands extended, shuffling piles of dried flesh, sinew, and teeth. At first Khedryn thought their veins and arteries were glowing, but no—the same filaments that lined the walls of the station also lined their bodies. It was if something had grown within them, taken them over.

They were humanoid, bipedal, but their condition did not allow him to identify their species. Shock stopped him in his tracks, and one of the corpses got a hand on his shoulder. As bony fingers sank into his flesh, he cursed, grunted against the pain, and punched the corpse in the face. Its head, already barely attached to a thick spine, flew off and slammed against the wall. The body collapsed at his feet. He drew both his blasters as he whirled and fired wildly. His first shot hit nothing but wall, but his second hit the thin, exposed rib cage of another corpse. It exploded into shards of bone and desiccated flesh. He threw himself against a wall and pulled the trigger as fast as he could, aiming at anything that moved.

When nothing else moved in the hallway, he picked his way through the carnage and ran aboard the supply ship. He remembered how to get to the cockpit and went directly for it. As he moved through the corridors and lifts, he flashed back on the events of the previous hours—being taken captive by the clones; the Umbaran; the little girl, Grace.

He hoped she was all right.

Once in the cockpit, he got the engines live and firing, but the ship's internal safeties prevented him from putting them on a loop that would result in an explosion. He opened the ship's internal network to the outside and raised R-6.

"Ar-Six, I'm on the supply ship and the engines are hot. I need you to crack the internal safeties so that I can blow the engines."

R-6 beeped a question.

"You have ten seconds, droid."

R-6 whooped in alarm. Khedryn watched the readout on the comp station as R-6 worked the system. The data scrolled past so fast that Khedryn could not read any of it. He turned to face the cockpit door, blasters at the ready, should the clones or the corpses show. Neither did, and R-6 had the safeties overridden in moments.

"Good job, Ar-Six," Khedryn said, and set the engines on a power loop that would eventually cause them to explode. The whole ship would go and, given its size, it would do enormous damage to the station.

"Jaden and Marr are en route," Khedryn said. "Get *Junker* ready to run."

The supply ship's engines began to spool up on their way to self-destruction. Khedryn sprinted back toward the station's lift. He encountered a single animated corpse, a straggler with an oversized skull and odd tusks. Without slowing, he blew it to shards with his blasters.

"And *stay* down," he said.

He saw the lift room ahead.

A buckle in the floor almost knocked him down. A scream resounded from deeper in the station, so filled with hate and rage that Khedryn covered his ears. The filaments in the walls glowed a hot red.

"We're coming up," said Jaden's voice over the comlink. "Mother is coming, too."

"Make it quick," Khedryn said. "The supply ship is ready to blow."

Jaden, Marr, Soldier, and Grace piled into the lift room. Mother's movement behind them caused the ground to shake. It was as if she were getting bigger with each passing moment, absorbing more and more of the station as she went.

"Get in and go," Jaden said. He used the Force to pull the door to the chamber closed and, holding it, backed up toward one of the control panels. Soldier scooped Grace up in his arms; the control panel's light scanned them both, the tube extended, adjusted its size, and up they went. Marr followed.

Mother slammed against the outer door. Her power drove Jaden a step backward, but he held the doors closed. Mother screamed again, a sound rich with hate, frustration, rage. The doors began to bulge inward.

The light on the control panel scanned Jaden, and the tube above him adjusted size, descended toward him.

He could no longer hold it. The door to the chamber burst open and Mother lurched into the room, her human torso even more bloated and discolored than before, the serpentine portion of her body now ten meters long.

Filaments burst out of the floor and walls and grasped for Jaden. He slashed them with his lightsaber as Mother roared. The tube scooped him up, and Mother's shriek trailed away as he streaked upward in the lift.

Khedryn sprinted into the room with the lifts. He went to the shafts, looked down but saw nothing. He waited there, heart racing, breath coming fast.

A vibration under his feet signaled the rise of the lifts. He went from one to another, watching for the sign of something coming up. In one of the lift tubes he saw a rapidly rising bulge and backed off as it expelled not Jaden or Marr but Soldier and Grace. Blood leaked from Soldier's nose and the side of his face looked as if he'd been hit with a brick. Burst capillaries in one of his eyes had turned it red.

"You!" Khedryn said, and fumbled for his blaster.

Soldier gestured with his free hand, tore the blaster from Khedryn's grasp, but did not ignite his lightsaber.

"I'm not your enemy," the clone said. "The Jedi and the Cerean are right behind us."

Before Khedryn could say anything, Soldier stepped forward and handed him back his blaster.

Khedryn looked at it, took it. "What happened?" he asked, knowing how stupid the question sounded.

"Weird things," Grace said, and smiled at him.

Khedryn could not help himself. He smiled in return. "I'm glad to see you," he said to her, and her grin turned shy.

The tube nearest Khedryn flexed, bulged, and spat out Marr. The Cerean's eyes looked as worried as Khedryn had ever seen them.

"What is it?" Khedryn said.

"Where's Jaden?"

"Not here yet."

"You started the autodestruct on the supply ship?"

Khedryn nodded. "What is going on? What is 'Mother'?"

As if in answer, the floor under them lurched, buckled. Grace squealed in alarm.

"A lie," Soldier said. "Mother is a lie."

Another lurch of the floor. Marr ignited his lightsaber. Soldier did the same. The tube on the far side of the room bulged and disgorged Jaden, his hair and eyebrows singed, his clothing burned, his breathing ragged.

The floor lurched again, nearly knocking all of them off their feet. Then it began to bulge upward, rising toward the ceiling. A scream of pure, unadulterated rage burst up from one of the shafts and set Khedryn's hair on end.

"Run!" Jaden said. "Run!"

Khedryn needed to hear nothing else. He turned, along with the rest of them, and sped for *Junker*.

Heat and smoke filled the dimly lit corridors. The filaments in the walls blinked through a series of colors, rapidly, crazily, the frenetic brain activity of a dying organism.

Jaden and Soldier led the flight, their yellow and red lightsabers cutting through the doors that didn't open at their approach. Soldier held the child in his free arm, her head buried in his neck and beard. Jaden used the Force to pull walls and doors together behind him, hoping to slow Mother. Mother shrieked behind them, and the impact of her body and power on the obstacles Jaden had put in her path sounded close, too close.

"Run!" Khedryn shouted. "Run!"

Another explosion sent them lurching, threw them all up against the wall, and knocked Soldier off his feet. Jaden and Marr pulled him upright and they ran on. The child was crying.

Ahead, the corridor split.

"*Junker*'s that way," Marr said, pointing to the left with his lightsaber.

"Where's the Umbaran's ship?" Soldier asked.

"That way," Marr said, nodding right. "Near your ship."

Soldier took Khedryn by the arm. "How long before the supply ship blows?"

Khedryn shook his arm free. "Moments. There's no time."

Behind them, Mother screamed her fury and pain. They could feel walls collapsing before her approach.

"She needs the meds," Soldier said, nodding at Grace. "I have to get aboard that ship."

"You could get them back on Fhost," Marr said.

"I'm not going back to Fhost," Soldier answered.

"Jaden?" Khedryn asked.

His mouth a hard line in the red glow of his lightsaber, Soldier turned to face Jaden. The Jedi stared into Soldier's gray eyes, the same eyes Jaden saw every morning when he looked in the mirror.

Jaden could not let him go, could he?

The soft cries of the child, her disease causing her flesh to visibly roil, made up his mind for him.

"Where will the two of you go?" Jaden asked him. "What will you do?"

"I don't know."

Jaden nodded; Soldier nodded.

"Go," Jaden said to him.

Without another word, and still cradling Grace in one of his arms, Soldier turned and ran for the Umbaran's ship. He must have used the Force to augment his speed, for he vanished in a blink.

"I don't think he can make it," Khedryn said. Not to the supply ship and then the Umbaran's ship.

"Maybe not," Jaden said. "But I had to let him try."

Another scream from Mother, another explosion in a distant part of the station, set Jaden's, Marr's, and Khedryn's feet to running.

"Have the ship ready to go, Ar-Six!" Khedryn said over his comlink, and the droid beeped agreement.

Ahead, they saw the docking tube, the open hatch of *Junker*'s airlock. They sprinted for it, but before they reached it a nest of filaments burst from the walls, squirming like snakes, and grabbed at them.

Jaden's blade was a blur as he cut through them, leaving them writhing and smoking on the floor. Marr did the same, and they kept moving. Jaden looked back and saw Mother's form filling the smoky corridor behind them.

"Go!" he said. "Go, go!"

He fell into the Force, gestured, and pulled the door nearest them closed.

Mother's shriek of frustration shook the walls.

He turned, darted onto *Junker* behind Khedryn and Marr, and closed the airlock hatch.

"Get us clear," he said to R-6 over the comlink.

Immediately *Junker* started to pull away from the docking tube. The tube stretched but did not release them. Filaments shot from its sides, grabbed at protuberances on *Junker*'s hull, tried to reel the ship back in. Through the viewport, Jaden could see the side of the station near where they had been docked pulsing, as more and more filaments gathered there, shooting out across the void to grip *Junker*. Jaden could feel Mother's presence just on the other side of the station's wall, waiting for them.

"Engines full!" Khedryn shouted into his comlink.

R-6 powered the freighter's engines to full and the ship strained against the station's grasp, against Mother's grip.

On the other side of the station, the supply ship exploded. There was an enormous ball of flame. Immediately, secondary explosions blossomed here and there on the station, growing in size and intensity, one after another rippling along its surface. Curtains of flame shot out into space. An explosion rocked the station near the tether and the part of the station in orbit lurched, severed from the tether, and began to fall toward the planet.

Meanwhile, the explosion that cut the tether spread

along its length toward the planet, a giant wick burning its way to the subsurface part of the station.

Jaden watched it all in horrified fascination, while *Junker*'s engines strained against the grasp of the filaments. The station fell planetward, dragging *Junker* with it. Marr, Khedryn, and Jaden stared out the viewport, their lives entirely dependent upon *Junker*'s engines.

"Come on, baby," Khedryn said. "Come on."

As one, ship and station fell toward the planet, picking up speed every second. Jaden could feel Mother's power pouring out of the station. The filaments held *Junker* like a net. The engines screamed, trying to keep both ship and station from falling.

"Divert everything to the engines!" Khedryn said to R-6. *"Everything!"*

The pitch of the engines changed, grew deeper; the lights dimmed as R-6 redirected all power but life support and artificial gravity to the engines.

The surface of the planet rushed up to meet them, to crush them, to bury them in fire and rock along with Mother.

All at once the filaments snapped and *Junker* sprang free, shooting into space like a blaster shot. The sudden acceleration was too much for the artificial gravity to compensate for immediately, and Jaden, Marr, and Khedryn slammed against the wall.

Jaden, his face pasted against the viewport, watched the station fall to the planet, the filaments squirming, trailing a wake of Mother's hate and rage.

The station struck the surface and silently flowered into a ball of fire. Mother's anger, her power, vanished in the flames. Secondary explosions below the surface veined the planet in orange lines, as the subsurface portion of the station blew.

* * *

Khedryn, Marr, Jaden, and R-6 crowded into *Junker*'s cockpit. Khedryn ran diagnostics—*Junker* seemed mostly intact, he was pleased to see—while Marr plotted coordinates for a jump to hyperspace.

To Khedryn, both of the Jedi—he now thought of Marr as a Jedi—seemed oddly reserved.

"Do you think they got clear in time?" he asked Jaden.

His question seemed to bring Jaden back from wherever his mind had been. The Jedi looked up and his eyes focused on Khedryn.

"Soldier?"

"And Grace," Khedryn said.

Jaden looked past him, out the cockpit, and into space. "I don't know. I think so. I hope so."

Khedryn hoped so, too.

Jaden cleared his throat, smiled, and stood. "I need to go report to the Order. Heading back to Fhost, Captain?"

Khedryn nodded. "Heading back to Fhost."

"After I finish the report, I'll throw on some caf," Jaden said. "Meet you both in the galley."

"Spike it with pulkay," Khedryn said. "We all deserve a drink."

Jaden just laughed as he walked out of the cockpit.

"I mean it," Khedryn said to his back. He did mean it. He needed a drink.

After he'd gone, Khedryn swung his seat toward Marr, and found the Cerean staring after Jaden, a worried look on his face.

"You all right?"

Marr smiled, but Khedryn knew it was forced. "Fine."

"What's with you two? You're both acting odd."

Marr fixed his gaze on Khedryn, the worry in his eyes magnified. "What do you mean 'odd'? Odd how?"

Khedryn sank back in his seat. "Ease up, Marr. I just mean that the two of you seem different. Probably just everything that happened. Relax."

But Marr did not relax. He stared after Jaden, his tension palpable to Khedryn.

"I didn't see anything odd in him," Marr said. "I think he's exactly the same. Exactly the same."

In the tiny confines of one of *Junker*'s lavatories, Jaden showered, toweled off, and stood before the small, polished metal mirror. His already narrow face looked drawn and his expression looked haggard, his gray eyes sunk deeply into their sockets and underscored by dark circles. A lot had happened over the past few days.

He needed to change the dressings on his wounds. But first he needed a shave.

He checked the sundries cabinet built into the wall and found a can of lather and an archaic razor Khedryn must have left there for passengers.

With the stink of the station washed from his body if not his mind, he methodically lathered his face and slowly pulled the razor down his cheeks and his throat, neatening the borders of his goatee.

As he did, his mind turned to Soldier, and he wondered how alike they were. They shared a similar biology, if not an absolutely identical one. They were, in a very true sense, brothers—twins even. And yet they had led very different lives and made very different choices.

People were not equations.

No. People were choices.

But how much did biology constrain the choices? Theoretically, Soldier could have turned from the dark side at any time. But didn't theory crash on the rocks of reality? Weren't Soldier's choices constrained by his biology, at least to some degree?

Weren't Jaden's?

He finished his shave, wiped off the lather, and stared at himself in the mirror. Something looked off. It took him a moment to realize what it was—a small scar he'd had on his right cheek since adolescence was gone. He'd cut himself with one of Uncle Orn's tools and it had not healed right.

"How could that be?" he muttered.

He put his face right next to the mirror, wondering if maybe it had just faded, but no, he didn't see it there at all. He stared at his image in the mirror a long time.

Uncomfortable possibilities started to swirl around in his mind. He tried to hold them at bay, but they kept rearing up in his consciousness. He chuckled, trying to laugh them away, but they lingered, stubborn.

"That's not possible," he said, denying something that he refused to name. He remembered his entire life. No one possessed the kind of technology it would require to transplant a lifetime of memories.

No, he was him. He could be no one else.

But he had been unconscious for a time after his fight with the Umbaran. He remembered how he had felt when he had awakened—the confusion, the inability to remember.

But all that was consistent with a head injury.

His eyes fell to his wounded fingers, the wounds opened anew.

Opened anew.

Marr had said as much, and Marr would not lie to him.

But Marr had eyed him strangely. Jaden had assumed it to be concern over his injuries, but couldn't it have been something else?

Couldn't it?

He looked at himself in the mirror, and he wondered.

* * *

Out in the far reaches of the system, Soldier studied the star charts in the Umbaran's scout flyer. They were in what the navicomp called the Unknown Regions. Indeed, all of space was an unknown region for Soldier, all of life.

He had met his clone. And seeing Jaden Korr had shown him what he could be.

He had sought purpose for decades, had thought he'd found it in Seer and their quest for Mother. But that had been a lie, a false hope born of desperation and loneliness. He had been alone even when he wasn't alone, different from the other clones, isolated, separate. Seer had seemed to understand his pain and had tried to give him a salve for it in their quest.

But Mother had been her quest, not his. His was . . . something else.

Grace sat curled up in the copilot's seat. She looked so fragile to him, so pale, so light, as if she might blow away in a strong wind. He had given her the meds. Her illness was controlled—he had saved enough from the supply ship to keep her symptom-free for years. During that time, he would protect her, raise her to have a better life than his, perhaps even find her a cure somewhere out there.

Yes, he had his purpose.

She opened her eyes, looked up at him, smiled. He smiled in return.

"It's dark in here," she said.

"This is as bright as the lighting allows," he said. The Umbaran must have designed it so. "We'll get it changed when we can."

"Where are we going?" she asked.

He thought about the answer a long while. "I don't know. We'll find a place, make a home there."

She seemed to accept that. Curling back up in the seat,

she was soon asleep once more. Her tiny snores made him smile.

Soldier sat in the dim cockpit of the ship, staring out at the limitless expanse of the Unknown Regions, a vast empty darkness broken by feeble points of light.

So much emptiness, he thought.

He picked a system from the navicomp and put in the coordinates.

He decided that he must focus on the lights.

With that, he engaged the hyperdrive.

Read on for an excerpt from
STAR WARS: FATE OF THE
JEDI:OUTCAST
by Aaron Allston

GALACTIC ALLIANCE DIPLOMATIC SHUTTLE,
HIGH CORUSCANT ORBIT

ONE BY ONE, THE STARS OVERHEAD BEGAN TO DISAPPEAR, swallowed by some enormous darkness interposing itself from above and behind the shuttle. Sharply pointed at its most forward position, broadening behind, the flood of blackness advanced, blotting out more and more of the unblinking starfield, until darkness was all there was to see.

Then, all across the length and breadth of the ominous shape, lights came on—blue and white running lights, tiny red hatch and security lights, sudden glows from within transparisteel viewports, one large rectangular whiteness limned by atmosphere shields. The lights showed the vast triangle to be the underside of an Imperial Star Destroyer, painted black, forbidding a moment ago, now comparatively cheerful in its proper running configuration. It was the *Gilad Pellaeon,* newly arrived from the Imperial Remnant, and its officers clearly knew how to put on a show.

Jaina Solo, sitting with the others in the dimly lit passenger compartment of the government VIP shuttle, watched the entire display through the overhead transparisteel canopy and laughed out loud.

The Bothan in the sumptuously padded chair next to hers gave her a curious look. His mottled red and tan fur twitched, either from suppressed irritation or embarrassment at Jaina's outburst. "What do you find so amusing?"

"Oh, both the obviousness of it and the skill with which it was performed. It's so very, *You used to think of us as dark and scary, but now we're just your stylish allies."* Jaina lowered her voice so that her next comment would not carry to the passengers in the seats behind. "The press will love it. That image will play on the holonews broadcasts constantly. Mark my words."

"Was that little show a Jagged Fel detail?"

Jaina tilted her head, considering. "I don't know. He could have come up with it, but he usually doesn't spend his time planning displays or events. When he does, though, they're usually pretty . . . effective."

The shuttle rose toward the *Gilad Pellaeon*'s main landing bay. In moments, it was through the square atmosphere barrier shield and drifting sideways to land on the deck nearby. The landing place was clearly marked—hundreds of beings, most wearing gray Imperial uniforms or the distinctive white armor of the Imperial stormtrooper, waited in the bay, and the one circular spot where none stood was just the right size for the Galactic Alliance shuttle.

The passengers rose as the shuttle settled into place. The Bothan smoothed his tunic, a cheerful blue decorated with a golden sliver pattern suggesting claws. "Time to go to work. You won't let me get killed, will you?"

Jaina let her eyes widen. "Is that what I was supposed to be doing here?" she asked in droll tones. "I should have brought my lightsaber."

The Bothan offered a long-suffering sigh and turned toward the exit.

They descended the shuttle's boarding ramp. With no duties required of her other than to keep alert and be the Jedi face at this preliminary meeting, Jaina was able to stand back and observe. She was struck with the unreality of it all. The niece and daughter of three of the most famous enemies of the Empire during the First Galactic Civil War of a few decades earlier, she was now witness to events that might bring the Galactic Empire—or Imperial Remnant, as it was called everywhere outside its own borders—into the Galactic Alliance on a lasting basis.

And at the center of the plan was the man, flanked by Imperial officers, who now approached the Bothan. Slightly under average size, though towering well above Jaina's diminutive height, he was dark-haired, with a trim beard and mustache that gave him a rakish look, and was handsome in a way that became more pronounced when he glowered. A scar on his forehead ran up into his hairline and seemed to continue as a lock of white hair from that point. He wore expensive but subdued black civilian garments, neck-to-toe, that would be inconspicuous anywhere on Coruscant but stood out in sharp relief to the gray and white uniforms, white armor, and colorful Alliance clothes surrounding him.

He had one moment to glance at Jaina. The look probably appeared neutral to onlookers, but for her it carried just a twinkle of humor, a touch of exasperation that the two of them had to put up with all these delays. Then an Alliance functionary, notable for his blandness, made introductions: "Imperial Head of State the most honorable Jagged Fel, may I present Senator Tiurrg Drey'lye of Bothawui, head of the Senate Unification Preparations Committee."

Jagged Fel took the Senator's hand. "I'm pleased to be working with you."

"And delighted to meet *you*. Chief of State Daala sends her compliments and looks forward to meeting you when you make planetfall."

Jag nodded. "And now, I believe, protocol insists that we open a bottle or a dozen of wine and make some preliminary discussion of security, introduction protocols, and so on."

"Fortunately about the wine, and regrettably about everything else, you are correct."

At the end of two full standard hours—Jaina knew from regular, surreptitious consultations of her chrono—Jag was able to convince the Senator and his retinue to accept a tour of the *Gilad Pellaeon*. He was also able to request a private consultation with the sole representative of the Jedi

Order present. Moments later, the gray-walled conference room was empty of everyone but Jag and Jaina.

Jag glanced toward the door. "Security seal, access limited to Jagged Fel and Jedi Jaina Solo, voice identification, activate." The door hissed in response as it sealed. Then Jag returned his attention to Jaina.

She let an expression of anger and accusation cross her face. "You're not fooling anyone, Fel. You're planning for an Imperial invasion of Alliance space."

Jag nodded. "I've been planning it for a while. Come here."

She moved to him, settled into his lap, and was suddenly but not unexpectedly caught in his embrace. They kissed urgently, hungrily.

Finally Jaina drew back and smiled at him. "This isn't going to be a routine part of your consultations with every Jedi."

"Uh, no. That would cause some trouble here and at home. But I actually *do* have business with the Jedi that does not involve the Galactic Alliance, at least not initially."

"What sort of business?"

"Whether or not the Galactic Empire joins with the Galactic Alliance, I think there ought to be an official Jedi presence in the Empire. A second Temple, a branch, an offshoot, whatever. Providing advice and insight to the Head of State."

"And protection?"

He shrugged. "Less of an issue. I'm doing all right. Two years in this position and not dead yet."

"Emperor Palpatine went nearly twenty-five years."

"I guess that makes him my hero."

Jaina snorted. "Don't even say that in jest . . . Jag, if the Remnant doesn't join the Alliance, I'm not sure the Jedi *can* have a presence without Alliance approval."

"The Order still keeps its training facility for youngsters in Hapan space. And the Hapans haven't rejoined."

"You sound annoyed. The Hapans still giving you trouble?"

"Let's not talk about *that*."

"Besides, moving the school back to Alliance space is just a matter of time, logistics, and finances; there's no question that it will happen. On the other hand, it's very likely that the government would withhold approval for a Jedi branch in the Remnant, just out of spite, if the Remnant doesn't join."

"Well, there's such a thing as an *unofficial* presence. And there's such a thing as rival schools, schismatic branches, and places for former Jedi to go when they can't be at the Temple."

Jaina smiled again, but now there was suspicion in her expression. "You just want to have this so *I'll* be assigned to come to the Remnant and set it up."

"That's a motive, but not the only one. Remember, to the Moffs and to a lot of the Imperial population, the Jedi have been bogeymen since Palpatine died. At the very least, I don't want them to be inappropriately afraid of the woman I'm in love with."

Jaina was silent for a moment. "Have we talked enough politics?"

"I think so."

"Good."

HORN FAMILY QUARTERS, KALLAD'S DREAM VACATION HOSTEL, CORUSCANT

Yawning, hair tousled, clad in a blue dressing robe, Valin Horn knew that he did not look anything like an experienced Jedi Knight. He looked like an unshaven, unkempt bachelor, which he also was. But here, in these rented quarters, there would be only family to see him—at least until he had breakfast, shaved, and dressed.

The Horns did not live here, of course. His mother, Mirax, was the anchor for the immediate family. Manager of a variety of interlinked businesses—trading, interplanetary finances, gambling and recreation, and, if rumors were true, still a little smuggling here and there—she maintained her home and business address on Corellia. Corran, her husband and Valin's father, was a Jedi Master, much of his life spent on missions away from the family, but his true home was where his heart resided, wherever Mirax lived. Valin and his sister, Jysella, also Jedi, lived wherever their missions sent them, and also counted Mirax as the center of the family.

Now Mirax had rented temporary quarters on Coruscant so the family could collect on one of its rare occasions, this time for the Unification Summit, where she and Corran would separately give depositions on the relationships among the Confederation states, the Imperial Remnant, and the Galactic Alliance as they related to trade and Jedi activities. Mirax had insisted that Valin and Jysella leave their Temple quarters and stay with their parents while these events were taking place, and few forces in the galaxy could stand before her decision—Luke Skywalker certainly knew better than to try.

Moving from the refresher toward the kitchen and dining nook, Valin brushed a lock of brown hair out of his eyes and grinned. Much as he might put up a public show of protest—the independent young man who did not need parents to direct his actions or tell him where to sleep—he hardly minded. It was good to see family. And both Corran and Mirax were better cooks than the ones at the Jedi Temple.

There was no sound of conversation from the kitchen, but there was some clattering of pans, so at least one of his parents must still be on hand. As he stepped from the hallway into the dining nook, Valin saw that it was his mother, her back to him as she worked at the stove. He pulled a chair from the table and sat. "Good morning."

"A joke, so early?" Mirax did not turn to face him, but her tone was cheerful. "No morning is good. I come light-years from Corellia to be with my family, and what happens? I have to keep Jedi hours to see them. Don't you know that I'm an executive? And a lazy one?"

"I forgot." Valin took a deep breath, sampling the smells

of breakfast. His mother was making hotcakes Corellian-style, nerf sausage links on the side, and caf was brewing. For a moment, Valin was transported back to his child-hood, to the family breakfasts that had been somewhat more common before the Yuuzhan Vong came, before Valin and Jysella had started down the Jedi path. "Where are Dad and Sella?"

"Your father is out getting some back-door information from other Jedi Masters for his deposition." Mirax pulled a plate from a cabinet and began sliding hotcakes and links onto it. "Your sister left early and wouldn't say what she was doing, which I assume either means it's Jedi business I can't know about or that she's seeing some man she doesn't *want* me to know about."

"Or both."

"Or both." Mirax turned and moved over to put the plate down before him. She set utensils beside it.

The plate was heaped high with food, and Valin recoiled from it in mock horror. "Stang, Mom, you're feeding your son, not a squadron of Gamorreans." Then he caught sight of his mother's face and he was suddenly no longer in a jok-ing mood.

This wasn't his mother.

Oh, the woman had Mirax's features. She had the round face that admirers had called "cute" far more often than "beautiful," much to Mirax's chagrin. She had Mirax's gen-erous, curving lips that smiled so readily and expressively, and Mirax's bright, lively brown eyes. She had Mirax's hair, a glossy black with flecks of gray, worn shoulder-length to fit readily under a pilot's helmet, even though she piloted far less often these days. She was Mirax to every freckle and dimple.

But she was not Mirax.

The woman, whoever she was, caught sight of Valin's confusion. "Something wrong?"

"Uh, no." Stunned, Valin looked down at his plate.

He had to think—logically, correctly, and *fast*. He might be in grave danger right now, though the Force currently gave him no indication of imminent attack. The true Mirax, wherever she was, might be in serious trouble or worse. Valin tried in vain to slow his heart rate and speed up his thinking processes.

Fact: Mirax had been here but had been replaced by an imposter. Presumably the real Mirax was gone; Valin could not sense anyone but himself and the imposter in the immediate vicinity. The imposter had remained behind for some reason that had to relate to Valin, Jysella, or Corran. It couldn't have been to capture Valin, as she could have done that with drugs or other methods while he slept, so the food was probably not drugged.

Under Not-Mirax's concerned gaze, he took a tentative bite of sausage and turned a reassuring smile he didn't feel toward her.

Fact: Creating an imposter this perfect must have taken a fortune in money, an incredible amount of research, and a volunteer willing to let her features be permanently carved into the likeness of another's. Or perhaps this was a clone, raised and trained for the purpose of simulating Mirax. Or maybe she was a droid, one of the very expensive, very rare human replica droids. Or maybe a shape-shifter. Whichever, the simulation was nearly perfect. Valin hadn't recognized the deception until . . .

Until *what*? What had tipped him off? He took another bite, not registering the sausage's taste or temperature, and maintained the face-hurting smile as he tried to recall the detail that had alerted him that this wasn't his mother.

He couldn't figure it out. It was just an instant realization, too fleeting to remember, too overwhelming to reject.

Would Corran be able to see through the deception? Would Jysella? Surely, they had to be able to. But what if they couldn't? Valin would accuse this woman and be thought insane.

Were Corran and Jysella even still at liberty? Still *alive*? At this moment, the Not-Mirax's colleagues could be spiriting the two of them away with the true Mirax. Or Corran and Jysella could be lying, bleeding, at the bottom of an access shaft, their lives draining away.

Valin couldn't think straight. The situation was too over-whelming, the mystery too deep, and the only person here who knew the answers was the one who wore the face of his mother.

He stood, sending his chair clattering backward, and fixed the false Mirax with a hard look. "Just a moment." He dashed to his room.

His lightsaber was still where he'd left it, on the night-stand beside his bed. He snatched it up and gave it a near-instantaneous examination. Battery power was still optimal; there was no sign that it had been tampered with.

He returned to the dining room with the weapon in his hand. Not-Mirax, clearly confused and beginning to look a little alarmed, stood by the stove, staring at him.

Valin ignited the lightsaber, its *snap-hiss* of activation startlingly loud, and held the point of the gleaming energy blade against the food on his plate. Hotcakes shriveled and blackened from contact with the weapon's plasma. Valin gave Not-Mirax an approving nod. "Flesh does the same thing under the same conditions, you know."

"Valin, what's *wrong?*"

"You may address me as Jedi Horn. You don't have the right to use my personal name." Valin swung the lightsaber around in a practice form, allowing the blade to come within a few centimeters of the glow rod fixture overhead, the wall, the dining table, and the woman with his mother's face. "You probably know from your research that the Jedi don't worry much about amputations."

Not-Mirax shrank back away from him, both hands on the stove edge behind her. "What?"

"We know that a severed limb can readily be replaced by a prosthetic that looks identical to the real thing. Prosthet-ics offer sensation and do everything flesh can. They're ideal substitutes in every way, except for requiring mainte-nance. So we don't feel too badly when we have to cut the arm or leg off a very bad person. But I assure you, that very bad person remembers the pain forever."

"Valin, I'm going to call your father now." Not-Mirax sidled toward the blue bantha-hide carrybag she had left on a side table.

Valin positioned the tip of his lightsaber directly beneath her chin. At the distance of half a centimeter, its containing force field kept her from feeling any heat from the blade, but a slight twitch on Valin's part could maim or kill her instantly. She froze.

"No, you're not. You know what you're going to do instead?"

Not-Mirax's voice wavered. "What?"

"You're going to *tell me what you've done with my mother!*" The last several words emerged as a bellow, driven by fear and anger. Valin knew that he looked as angry as he sounded; he could feel blood reddening his face, could even see redness begin to suffuse everything in his vision.

"Boy, put the blade down." Those were not the woman's words. They came from behind. Valin spun, bringing his blade up into a defensive position.

In the doorway stood a man, middle-aged, clean-shaven, his hair graying from brown. He was of below-average height, his eyes a startling green. He wore the brown robes of a Jedi. His hands were on his belt, his own lightsaber still dangling from it.

He was Valin's father, Jedi Master Corran Horn. But he wasn't, any more than the woman behind Valin was Mirax Horn.

Valin felt a wave of despair wash over him. *Both* parents replaced. Odds were growing that the real Corran and Mirax were already dead.

Yet Valin's voice was soft when he spoke. "They may have made you a virtual double for my father. But they can't have given you his expertise with the lightsaber."

"You don't want to do what you're thinking about, son."

"When I cut you in half, that's all the proof anyone will ever need that you're not the real Corran Horn."

Valin lunged.